EDITH WHARTON

(1862–1937) was born in New York, the daughter of Lucretia Rhinelander and George Frederic Jones. In 1885 she married a Boston socialite, Edward Robbins Wharton and lived with him in Newport, Rhode Island, frequently travelling to Europe where she became friendly with Henry James. But her marriage was an unhappy one and Edith turned to writing. Her first novel, *The Valley of Decision*, appeared in 1902. She went on to publish an average of more than a book a year for the rest of her life. Her first critical and popular success came with *The House of Mirth* (1905). Then followed her richest period of literary activity which included *The Fruit of the Tree* (1907), *Madame de Treymes* (1907) and *The Reef* (1912). Her husband's mental health steadily declined and in 1910, when they had moved permanently to France, the marriage finally broke up, ending in divorce in 1913.

Edith Wharton's writing was largely abandoned during the First World War. She threw herself into war work for which she was awarded the Cross of the Legion d'Honneur and the Order of Leopold. After the war she moved to an eighteenth-century villa north of Paris, and spent her winters in a converted monastery on the Riviera. *The Age of Innocence* won the Pulitzer Prize in the year it was published, 1920, and was made into a major film directed by Martin Scorcese, starring Daniel Day Lewis, Winona Ryder and Michele Pfeiffer in 1993. She was the first woman to receive a Doctorate of Letters from Yale University and in 1930 she became a member of the American Academy of Arts and Letters. One of America's greatest novelists, Edith Wharton died in France at the age of seventy-five.

Virago also publishes *The Reef*, *Roman Fever*, *Ethan Frome*, *The Fruit of the Tree*, *Madame de Treymes*, *Old New York*, *The Mother's Recompense*, *The Children*, *Hudson River Bracketed*, *The Gods Arrive*, *The House of Mirth*, *The Age of Innocence* and *The Custom of the Country*.

VIRAGO
MODERN
CLASSIC
NUMBER
398

Edith Wharton

THE
GLIMPSES OF
THE MOON

With an introduction by Claire Preston

Published by VIRAGO PRESS Limited 1995
20 Vauxhall Bridge Road, London SW1V 2SA

Reprinted 1995

First published by D. Appleton & Company in New York
and London, 1922

Introduction Copyright © Claire Preston 1994

*A CIP record for this book
is available from the British Library.*

Printed and bound in Great Britain by
Cox & Wyman Ltd, Reading, Berkshire

INTRODUCTION

'Nothing more competent than this book could possibly be imagined,' said Rebecca West disdainfully of *The Glimpses of the Moon*. Her review,* which could hardly contain its contempt for the novel and its characters, was only more acidulated than others in its reckoning of Edith Wharton's 1922 bestseller. Opinion ranged from despair ('cheap and common'), irritation ('frightfully repetitious'), disbelief (an 'improbable jambalaya'), and condescension ('a peculiarly affecting example of . . . all the dangers the novelist . . . is likely to encounter'), to pompous outrage ('we would recommend nobody to buy it or to read it'). But the novel turned out to be one of those regular instances of a critical disaster which is also a commercial triumph. It sold hugely; a successful film of it appeared a few years later.

Part of the trouble was its timing. *The Glimpses of the Moon* followed *The Age of Innocence* (1921), which had just won the Pulitzer Prize for the previous year; Wharton had the difficult task of matching this widely acclaimed novel, an act almost impossible to follow. *Glimpses*, in any case, is not the same kind of work, and unlike its predecessor, which was written within a year, it had a long gestation during the years 1916 to 1921; it was written alongside *A Son at the Front* (1923) and her unfinished novel *Literature*, and all three were offered to her publishers. What the publishers wanted, however, was another *House of Mirth* (1905), and although the original proposal for *Glimpses* does not resemble that earlier novel, the finished product has distinct similarities to it, as if Wharton had yielded to market pressure. It is, therefore, really an *earlier* novel than *The Age of Innocence*, and its concerns are not clearly related to those of that masterpiece.

Other reasons for its critical failure may have been recognised by Wharton herself before she ever finished the novel. Writing to Sinclair Lewis in 1922, she observed that 'irony

---

* This piece, by the way, is remarkable in its constant ungenerous comparisons of Wharton to what West thinks of as the really important writers of the day, every one of whom is now either forgotten or relegated to the third rank. She also incorrectly cites Donne as the source of the title, when it is in fact from *Hamlet*.

seems to have become as unintelligible as Chinese' to the American reading public. She admired most in Lewis's work his 'balancing . . . over the sloppy abyss of sentimentality'. The antagonistic reviewers of *Glimpses* are mainly those who fail to detect anything but a sincere regard for its characters, and who, missing her ironical strokes altogether, complain of her 'immorality' in depicting so clearly the vapidity of the post-war international set.

What Wharton was trying to accomplish – though not with complete success – was, as she explained to Bernard Berenson during the composition of it, the 'adventures of a young couple who believe themselves to be completely affranchis & up-to-date, but are continually tripped up by obsolete sensibilities, & discarded ideals – A difficult subject . . .'

The story of this 'difficult subject' is simple; even, by Wharton's own reckoning, slight. Two attractive but impecunious young American socialites fall in love and decide to embark on the apparently mad exercise of marrying for this reason alone, without money or prospects more substantial than their popularity and their ability to extract favours, cash, the use of houses, and presents from their exceedingly rich friends. Since this has always been their *modus vivendi*, there is nothing especially remarkable in the assumption that they should succeed, at least for a while; the fascination lies in the manner in which the attempt is reduced to a kind of science, the science, as Susy calls it, of 'managing', of performing little services (often furtive) for generous benefactors. Their marriage, Nick and Susy agree, shall continue only as long as their wedding cheques can be made to last, or until one of them gets a better offer.

The adventure goes blissfully enough for most of a year in Italy; however, Susy is to some extent heedless of the moral quagmire into which 'managing' must lead her; and Nick, when he discovers that she has been helping an especially beneficent friend deceive her husband, leaves her in passionate disillusionment. The remainder of the story, during which they each nearly take up with new (and hideously rich) partners, is spent in self-examination which leads, finally, to their reunion.

Susy Lansing is distinctly the more interesting of the pair, probably because she is more honest with herself. Susy's meditations on her situation have a clarity and cynicism which her husband's lack. About

> people with a balance . . . the people one always had to put oneself out for, she knew nearly all that there was to know . . . and judged them with the contemptuous lucidity of nearly twenty years dependence.

Susy knows all that there is to know about accepting lifts and vacations, last year's dresses, presents and dinner invitations, in return for strategic flirtations, stylish conversation, and a decorative appearance in the houses of her friends. She recognises and bitterly resents 'the blessed moral freedom that wealth confers', and admires the fortitude of the Fulmers, down-at-heel members of their set who prefer their painting, their music, their unruly troop of children, and above all, each other, in a small cottage in New Hampshire, to the better prospects they might have enjoyed had they married for money instead of love. For Nick the Fulmers are 'an awful object-lesson in what happened to young people who lost their heads'.

Nick is at first fascinated by Susy's ability to make ends meet by ingenious contrivances, so different from his careless code of 'mays' and 'mustn'ts'. During their first, troth-plighting discussion of their future, his heightened romantic sensibility ('Lansing could not see the view at their feet for the stir of the brown lashes on her cheek') is woven together with the monetary accounting to which Susy's thoughts always return ('Cheques, my dear, nothing but cheques'). There is frequent reference to Susy's 'almost masculine' regard for her promises and word of honour, and it is as though Nick is infatuated with someone whose delicate femininity is matched with a seemingly male determination and practicality which he himself lacks. Although both have long since taken the measure of the world, and know 'just what it was worth to them and for what reasons', it is Susy whose plain reckoning of Nick on first meeting him is 'I'd rather have a husband like that than a steam-yacht!', and Nick who allows himself to be deluded about the nature of their existence together ('he had taken care not to ask') until the evidence of her compromises becomes too plain for him to ignore.

Nick, as his wife quickly recognises, adheres to a standard of conduct higher than hers. His bachelor flat shows her that he has never accepted a present, or, as he later declares, 'done people's dirty work for them'. At one point, before their marriage, a patroness of Susy's who fancies Nick asks her to give him up; this she does for a time, citing 'a business arrangement'. When Nick can hardly be made to understand the nature of this claim on her, Susy exclaims, 'You talk like the hero of a novel – the kind my governess used to read.'

This is the central complication: both of them are devoted to a life of ease and beautiful things, and are content to be offered proximity to them. Susy 'loved luxury: splendid things always made her feel handsome and high ceilings arrogant.' She also hopes to make everything easy and pleasant for Nick. Nick, for his part, has had a recent five months in India for the price of going with rich bores; 'But it was my only chance – and what the deuce is one to do?' As Nick himself says, 'there were things a fellow put up with . . . there were other things he wouldn't traffic in at any price. But for a woman . . . the temptations might be greater, the cost considerably higher, the dividing line between "mays" and "mustn'ts" more fluctuating and less sharply drawn.' But because all the arrangements for their married existence have been made by Susy, they are made on her terms rather than on his; his enjoyment of their magical honeymoon in Como and Venice has equalled hers, but he has not bothered to enquire how it has all been managed. 'If there were certain links in the chain . . . certain arrangements and contrivances that still needed further elucidation, why, he was lazily resolved to clear them up with her some day.' Nick, we are often reminded, has determined to live in the present, to disregard the future; 'he had thought it rather fine to be able to give himself so intensely to the fullness of each moment instead of hurrying past it . . .' Nick *is* like the hero of a novel in his elevated discriminations, but he cannot accept the consequences of his irresponsibility. He affects high ideals, scorns the very world he is content to inhabit.

Like Susy, Nick is a lifelong social parasite, a sort of parlour intellectual, who 'writes'. His book, *The Pageant of Alexander*, the putative project which will establish him in the world of letters and earn their keep, is as fanciful as the income he expects it to produce. 'He liked writing descriptions, and vaguely felt that under the guise of fiction he could develop his theory of Oriental influences in Western art at the expense of less learning than if he had tried to put his ideas into an essay. He knew enough of his subject to know that he did not know enough to write about it . . .' Wharton's scorn for the dilettante is palpable in this passage: she, who kept a rigorous daily writing schedule, whose books have *plot* above all else, who *had* written well on art, but not under the guise of fiction, makes her young man a moral, as well as a literary, lightweight, of finely enunciated principles which nonetheless do no work in his marriage other than to allow him to leave it with a clear conscience. Lacking the sort of self-knowledge that gains his wife our respect, Nick is little more than a lazy, high-toned young prig.

When he leaves her, rather than earn his crust in Grub Street or closet himself in some shabby room with his book, he battens on the Mortimer Hickses, Wharton's culture-mad prairie plutocrats from Apex City. Cruising in their majestic steam-yacht past the landscapes of the Old World, these midwestern millionaires are both more gullible and yet more attractive than the attenuated, purposeless vagrants of the international social scene from which Nick and Susy derive. Nick is taken on as cultural guide and social arbiter to the Hickses, whose blunt and commanding daughter Coral, as he is already aware, is in love with him. Nick's attitude towards this family is an unpleasant mixture of gratitude for their subsidy and condescension toward their naive enthusiasm; still, he is not above taking their generous cheques and contemplating a luxurious future with Coral. His reiterated determination to leave the Hicks entourage because 'he liked them too well' to take their money begins to seem preposterous, his conviction not to return to Susy because *she* could not be expected to live the self-supported life ('two rooms and no servant'), incredible.

The architecture of the story (the 'competence' to which West refers) is almost operatically neat; the tale and its characters, superficially rather sentimental, are subservient to thematic and structural considerations, and it may be this that offended the reviewers. We are offered, for example, a pair of young women (Susy and Coral); contrasting kinds of small children (Clarissa Vanderlyn and the Fulmers); contiguous scenes set in hotels of the same name in separate European cities; duet-like but separated conversations about jewels and arranged marriages; a sudden and unexpected inheritance of a vast fortune and a title for one of the subordinate characters; one or two neat ironies in the whirligig of adultery and country houses; all these features seem got up from the fanciful landscape of romance, not of realism. Yet each obeys Wharton's stern theme: the opening idyll by Lake Como, with its luscious evocation of the moon and June, is punctured by a cigar-stealing incident which reduces the heroine to the kind of tourist who swipes towels from hotels; the doll-like, preternaturally wise, neglected, and rich Clarissa crows over her new pearl necklace that she has been given it 'because I said I'd rather have it than a book', disclosed for what she is – a victim of her own moneyed childhood.

With its apparently contrived symmetries and coincidences, the plot sets off certain unassailable and often uncomfortable truths as brilliantly as the jewellers in this book re-set precious stones. Susy is caught assisting Clarrisa's mother in her amours; 'you accept things theoretically – and then when they happen . . .' she says, facing down Nick's hypocrisy; 'doesn't our being together depend on what we can get out of people? And hasn't there always got to be some give-and-take? Did you ever in your life get anything for nothing?' Much later, Susy makes the sickening discovery that Ellie Vanderlyn proposes a divorce from Clarissa's very rich father, in order to marry the even richer lover whom

Susy assisted her in entertaining: 'I think you're abominable,' she exclaimed, 'with Clarissa . . . and all the money you can possibly want . . .', to which Ellie replies, 'But you simply don't know what you're talking about. *As if anybody ever had all the money they wanted!*'

Wharton considers the impossible collision between want and principles. To be able to exercise the latter, Nick and Susy think, they must be above worrying about the former. To both of them, at first, being above financial concerns means being very well off. But the movement of the book is rather toward the simpler conclusion which all but the very rich can imagine: to be financially content you must set your sights, like the Fulmers, very low, in order that you may set your values high. As someone says at one point, the profits from Nick's intended literary efforts would not keep Susy in hats for a season; and when Susy turns down her rich suitor, she wanders the streets of Paris admiring 'the tired independent faces' of the working women and the material heedlessness of a wimpled nun on her way to visit the poor, comparing their expenses to 'the necessities that enslaved her' ('so much for her dresses, so much for her cigarettes, so much for bridge and cabs and tips').

Reconciliation is bought by Susy for them both. It is she who finds her way toward the 'higher' standard of her husband. Certainly he too has endured some soul-searching in the months of their separation, but his decision to seek her out is finally actuated by ordinary and unexamined longing, which overrides his scruples about her behaviour; quite simply, he finds he can't do without her. Her decision to be with him develops out of a genuine process of growth and realisation, a process which occupies two-thirds of the book. As with most Wharton novels, the woman's path is the more complex and interesting; and it is Susy's which must interest us over Nick's. Susy has had to be more adept at managing because she is the more vulnerable; a woman in her position cannot afford the luxury of Nick's scruples. Her subsequent sentimental education in an apparently masculine code is not, though, a weak capitulation by Wharton to traditional expectations. That Susy eventually recalls herself from the slough is a measure of her versatility and imagination. Susy learns exactly what she won't traffic in at any price, and actually becomes the better person her husband is always describing. It is a journey Nick never makes, or needs to make.

Susy's way toward self-sufficiency and contentment lies with children. It was in this period that Wharton started to be noticeably interested in the young, who often represent for her a kind of distilled sensibility and wisdom which is not yet occluded by the wearinesses of adult proprieties. Perhaps recollecting her own rather peculiar childhood of solitary literary pursuits, Wharton's children are nearly always intelligent, canny, and utterly undeceived by their elders. In *The Children* (1928), the hilariously varied group of 'steps' and 'halfs' have a sort of brutal instinct for survival, which usually means getting all they can from current circumstances, in the form of affection, attention, good dinners, and presents.

The children of *The Glimpses of the Moon* are near relations. Early in the story, Susy and Nick stay in the Venetian palazzo of the absent Vanderlyns, where the eight-year-old Vanderlyn daughter has been left with the servants. On the first morning, Susy awakes to find little Clarissa has come in with the breakfast tray; the girl assumes Susy is recently divorced. 'What in the world made you think so?' the newly-wed Susy asks. 'Because you look so awfully happy,' Clarissa replies, with the horrifying logic of her class. It is Clarissa who receives a pearl necklace, bought for her on the proceeds of her mother's adultery; in her infant delight she mimics the fierce acquisitiveness of her parents and their set. Susy wakens to the pathos of Clarissa's position, and intermittently attempts to give her the attention she should be receiving from her truant parents.

It is not, however, until she is asked to look after the five Fulmer children for a summer that she starts to understand what living on one's own terms may mean. Bereft of Nick by this stage, she turns up in Versailles to be sheltered by yet another rich friend, who proposes that Susy manage the Fulmer children while the friend travels with their painter-father, whom she has taken up as her own pet genius. For the first time in her life, Susy refuses to co-operate; her sense of independence and honour are changing: 'Nick had ... waked in her again something which had lain unconscious under years of accumulated indifference ... It was almost ... as if he had left her with a child.' Out of a job, so to speak, and with nowhere much to go, Susy consults with Fulmer's wife, Grace, a violinist who is simultaneously being championed by a rival socialite. Grace also asks Susy to look after the children so that she can go to England to play in concerts; this time, Susy accepts, moving to an obscure Parisian district where she performs all the offices of a mother for the demanding and energetic family. It is here, in the end, that she is found by Nick, looking (melodramatically) poor and motherly, and utterly unlike a social butterfly.

This biggest service, of all her canny services to her friends, is rendered to the one friend who can do nothing material for her, who is herself dependent on the rich for her opportunities. It is a service which Susy at first undertakes as a way of bludgeoning the insistent longing for her husband, but which she comes to see as an education; it gives her 'the sense of being herself mothered, of taking her first steps in the life of immaterial values which had begun to seem so much more substantial than any she had known'. The slightly improbable precocity of the Fulmer children (all under twelve, they like Shakespeare and art galleries) serves to remind Susy of the world in which all but her rich friends find their dreams: 'However inadequate Grace Fulmer's bringing-up of her increasing tribe had been, they had heard in her company nothing trivial or dull: good music, good books and good talk had been their daily food ...' Clarissa Vanderlyn's 'hard little appetite' for necklaces is vividly compared to the Fulmers' persistent requests to be read to or be told stories. Susy wonders that Nick's influence, and their parting, 'should have done less to mature and steady her than these few weeks in a house full of children.'

Susy has done nothing very culpable in the course of the novel, nothing to merit the misery Nick puts her through. She has married for love, kept her word and her bargain, behaved like a brick about the dissolution of her marriage. She has played by the rules, including those 'hideous intricacies of managing' which have made their life together possible, from which her more delicate husband profits but which he prefers not to recognise. The customary roles are reversed: Nick is the shrinking and unworldly partner, who leaves the nasty business of money and accounts to his wife; who is half attracted to the handsome, 'massive', straight-talking Coral Hicks, the midwestern heiress who even has a faint moustache. Wharton does not admire such ethereal, red-and-white virtue as Nick's is. Her most powerful characters are cousin-german to Susy, and are all female; perhaps she most nearly resembles Undine Spragg, the ruthless social mountaineer in *The Custom of the Country*.

The Glimpses of the Moon, like many of Wharton's fictions, moves among vastly endowed patrician New Yorkers, or expatriate *nouveaux riches* in their perpetual wanderings and thrill-seekings, their codes of honour and of money; often her principals, like Susy and Nick, are uneasy in the barbarian world of the American tribal rich. The solutions discovered by Lawrence Selden and Lily Bart, Newland Archer and Ellen Olenska, Kate Clephane, or Ralph Marvell, are as various and extreme as disappointment and death. Wharton was not inclined to cheerful endings: they do not sort with the sordid but inevitable accommodations, or with the emotional anaesthesia required by that world. Susy, like the rest, acknowledges her social reality and is not afraid of owning up to her compromises; almost singularly, however, she finally leaves them behind. This is as near a happy resolution as Wharton ever came.

Wharton was in her time charged with being cold, with being interested in her characters only as a naturalist in his insect specimens. Curiously, though, this novel was regarded by some as a clumsy attempt at sentimentalism by a writer whose natural *métier* was detached and ironical. For those who already disliked Mrs Wharton's books, *Glimpses* was a bonanza: if her irony and coldness had been 'un- womanly', her warmth in *Glimpses* was derided as all too predictably feminine. But it is quite wrong to read the story in this way:

sentimentality is a trait associated almost ex- clusively with
Nick Lansing. In any case, one can almost never look for or
expect to develop 'sympathy' with character in Wharton's
work, where *design* is often more important; it is the ironist,
not the sentimentalist, who so brilliantly records the
hieroglyphic worlds of her chosen groups. There is an
instructive comparison to be made here with Fitzgerald,
whose theme of idealistic detachment in *Tender is the Night*
is far more rigorously handled in *Glimpses*, and whose
affection for the Patches muddies the otherwise crystalline
The Beautiful and the Damned. By contrast, Wharton usually
lingers, as one reviewer of *Glimpses* put it, 'on unpleasant
people'. The spiritual dilemma of a Newland Archer and the
overriding and fatal social necessities of a Lily Bart may be
deeply affecting; but they are no less glacial, no less designed
and patterned than the insatiable material appetite of an
Undine Spragg, or the pragmatic solution of a Charity Royall.
The choreographed tale of Nick and Susy Lansing is like
these – fascinating and elegant in its stark opposition of
wealth and ideals.

Like the ironical Charlie Strefford – the character in
Glimpses most like the naturalist, most willing to dissect the
social condition – Wharton cannot afford to become too fond
of her specimens. Like Strefford, she is 'in the show, and yet
outside of it'. But Strefford's downfall occurs when Susy
sadly discovers that after all, he is really more interested in
the scandals he retails than in his satires on them. Of this we
cannot accuse Edith Wharton.

Claire Preston, Cambridge, 1994

PART I

THE GLIMPSES OF
THE MOON

I

IT rose for them—their honey-moon—over the
waters of a lake so famed as the scene of romantic raptures that they were rather proud
of not having been afraid to choose it as the setting of their own.

"It required a total lack of humour, or as great
a gift for it as ours, to risk the experiment," Susy
Lansing opined, as they hung over the inevitable
marble balustrade and watched their tutelary orb
roll its magic carpet across the waters to their
feet.

"Yes—or the loan of Strefford's villa," her
husband emended, glancing upward through the
branches at a long low patch of paleness to which
the moonlight was beginning to give the form of a
white house-front.

"Oh, come—when we'd five to choose from. At
least if you count the Chicago flat."

"So we had—you wonder!" He laid his hand
on hers, and his touch renewed the sense of mar-
velling exultation which the deliberate survey of
their adventure always roused in her. . . . It
was characteristic that she merely added, in her

1

steady laughing tone: "Or, not counting the flat—for I hate to brag—just consider the others: Violet Melrose's place at Versailles, your aunt's villa at Monte Carlo—*and* a moor!"

She was conscious of throwing in the moor tentatively, and yet with a somewhat exaggerated emphasis, as if to make sure that he shouldn't accuse her of slurring it over. But he seemed to have no desire to do so. "Poor old Fred!" he merely remarked; and she breathed out carelessly: "Oh, well—"

His hand still lay on hers, and for a long interval, while they stood silent in the enveloping loveliness of the night, she was aware only of the warm current running from palm to palm, as the moonlight below them drew its line of magic from shore to shore.

Nick Lansing spoke at last. "Versailles in May would have been impossible: all our Paris crowd would have run us down within twenty-four hours. And Monte Carlo is ruled out because it's exactly the kind of place everybody expected us to go. So —with all respect to you—it wasn't much of a mental strain to decide on Como."

His wife instantly challenged this belittling of her capacity. "It took a good deal of argument to convince you that we could face the ridicule of Como!"

"Well, I should have preferred something in a lower key; at least I thought I should till we got here. Now I see that this place is idiotic unless

one is perfectly happy; and that then it's—as good
as any other."

She sighed out a blissful assent. "And I must
say that Streffy has done things to a turn. Even
the cigars—*who* do you suppose gave him those
cigars?" She added thoughtfully: "You'll miss
them when we have to go."

"Oh, I say, don't let's talk to-night about going.'
'Aren't we outside of time and space . . . ?
Smell that guinea-a-bottle stuff over there: what
is it? Stephanotis?"

"Y-yes. . . . I suppose so. Or gardenias. . . .
Oh, the fire-flies! Look . . . there, against that
splash of moonlight on the water. Apples of
silver in a net-work of gold. . . ." They leaned
together, one flesh from shoulder to finger-tips,
their eyes held by the snared glitter of the ripples.

"I could bear," Lansing remarked, "even a
nightingale at this moment. . . ."

A faint gurgle shook the magnolias behind them,
and a long liquid whisper answered it from the
thicket of laurel above their heads.

"It's a little late in the year for them: they're
ending just as we begin."

Susy laughed. "I hope when our turn comes we
shall say good-bye to each other as sweetly."

It was in her husband's mind to answer:
"They're not saying good-bye, but only settling
down to family cares." But as this did not happen to be in his plan, or in Susy's, he merely
echoed her laugh and pressed her closer.

The spring night drew them into its deepening embrace. The ripples of the lake had gradually widened and faded into a silken smoothness, and high above the mountains the moon was turning from gold to white in a sky powdered with vanishing stars. Across the lake the lights of a little town went out, one after another, and the distant shore became a floating blackness. A breeze that rose and sank brushed their faces with the scents of the garden; once it blew out over the water a great white moth like a drifting magnolia petal. The nightingales had paused and the trickle of the fountain behind the house grew suddenly insistent.

When Susy spoke it was in a voice languid with visions. "I have been thinking," she said, "that we ought to be able to make it last at least a year longer."

Her husband received the remark without any sign of surprise or disapprobation; his answer showed that he not only understood her, but had been inwardly following the same train of thought.

"You mean," he enquired after a pause, "without counting your grandmother's pearls?"

"Yes—without the pearls."

He pondered a while, and then rejoined in a tender whisper: "Tell me again just how."

"Let's sit down, then. No, I like the cushions best."

He stretched himself in a long willow chair, and she curled up on a heap of boat-cushions and leaned her head against his knee. Just above her, when she lifted her lids, she saw bits of moon-flooded sky incrusted like silver in a sharp black patterning of plane-boughs. All about them breathed of peace and beauty and stability, and her happiness was so acute that it was almost a relief to remember the stormy background of bills and borrowing against which its frail structure had been reared. "People with a balance can't be as happy as all this," Susy mused, letting the moonlight filter through her lazy lashes.

People with a balance had always been Susy Branch's bugbear; they were still, and more dangerously, to be Susy Lansing's. She detested them, detested them doubly, as the natural enemies of mankind and as the people one always had to put one's self out for. The greater part of her life having been passed among them, she knew nearly all that there was to know about them, and judged them with the contemptuous lucidity of nearly twenty years of dependence. But at the present moment her animosity was diminished not only by the softening effect of love but by the fact that she had got out of those very people more—yes, ever so much more—than she and Nick, in their hours of most reckless planning, had ever dared to hope for.

"After all, we owe them *this!*" she mused.

Her husband, lost in the drowsy beatitude of the hour, had not repeated his question; but she was still on the trail of the thought he had started. A year—yes, she was sure now that with a little

management they could have a whole year of it!
"It" was their marriage, their being together,
and away from bores and bothers, in a comrade-
ship of which both of them had long ago guessed
the immediate pleasure, but she at least had never
imagined the deeper harmony.

It was at one of their earliest meetings—at one
of the heterogeneous dinners that the Fred Gillows tried to think "literary"—that the young
man who chanced to sit next to her, and of whom
it was vaguely rumoured that he had "written,"
had presented himself to her imagination as the
sort of luxury to which Susy Branch, heiress,
might conceivably have treated herself as a crowning folly. Susy Branch, pauper, was fond of picturing how this fancied double would employ her
millions: it was one of her chief grievances
against her rich friends that they disposed of
theirs so unimaginatively.

"I'd rather have a husband like that than
a steam-yacht!" she had thought at the end of her
talk with the young man who had written, and as
to whom it had at once been clear to her that nothing his pen had produced, or might hereafter set
down, would put him in a position to offer his wife
anything more costly than a row-boat.

"His wife—! As if he could ever have one!
For he's not the kind to marry for a yacht
either." In spite of her past, Susy had preserved
enough inner independence to detect the latent
signs of it in others, and also to ascribe it impul-

sively to those of the opposite sex who happened to interest her. She had a natural contempt for people who gloried in what they need only have endured. She herself meant eventually to marry, because one couldn't forever hang on to rich people; but she was going to wait till she found some one who combined the maximum of wealth with at least a minimum of companionableness.

She had at once perceived young Lansing's case to be exactly the opposite: he was as poor as he could be, and as companionable as it was possible to imagine. She therefore decided to see as much of him as her hurried and entangled life permitted; and this, thanks to a series of adroit adjustments, turned out to be a good deal. They met frequently all the rest of that winter; so frequently that Mrs. Fred Gillow one day abruptly and sharply gave Susy to understand that she was "making herself ridiculous."

"Ah—" said Susy with a long breath, looking her friend and patroness straight in the painted eyes.

"Yes," cried Ursula Gillow in a sob, "before you interfered Nick liked me awfully . . . and, of course, I don't want to reproach you . . . but when I think. . . ."

Susy made no answer. How could she, when *she* thought? The dress she had on had been given her by Ursula; Ursula's motor had carried her to the feast from which they were both returning. She counted on spending the following August

with the Gillows at Newport . . . and the only alternative was to go to California with the Bockheimers, whom she had hitherto refused even to
dine with.

"Of course, what you fancy is perfect nonsense,
Ursula; and as to my interfering—" Susy hesitated, and then murmured: "But if it will make
you any happier I'll arrange to see him
less often. . . ." She sounded the lowest depths
of subservience in returning Ursula's tearful
kiss. . . .

Susy Branch had a masculine respect for her
word; and the next day she put on her most becoming hat and sought out young Mr. Lansing in
his lodgings. She was determined to keep her
promise to Ursula; but she meant to look her best
when she did it.

She knew at what time the young man was likely
to be found, for he was doing a dreary job on a
popular encyclopædia (V to X), and had told her
what hours were dedicated to the hateful task.
"Oh, if only it were a novel!" she thought as she
mounted his dingy stairs; but immediately reflected that, if it were the kind that she could bear
to read, it probably wouldn't bring him in much
more than his encyclopædia. Miss Branch had
her standards in literature. . . .

The apartment to which Mr. Lansing admitted
her was a good deal cleaner, but hardly less dingy,
than his staircase. Susy, knowing him to be addicted to Oriental archæology, had pictured him

in a bare room adorned by a single Chinese bronze of flawless shape, or by some precious fragment of Asiatic pottery. But such redeeming features were conspicuously absent, and no attempt had been made to disguise the decent indigence of the bed-sitting-room.

Lansing welcomed his visitor with every sign of pleasure, and with apparent indifference as to what she thought of his furniture. He seemed to be conscious only of his luck in seeing her on a day when they had not expected to meet. This made Susy all the sorrier to execute her promise, and the gladder that she had put on her prettiest hat; and for a moment or two she looked at him in silence from under its conniving brim.

Warm as their mutual liking was, Lansing had never said a word of love to her; but this was no deterrent to his visitor, whose habit it was to speak her meaning clearly when there were no reasons, worldly or pecuniary, for its concealment. After a moment, therefore, she told him why she had come; it was a nuisance, of course, but he would understand. Ursula Gillow was jealous, and they would have to give up seeing each other.

The young man's burst of laughter was music to her; for, after all, she had been rather afraid that being devoted to Ursula might be as much in his day's work as doing the encyclopædia.

"But I give you my word it's a raving-mad mistake! And I don't believe she ever meant *me*, to begin with—" he protested; but Susy, her common-sense returning with her reassurance, promptly cut short his denial.

"You can trust Ursula to make herself clear on such occasions. And it doesn't make any difference what *you* think. All that matters is what *she* believes."

"Oh, come! I've got a word to say about that too, haven't I?"

Susy looked slowly and consideringly about the room. There was nothing in it, absolutely nothing, to show that he had ever possessed a spare dollar—or accepted a present.

"Not as far as I'm concerned," she finally pronounced.

"How do you mean? If I'm as free as air—?"

"I'm not."

He grew thoughtful. "Oh, then, of course—. It only seems a little odd," he added drily, "that in that case, the protest should have come from Mrs. Gillow."

"Instead of coming from my millionaire bridegroom? Oh, I haven't any; in that respect I'm as free as you."

"Well, then—? Haven't we only got to stay free?"

Susy drew her brows together anxiously. It was going to be rather more difficult than she had supposed.

"I said I was as free in that respect. I'm not going to marry—and I don't suppose you are?"

"God, no!" he ejaculated fervently.

"But that doesn't always imply complete freedom. . . ."

He stood just above her, leaning his elbow against the hideous black marble arch that framed his fireless grate. As she glanced up she saw his face harden, and the colour flew to hers.

"Was that what you came to tell me?" he asked.

"Oh, you don't understand—and I don't see why you don't, since we've knocked about so long among exactly the same kind of people." She stood up impulsively and laid her hand on his arm. "I do wish you'd help me—!"

He remained motionless, letting the hand lie untouched.

"Help you to tell me that poor Ursula was a pretext, but that there *is* someone who—for one reason or another—really has a right to object to your seeing me too often?"

Susy laughed impatiently. "You talk like the hero of a novel—the kind my governess used to read. In the first place I should never recognize that kind of right, as you call it—never!"

"Then what kind do you?" he asked with a clearing brow.

"Why—the kind I suppose you recognize on the part of your publisher." This evoked a hollow laugh from him. "A business claim, call it," she pursued. "Ursula does a lot for me: I live on her for half the year. This dress I've got on now is one she gave me. Her motor is going to take me to a dinner to-night. I'm going to spend next summer with her at Newport. . . . If I don't, I've got to go to California with the Bockheimers—so good-bye."

Suddenly in tears, she was out of the door and down his steep three flights before he could stop her—though, in thinking it over, she didn't even remember if he had tried to. She only recalled having stood a long time on the corner of Fifth Avenue, in the harsh winter radiance, waiting till a break in the torrent of motors laden with fashionable women should let her cross, and saying to herself: "After all, I might have promised Ursula . . . and kept on seeing him. . . ."

Instead of which, when Lansing wrote the next day entreating a word with her, she had sent back a friendly but firm refusal; and had managed soon afterward to get taken to Canada for a fort-night's ski-ing, and then to Florida for six weeks in a house-boat. . . .

As she reached this point in her retrospect the remembrance of Florida called up a vision of moonlit waters, magnolia fragrance and balmy airs; merging with the circumambient sweetness, it laid a drowsy spell upon her lids. Yes, there had been a bad moment: but it was over; and she was here, safe and blissful, and with Nick; and this was his knee her head rested on, and they had a year ahead of them . . . a whole year. . . . "Not counting the pearls," she murmured, shutting her eyes. . . .

II

LANSING threw the end of Strefford's expensive cigar into the lake, and bent over his wife. Poor child! She had fallen asleep. . . . He leaned back and stared up again at the silver-flooded sky. How queer—how inexpressibly queer—it was to think that that light was shed by his honey-moon! A year ago, if anyone had predicted his risking such an adventure, he would have replied by asking to be locked up at the first symptoms. . . .

There was still no doubt in his mind that the adventure was a mad one. It was all very well for Susy to remind him twenty times a day that they had pulled it off—and so why should he worry? Even in the light of her far-seeing cleverness, and of his own present bliss, he knew the future would not bear the examination of sober thought. And as he sat there in the summer moonlight, with her head on his knee, he tried to recapitulate the successive steps that had landed them on Streffy's lake-front.

On Lansing's side, no doubt, it dated back to his leaving Harvard with the large resolve not to miss anything. There stood the evergreen Tree of Life, the Four Rivers flowing from its foot; and on every one of the four currents he meant to

launch his little skiff. On two of them he had not
gone very far, on the third he had nearly stuck in
the mud; but the fourth had carried him to the
very heart of wonder. It was the stream of his
lively imagination, of his inexhaustible interest in
every form of beauty and strangeness and folly.
On this stream, sitting in the stout little craft of
his poverty, his insignificance and his independence, he had made some notable voyages. . . .
And so, when Susy Branch, whom he had sought
out through a New York season as the prettiest
and most amusing girl in sight, had surprised
him with the contradictory revelation of her
modern sense of expediency and her old-fashioned
standard of good faith, he had felt an irresistible
desire to put off on one more cruise into the unknown.

It was of the essence of the adventure that,
after her one brief visit to his lodgings, he should
have kept his promise and not tried to see her
again. Even if her straightforwardness had not
roused his emulation, his understanding of her
difficulties would have moved his pity. He knew
on how frail a thread the popularity of the penniless hangs, and how miserably a girl like Susy
was the sport of other people's moods and whims.
It was a part of his difficulty and of hers that to
get what they liked they so often had to do what
they disliked. But the keeping of his promise was
a greater bore than he had expected. Susy
Branch had become a delightful habit in a life

where most of the fixed things were dull, and her disappearance had made it suddenly clear to him that his resources were growing more and more limited. Much that had once amused him hugely now amused him less, or not at all: a good part of his world of wonder had shrunk to a village peep-show. And the things which had kept their stimulating power—distant journeys, the enjoyment of art, the contact with new scenes and strange societies—were becoming less and less attainable. Lansing had never had more than a pittance; he had spent rather too much of it in his first plunge into life, and the best he could look forward to was a middle-age of poorly-paid hackwork, mitigated by brief and frugal holidays. He knew that he was more intelligent than the average, but he had long since concluded that his talents were not marketable. Of the thin volume of sonnets which a friendly publisher had launched for him, just seventy copies had been sold; and though his essay on "Chinese Influences in Greek Art" had created a passing stir, it had resulted in controversial correspondence and dinner invitations rather than in more substantial benefits. There seemed, in short, no prospect of his ever earning money, and his restricted future made him attach an increasing value to the kind of friendship that Susy Branch had given him. Apart from the pleasure of looking at her and listening to her—of enjoying in her what others less discriminatingly but as liberally ap-

preciated—he had the sense, between himself and
her, of a kind of free-masonry of precocious tolerance and irony. They had both, in early youth,
taken the measure of the world they happened to
live in: they knew just what it was worth to them
and for what reasons, and the community of these
reasons lent to their intimacy its last exquisite
touch. And now, because of some jealous whim
of a dissatisfied fool of a woman, as to whom he
felt himself no more to blame than any young
man who has paid for good dinners by good
manners, he was to be deprived of the one complete companionship he had ever known. . . .

His thoughts travelled on. He recalled the long
dull spring in New York after his break with
Susy, the weary grind on his last articles, his listless speculations as to the cheapest and least bor-
ing way of disposing of the summer; and then the
amazing luck of going, reluctantly and at the last
minute, to spend a Sunday with the poor Nat
Fulmers, in the wilds of New Hampshire, and of
finding Susy there—Susy, whom he had never
even suspected of knowing anybody in the Fulmers' set!

She had behaved perfectly—and so had he—
but they were obviously much too glad to see each
other. And then it was unsettling to be with her
in such a house as the Fulmers', away from the
large setting of luxury they were both used to,
in the cramped cottage where their host had his
studio in the verandah, their hostess practised her

violin in the dining-room, and five ubiquitous children sprawled and shouted and blew trumpets and put tadpoles in the water-jugs, and the mid-day dinner was two hours late—and proportionately bad—because the Italian cook was posing for Fulmer.

Lansing's first thought had been that meeting Susy in such circumstances would be the quickest way to cure them both of their regrets. The case of the Fulmers was an awful object-lesson in what happened to young people who lost their heads; poor Nat, whose pictures nobody bought, had gone to seed so terribly—and Grace, at twenty-nine, would never again be anything but the woman of whom people say, "I can remember her when she was lovely."

But the devil of it was that Nat had never been such good company, or Grace so free from care and so full of music; and that, in spite of their disorder and dishevelment, and the bad food and general crazy discomfort, there was more amusement to be got out of their society than out of the most opulently staged house-party through which Susy and Lansing had ever yawned their way.

It was almost a relief to the young man when, on the second afternoon, Miss Branch drew him into the narrow hall to say: "I really can't stand the combination of Grace's violin and little Nat's motor-horn any longer. Do let us slip out till the duet is over."

"How do *they* stand it, I wonder?" he basely, echoed, as he followed her up the wooded path behind the house.

"It might be worth finding out," she rejoined with a musing smile.

But he remained resolutely sceptical. "Oh, give them a year or two more and they'll collapse—! His pictures will never sell, you know. He'll never even get them into a show."

"I suppose not. And she'll never have time to do anything worth while with her music."

They had reached a piny knoll high above the ledge on which the house was perched. All about them stretched an empty landscape of endless featureless wooded hills. "Think of sticking here all the year round!" Lansing groaned.

"I know. But then think of wandering over the world with some people!"

"Oh, Lord, yes. For instance, my trip to India with the Mortimer Hickses. But it was my only chance—and what the deuce is one to do?"

"I wish I knew!" she sighed, thinking of the Bockheimers; and he turned and looked at her.

"Knew what?"

"The answer to your question. What *is* one to do—when one sees both sides of the problem? Or, every possible side of it, indeed?"

They had seated themselves on a commanding rock under the pines, but Lansing could not see the view at their feet for the stir of the brown lashes on her cheek.

"You mean: Nat and Grace may after all be having the best of it?"

"How can I say, when I've told you I see all the sides? Of course," Susy added hastily, "*I* couldn't live as they do for a week. But it's wonderful how little it's dimmed them."

"Certainly Nat was never more coruscating. And she keeps it up even better." He reflected. "We do them good, I daresay."

"Yes—or they us. I wonder which?"

After that, he seemed to remember that they sat a long time silent, and that his next utterance was a boyish outburst against the tyranny of the existing order of things, abruptly followed by the passionate query why, since he and she couldn't alter it, and since they both had the habit of looking at facts as they were, they wouldn't be utter fools not to take their chance of being happy in the only way that was open to them? To this challenge he did not recall Susy's making any definite answer; but after another interval, in which all the world seemed framed in a sudden kiss, he heard her murmur to herself in a brooding tone: "I don't suppose it's ever been tried before; but we might—." And then and there she had laid before him the very experiment they had since hazarded. . . .

She would have none of surreptitious bliss, she began by declaring; and she set forth her reasons with her usual lucid impartiality. In the first place, she should have to marry some day, and when she made the bargain she meant it to be an honest one; and secondly, in the matter of love, she would never give herself to anyone she did not really care for, and if such happiness ever came to her she did not want it shorn of half its brightness by the need of fibbing and plotting and dodging.

"I've seen too much of that kind of thing. Half the women I know who've had lovers have had them for the fun of sneaking and lying about it; but the other half have been miserable. And I should be miserable."

It was at this point that she unfolded her plan. Why shouldn't they marry; belong to each other openly and honourably, if for ever so short a time, and with the definite understanding that whenever either of them got the chance to do better he or she should be immediately released? The law of their country facilitated such exchanges, and society was beginning to view them as indulgently as the law. As Susy talked, she warmed to her theme and began to develop its endless possibilities.

"We should really, in a way, help more than we should hamper each other," she ardently explained. "We both know the ropes so well; what one of us didn't see the other might—in the way of opportunities, I mean. And then we should be a novelty as married people. We're both rather unusually popular—why not be frank?—and it's such a blessing for dinner-givers to be able to

count on a couple of whom neither one is a blank.
Yes, I really believe we should be more than twice
the success we are now; at least," she added with
a smile, "if there's that amount of room for im-
provement. I don't know how you feel; a man's
popularity is so much less precarious than a girl's
—but I know it would furbish me up tremend-
ously to reappear as a married woman." She
glanced away from him down the long valley at
their feet, and added in a lower tone: "And I
should like, just for a little while, to feel I had
something in life of my very own—something
that nobody had lent me, like a fancy-dress or a
motor or an opera cloak."

The suggestion, at first, had seemed to Lansing
as mad as it was enchanting: it had thoroughly
frightened him. But Susy's arguments were irre-
futable, her ingenuities inexhaustible. Had he
ever thought it all out? She asked. No. Well,
she had; and would he kindly not interrupt? In
the first place, there would be all the wedding-
presents. Jewels, and a motor, and a silver dinner service, did she mean? Not a bit of it! She
could see he'd never given the question proper
thought. Cheques, my dear, nothing but cheques
—she undertook to manage that on her side: she
really thought she could count on about fifty, and
she supposed he could rake up a few more? Well,
all that would simply represent pocket-money!
For they would have plenty of houses to live in:
he'd see. People were always glad to lend their

house to a newly-married couple. It was such fun to pop down and see them: it made one feel romantic and jolly. All they need do was to accept the houses in turn: go on honey-mooning for a year! What was he afraid of? Didn't he think they'd be happy enough to want to keep it up? And why not at least try—get engaged, and then see what would happen? Even if she was all wrong, and her plan failed, wouldn't it have been rather nice, just for a month or two, to fancy they were going to be happy? "I've often fancied it all by myself," she concluded; "but fancying it with you would somehow be so awfully different. . . ."

That was how it began: and this lakeside dream was what it had led up to. Fantastically improbable as they had seemed, all her previsions had come true. If there were certain links in the chain that Lansing had never been able to put his hand on, certain arrangements and contrivances that still needed further elucidation, why, he was lazily resolved to clear them up with her some day; and meanwhile it was worth all the past might have cost, and every penalty the future might exact of him, just to be sitting here in the silence and sweetness, her sleeping head on his knee, clasped in his joy as the hushed world was clasped in moonlight.

He stooped down and kissed her. "Wake up," he whispered, "it's bed-time."

III

THEIR month of Como was within a few hours of ending. Till the last moment they had hoped for a reprieve; but the accommodating Streffy had been unable to put the villa at their disposal for a longer time, since he had had the luck to let it for a thumping price to some beastly bounders who insisted on taking possession at the date agreed on.

Lansing, leaving Susy's side at dawn, had gone down to the lake for a last plunge; and swimming homeward through the crystal light he looked up at the garden brimming with flowers, the long low house with the cypress wood above it, and the window behind which his wife still slept. The month had been exquisite, and their happiness as rare, as fantastically complete, as the scene before him. He sank his chin into the sunlit ripples and sighed for sheer content. . . .

It was a bore to be leaving the scene of such complete well-being, but the next stage in their progress promised to be hardly less delightful. Susy was a magician: everything she predicted came true. Houses were being showered on them; on all sides he seemed to see beneficent spirits. winging toward them, laden with everything from a *piano nobile* in Venice to a camp in the Adiron-

dacks. For the present, they had decided on the
former. Other considerations apart, they dared
not risk the expense of a journey across the At-
lantic; so they were heading instead for the
Nelson Vanderlyns' palace on the Giudecca.
They were agreed that, for reasons of expediency,
it might be wise to return to New York for the
coming winter. It would keep them in view, and
probably lead to fresh opportunities; indeed, Susy
already had in mind the convenient flat that she
was sure a migratory cousin (if tactfully handled,
and assured that they would not overwork her
cook) could certainly be induced to lend them.
Meanwhile the need of making plans was still remote; and if there was one art in which young
Lansing's twenty-eight years of existence had
perfected him it was that of living completely and
unconcernedly in the present. . . .

If of late he had tried to look into the future
more insistently than was his habit, it was only
because of Susy. He had meant, when they
married, to be as philosophic for her as for himself; and he knew she would have resented above
everything his regarding their partnership as a
reason for anxious thought. But since they had
been together she had given him glimpses of her
past that made him angrily long to shelter and defend her future. It was intolerable that a spirit
as fine as hers should be ever so little dulled or
diminished by the kind of compromises out of
which their wretched lives were made. For him-

self, he didn't care a hang: he had composed for
his own guidance a rough-and-ready code, a short
set of "mays" and "mustn'ts" which immensely
simplified his course. There were things a fellow
put up with for the sake of certain definite and
otherwise unattainable advantages; there were
other things he wouldn't traffic with at any price.
But for a woman, he began to see, it might be different. The temptations might be greater, the
cost considerably higher, the dividing line between
the "mays" and "mustn'ts" more fluctuating and
less sharply drawn. Susy, thrown on the world
at seventeen, with only a weak wastrel of a father
to define that treacherous line for her, and with
every circumstance soliciting her to overstep it,
seemed to have been preserved chiefly by an in-
nate scorn of most of the objects of human folly.
"Such trash as he went to pieces for," was her
curt comment on her parent's premature demise:
as though she accepted in advance the necessity
of ruining one's self for something, but was resolved to discriminate firmly between what was
worth it and what wasn't.

This philosophy had at first enchanted Lansing;
but now it began to rouse vague fears. The fine
armour of her fastidiousness had preserved her
from the kind of risks she had hitherto been exposed to; but what if others, more subtle, found
a joint in it? Was there, among her delicate discriminations, any equivalent to his own rules?
Might not her taste for the best and rarest be the

very instrument of her undoing; and if something that wasn't "trash" came her way, would she hesitate a second to go to pieces for it?

He was determined to stick to the compact that they should do nothing to interfere with what each referred to as the other's "chance"; but what if, when hers came, he couldn't agree with her in recognizing it? He wanted for her, oh, so passionately, the best; but his conception of that best had so insensibly, so subtly been transformed in the light of their first month together!

His lazy strokes were carrying him slowly shoreward; but the hour was so exquisite that a few yards from the landing he laid hold of the mooring rope of Streffy's boat and floated there, following his dream. . . . It was a bore to be leaving; no doubt that was what made him turn things inside-out so uselessly. Venice would be delicious, of course; but nothing would ever again be as sweet as this. And then they had only a year of security before them; and of that year a month was gone.

Reluctantly he swam ashore, walked up to the house, and pushed open a window of the cool painted drawing-room. Signs of departure were already visible. There were trunks in the hall, tennis rackets on the stairs; on the landing, the cook Giulietta had both arms around a slippery hold-all that refused to let itself be strapped. It all gave him a chill sense of unreality, as if the past month had been an act on the stage, and its setting were being folded away and rolled into the wings to make room for another play in which he and Susy had no part.

By the time he came down again, dressed and hungry, to the terrace where coffee awaited him, he had recovered his usual pleasant sense of security. Susy was there, fresh and gay, a rose in her breast and the sun in her hair: her head was bowed over Bradshaw, but she waved a fond hand across the breakfast things, and presently looked up to say: "Yes, I believe we can just manage it."

"Manage what?"

"To catch the train at Milan—if we start in the motor at ten sharp."

He stared. "The motor? What motor?"

"Why, the new people's—Streffy's tenants. He's never told me their name, and the chauffeur says he can't pronounce it. The chauffeur's is Ottaviano, anyhow; I've been making friends with him. He arrived last night, and he says they're not due at Como till this evening. He simply jumped at the idea of running us over to Milan."

"Good Lord—" said Lansing, when she stopped.

She sprang up from the table with a laugh. "It will be a scramble; but I'll manage it, if you'll go up at once and pitch the last things into your trunk."

"Yes; but look here—have you any idea what it's going to cost?"

She raised her eyebrows gaily. "Why, a good deal less than our railway tickets. Ottaviano's got a sweetheart in Milan, and hasn't seen her for six months. When I found that out I knew he'd be going there anyhow."

It was clever of her, and he laughed. But why was it that he had grown to shrink from even such harmless evidence of her always knowing how to "manage"? "Oh, well," he said to himself, "she's right: the fellow would be sure to be going to Milan."

Upstairs, on the way to his dressing room, he found her in a cloud of finery which her skilful hands were forcibly compressing into a last portmanteau. He had never seen anyone pack as cleverly as Susy: the way she coaxed reluctant things into a trunk was a symbol of the way she fitted discordant facts into her life. "When I'm rich," she often said, "the thing I shall hate most will be to see an idiot maid at my trunks."

As he passed, she glanced over her shoulder, her face pink with the struggle, and drew a cigar-box from the depths. "Dearest, do put a couple of cigars into your pocket as a tip for Ottaviano."

Lansing stared. "Why, what on earth are you doing with Streffy's cigars?"

"Packing them, of course. . . . You don't suppose he meant them for those other people?" She gave him a look of honest wonder.

"I don't know whom he meant them for—but they're not ours. . . ."

She continued to look at him wonderingly. "I don't see what there is to be solemn about. The cigars are not Streffy's either . . . you may be sure he got them out of some bounder. And there's nothing he'd hate more than to have them passed on to another."

"Nonsense. If they're not Streffy's they're much less mine. Hand them over, please, dear."

"Just as you like. But it does seem a waste; and, of course, the other people will never have one of them. . . . The gardener and Giulietta's lover will see to that!"

Lansing looked away from her at the waves of lace and muslin from which she emerged like a rosy Nereid. "How many boxes of them are left?"

"Only four."

"Unpack them, please."

Before she moved there was a pause so full of challenge that Lansing had time for an exasperated sense of the disproportion between his anger and its cause. And this made him still angrier.

She held out a box. "The others are in your suit-case downstairs. It's locked and strapped."

"Give me the key, then."

"We might send them back from Venice, mightn't we? That lock is so nasty: it will take you half an hour."

"Give me the key, please." She gave it.

He went downstairs and battled with the lock, for the allotted half-hour, under the puzzled eyes of Giulietta and the sardonic grin of the chauffeur, who now and then, from the threshold, politely reminded him how long it would take to get to Milan. Finally the key turned, and Lansing, broken-nailed and perspiring, extracted the cigars and stalked with them into the deserted drawing room. The great bunches of golden roses that he and Susy had gathered the day before were dropping their petals on the marble embroidery of the floor, pale camellias floated in the alabaster *tazzas* between the windows, haunting scents of the garden blew in on him with the breeze from the lake. Never had Streffy's little house seemed so like a nest of pleasures. Lansing laid the cigar boxes on a console and ran upstairs to collect his last possessions. When he came down again, his wife, her eyes brilliant with achievement, was seated in their borrowed chariot, the luggage cleverly stowed away, and Giulietta and the gardener kissing her hand and weeping out inconsolable farewells.

"I wonder what she's given *them?*" he thought, as he jumped in beside her and the motor whirled them through the nightingale-thickets to the gate.

IV

CHARLIE STREFFORD'S villa was like a nest in a rose-bush; the Nelson Vanderlyns' palace called for loftier analogies.

Its vastness and splendour seemed, in comparison, oppressive to Susy. Their landing, after dark, at the foot of the great shadowy staircase, their dinner at a dimly-lit table under a ceiling weighed down with Olympians, their chilly evening in a corner of a drawing room where minuets should have been danced before a throne, contrasted with the happy intimacies of Como as their sudden sense of disaccord contrasted with the mutual confidence of the day before.

The journey had been particularly jolly: both Susy and Lansing had had too long a discipline in the art of smoothing things over not to make a special effort to hide from each other the ravages of their first disagreement. But, deep down and invisible, the disagreement remained; and compunction for having been its cause gnawed at Susy's bosom as she sat in her tapestried and vaulted bedroom, brushing her hair before a tarnished mirror.

"I thought I liked grandeur; but this place is really out of scale," she mused, watching the reflection of a pale hand move back and forward in the dim recesses of the mirror.

"And yet," she continued, "Ellie Vanderlyn's hardly half an inch taller than I am; and she certainly isn't a bit more dignified. . . . I wonder if it's because I feel so horribly small to-night that the place seems so horribly big."

She loved luxury: splendid things always made her feel handsome and high ceilings arrogant; she did not remember having ever before been oppressed by the evidences of wealth.

She laid down the brush and leaned her chin on her clasped hands. . . . Even now she could not understand what had made her take the cigars. She had always been alive to the value of her inherited scruples: her reasoned opinions were unusually free, but with regard to the things one couldn't reason about she was oddly tenacious. And yet she had taken Streffy's cigars! She had taken them—yes, that was the point—she had taken them for Nick, because the desire to please him, to make the smallest details of his life easy and agreeable and luxurious, had become her absorbing preoccupation. She had committed, for him, precisely the kind of little baseness she would most have scorned to commit for herself; and, since he hadn't instantly felt the difference, she would never be able to explain it to him.

She stood up with a sigh, shook out her loosened hair, and glanced around the great frescoed room. The maid-servant had said something about the

Signora's having left a letter for her; and there it lay on the writing-table, with her mail and Nick's; a thick envelope addressed in Ellie's childish scrawl, with a glaring "Private" dashed across the corner.

"What on earth can she have to say, when she hates writing so?" Susy mused.

She broke open the envelope, and four or five stamped and sealed letters fell from it. All were addressed, in Ellie's hand, to Nelson Vanderlyn Esqre; and in the corner of each was faintly pencilled a number and a date: one, two, three, four— with a week's interval between the dates.

"Goodness—" gasped Susy, understanding.

She had dropped into an armchair near the table, and for a long time she sat staring at the numbered letters. A sheet of paper covered with Ellie's writing had fluttered out among them, but she let it lie; she knew so well what it would say! She knew all about her friend, of course; except poor old Nelson, who didn't? But she had never imagined that Ellie would dare to use her in this way. It was unbelievable . . . she had never pictured anything so vile. . . . The blood rushed to her face, and she sprang up angrily, half minded to tear the letters in bits and throw them all into the fire.

She heard her husband's knock on the door between their rooms, and swept the dangerous packet under the blotting-book.

"Oh, go away, please, there's a dear," she

called out; "I haven't finished unpacking, and everything's in such a mess." Gathering up Nick's papers and letters, she ran across the room and thrust them through the door. "Here's something to keep you quiet," she laughed, shining in on him an instant from the threshold.

She turned back feeling weak with shame. Ellie's letter lay on the floor: reluctantly she stooped to pick it up, and one by one the expected phrases sprang out at her.

"One good turn deserves another. . . . Of course you and Nick are welcome to stay all summer. . . . There won't be a particle of expense for you—the servants have orders. . . . If you'll just be an angel and post these letters yourself. . . . It's been my only chance for such an age; when we meet I'll explain everything. And in a month at latest I'll be back to fetch Clarissa. . . ."

Susy lifted the letter to the lamp to be sure she had read aright. To fetch Clarissa! Then Ellie's child was here? Here, under the roof with them, left to their care? She read on, raging. "She's so delighted, poor darling, to know you're coming. I've had to sack her beastly governess for impertinence, and if it weren't for you she'd be all alone with a lot of servants I don't much trust. So for pity's sake be good to my child, and forgive me for leaving her. She thinks I've gone to take a cure; and she knows she's not to tell her Daddy that I'm away, because it would only worry him if he thought I was ill. She's perfectly to be

trusted; you'll see what a clever angel she is...."
And then, at the bottom of the page, in a last
slanting postscript: "Susy darling, if you've ever
owed me anything in the way of kindness, you
won't, on your sacred honour, say a word of this
to any one, even to Nick. *And I know I can count
on you to rub out the numbers.*"

Susy sprang up and tossed Mrs. Vanderlyn's
letter into the fire: then she came slowly back to
the chair. There, at her elbow, lay the four fatal
envelopes; and her next affair was to make up her
mind what to do with them.

To destroy them on the spot had seemed, at first
thought, inevitable: it might be saving Ellie as
well as herself. But such a step seemed to Susy
to involve departure on the morrow, and this in
turn involved notifying Ellie, whose letter she had
vainly scanned for an address. Well—perhaps
Clarissa's nurse would know where one could
write to her mother; it was unlikely that even Ellie would go off without assuring some means of
communication with her child. At any rate, there
was nothing to be done that night: nothing but to
work out the details of their flight on the morrow,
and rack her brains to find a substitute for the
hospitality they were rejecting. Susy did not disguise from herself how much she had counted on
the Vanderlyn apartment for the summer: to be
able to do so had singularly simplified the future.
She knew Ellie's largeness of hand, and had been
sure in advance that as long as they were her

guests their only expense would be an occasional present to the servants. And what would the alternative be? She and Lansing, in their endless talks, had so lived themselves into the vision of indolent summer days on the lagoon, of flaming hours on the beach of the Lido, and evenings of music and dreams on their broad balcony above the Giudecca, that the idea of having to renounce these joys, and deprive her Nick of them, filled Susy with a wrath intensified by his having confided in her that when they were quietly settled in Venice he "meant to write." Already nascent in her breast was the fierce resolve of the author's wife to defend her husband's privacy and facilitate his encounters with the Muse. It was abominable, simply abominable, that Ellie Vanderlyn should have drawn her into such a trap!

Well—there was nothing for it but to make a clean breast of the whole thing to Nick. The trivial incident of the cigars—how trivial it now seemed!—showed her the kind of stand he would take, and communicated to her something of his own uncompromising energy. She would tell him the whole story in the morning, and try to find a way out with him: Susy's faith in her power of finding a way out was inexhaustible. But suddenly she remembered the adjuration at the end of Mrs. Vanderlyn's letter: "If you're ever owed me anything in the way of kindness, you won't, on your sacred honour, say a word to Nick. . . ."

It was, of course, exactly what no one had the

right to ask of her: if indeed the word "right"
could be used in any conceivable relation to this
coil of wrongs. But the fact remained that, in the
way of kindness, she did owe much to Ellie; and
that this was the first payment her friend had ever
exacted. She found herself, in fact, in exactly the
same position as when Ursula Gillow, using the
same argument, had appealed to her to give up
Nick Lansing. Yes, Susy reflected; but then Nelson Vanderlyn had been kind to her too; and the
money Ellie had been so kind with was Nelson's.
. . . The queer edifice of Susy's standards tottered on its base—she honestly didn't know where
fairness lay, as between so much that was foul.

The very depth of her perplexity puzzled her.
She had been in "tight places" before; had indeed
been in so few that were not, in one way or another, constricting! As she looked back on her
past it lay before her as a very network of perpetual concessions and contrivings. But never before had she had such a sense of being tripped up,
gagged and pinioned. The little misery of the
cigars still galled her, and now this big humiliation superposed itself on the raw wound. Decidedly, the second month of their honey-moon was
beginning cloudily. . . .

She glanced at the enamelled travelling-clock
on her dressing table—one of the few wedding-
presents she had consented to accept in kind—and
was startled at the lateness of the hour. In a moment Nick would be coming; and an uncomfortable

sensation in her throat warned her that through sheer nervousness and exasperation she might blurt out something ill-advised. The old habit of being always on her guard made her turn once more to the looking-glass. Her face was pale and haggard; and having, by a swift and skilful application of cosmetics, increased its appearance of fatigue, she crossed the room and softly opened her husband's door.

He too sat by a lamp, reading a letter which he put aside as she entered. His face was grave, and she said to herself that he was certainly still thinking about the cigars.

"I'm very tired, dearest, and my head aches so horribly that I've come to bid you good-night." Bending over the back of his chair, she laid her arms on his shoulders. He lifted his hands to clasp hers, but, as he threw his head back to smile up at her she noticed that his look was still serious, almost remote. It was as if, for the first time, a faint veil hung between his eyes and hers.

"I'm so sorry: it's been a long day for you," he said absently, pressing his lips to her hands.

She felt the dreaded twitch in her throat.

"Nick!" she burst out, tightening her embrace, "before I go, you've got to swear to me on your honour that you *know* I should never have taken those cigars for myself!"

For a moment he stared at her, and she stared back at him with equal gravity; then the same irresistible mirth welled up in both, and Susy's compunctions were swept away on a gale of laughter.

When she woke the next morning the sun was pouring in between her curtains of old brocade, and its refraction from the ripples of the Canal was drawing a network of golden scales across the vaulted ceiling. The maid had just placed a tray on a slim marquetry table near the bed, and over the edge of the tray Susy discovered the small serious face of Clarissa Vanderlyn. At the sight of the little girl all her dormant qualms awoke.

Clarissa was just eight, and small for her age: her little round chin was barely on a level with the tea-service, and her clear brown eyes gazed at Susy between the ribs of the toast-rack and the single tea-rose in an old Murano glass. Susy had not seen her for two years, and she seemed, in the interval, to have passed from a thoughtful infancy to complete ripeness of feminine experience. She was looking with approval at her mother's guest.

"I'm so glad you've come," she said in a small sweet voice. "I like you so very much. I know I'm not to be often with you; but at least you'll have an eye on me, won't you?"

"An eye on you! I shall never want to have it off you, if you say such nice things to me!" Susy laughed, leaning from her pillows to draw the little girl up to her side.

Clarissa smiled and settled herself down comfortably on the silken bedspread. "Oh, I know

I'm not to be always about, because you're just married; but *could* you see to it that I have my meals regularly?"

"Why, you poor darling! Don't you always?"

"Not when mother's away on these cures. The servants don't always obey me: you see I'm so little for my age. In a few years, of course, they'll have to—even if I don't grow much," she added judiciously. She put out her hand and touched the string of pearls about Susy's throat. "They're small, but they're very good. I suppose you don't take the others when you travel?"

"The others? Bless you! I haven't any others —and never shall have, probably."

"No other pearls?"

"No other jewels at all."

Clarissa stared. "Is that *really* true?" she asked, as if in the presence of the unprecedented.

"Awfully true," Susy confessed. "But I think I can make the servants obey me all the same."

This point seemed to have lost its interest for Clarissa, who was still gravely scrutinizing her companion. After a while she brought forth another question.

"Did you have to give up all your jewels when you were divorced?"

"Divorced—?" Susy threw her head back against the pillows and laughed. "Why, what are you thinking of? Don't you remember that I wasn't even married the last time you saw me?"

"Yes; I do. But that was two years ago." The

little girl wound her arms about Susy's neck and leaned against her caressingly. "Are you going to be soon, then? I'll promise not to tell if you don't want me to."

"Going to be divorced? Of course not! What in the world made you think so?"

"Because you look so awfully happy," said Clarissa Vanderlyn simply.

V

IT was a trifling enough sign, but it had remained in Susy's mind: that first morning in Venice Nick had gone out without first coming in to see her. She had stayed in bed late, chatting with Clarissa, and expecting to see the door open and her husband appear; and when the child left, and she had jumped up and looked into Nick's room, she found it empty, and a line on his dressing table informed her that he had gone out to send a telegram.

It was lover-like, and even boyish, of him to think it necessary to explain his absence; but why, had he not simply come in and told her? She instinctively connected the little fact with the shade of preoccupation she had noticed on his face the night before, when she had gone to his room and found him absorbed in a letter; and while she dressed she had continued to wonder what was in the letter, and whether the telegram he had hurried out to send was an answer to it.

She had never found out. When he reappeared, handsome and happy as the morning, he proffered no explanation; and it was part of her life-long policy not to put uncalled-for questions. It was not only that her jealous regard for her own freedom was matched by an equal respect for that of others; she had steered too long among the social reefs and shoals not to know how narrow is the passage that leads to peace of mind, and she was determined to keep her little craft in mid-channel. But the incident had lodged itself in her memory, acquiring a sort of symbolic significance, as of a turning-point in her relations with her husband. Not that these were less happy, but that she now beheld them, as she had always formerly beheld such joys, as an unstable islet in a sea of storms. Her present bliss was as complete as ever, but it was ringed by the perpetual menace of all she knew she was hiding from Nick, and of all she suspected him of hiding from her. . . .

She was thinking of these things one afternoon about three weeks after their arrival in Venice. It was near sunset, and she sat alone on the balcony, watching the cross-lights on the water weave their pattern above the flushed reflection of old palace-basements. She was almost always alone at that hour. Nick had taken to writing in the afternoons—he had been as good as his word, and so, apparently, had the Muse—and it was his habit to join his wife only at sunset, for a late row on the lagoon. She had taken Clarissa, as usual, to the Giardino Pubblico, where that obliging child had politely but indifferently "played"—Clarissa joined in the diversions of her age as if conforming to an obsolete tradition—and had brought her back for a music lesson, echoes of which now drifted down from a distant window.

Susy had come to be extremely thankful for

Clarissa. But for the little girl, her pride in her husband's industry might have been tinged with a faint sense of being at times left out and forgotten; and as Nick's industry was the completest justification for their being where they were, and for her having done what she had, she was grateful to Clarissa for helping her to feel less alone. Clarissa, indeed, represented the other half of her justification: it was as much on the child's account as on Nick's that Susy had held her tongue, remained in Venice, and slipped out once a week to post one of Ellie's numbered letters. A day's experience of the Palazzo Vanderlyn had convinced Susy of the impossibility of deserting Clarissa. Long experience had shown her that the most crowded households often contain the loneliest nurseries, and that the rich child is exposed to evils unknown to less pampered infancy; but hitherto such things had merely been to her one of the uglier bits in the big muddled pattern of life. Now she found herself feeling where before she had only judged: her precarious bliss came to her charged with a new weight of pity.

She was thinking of these things, and of the approaching date of Ellie Vanderlyn's return, and of the searching truths she was storing up for that lady's private ear, when she noticed a gondola turning its prow toward the steps below the balcony. She leaned over, and a tall gentleman in shabby clothes, glancing up at her as he jumped out, waved a mouldy Panama in joyful greeting.

"Streffy!" she exclaimed as joyfully; and she was half-way down the stairs when he ran up them followed by his luggage-laden boatman.

"It's all right, I suppose?—Ellie said I might come," he explained in a shrill cheerful voice; "and I'm to have my same green room with the parrot-panels, because its furniture is already so frightfully stained with my hair-wash."

Susy was beaming on him with the deep sense of satisfaction which his presence always produced in his friends. There was no one in the world, they all agreed, half as ugly and untidy and delightful as Streffy; no one who combined such outspoken selfishness with such imperturbable good humour; no one who knew so well how to make you believe he was being charming to you when it was you who were being charming to him.

In addition to these seductions, of which none estimated the value more accurately than their possessor, Strefford had for Susy another attraction of which he was probably unconscious. It was that of being the one rooted and stable being among the fluid and shifting figures that composed her world. Susy had always lived among people so denationalized that those one took for Russians generally turned out to be American, and those one was inclined to ascribe to New York proved to have originated in Rome or Bucharest. These cosmopolitan people, who, in countries not their own, lived in houses as big as hotels, or in hotels where the guests were as international as the waiters, had inter-married, inter-loved and inter-divorced each other over the whole face of Europe, and according to every code that attempts to regulate human ties. Strefford, too, had his home in this world, but only one of his homes. The other, the one he spoke of, and probably thought of, least often, was a great dull English country-house in a northern county, where a life as monotonous and self-contained as his own was chequered and dispersed had gone on for generation after generation; and it was the sense of that house, and of all it typified even to his vagrancy and irreverence, which, coming out now and then in his talk, or in his attitude toward something or somebody, gave him a firmer outline and a steadier footing than the other marionettes in the dance. Superficially so like them all, and so eager to outdo them in detachment and adaptability, ridiculing the prejudices he had shaken off, and the people to whom he belonged, he still kept, under his easy pliancy, the skeleton of old faiths and old fashions. "He talks every language as well as the rest of us," Susy had once said of him, "but at least he talks one language better than the others"; and Strefford, told of the remark, had laughed, called her an idiot, and been pleased.

As he shambled up the stairs with her, arm in arm, she was thinking of this quality with a new appreciation of its value. Even she and Lansing, in spite of their unmixed Americanism, their substantial background of old-fashioned cousinships

in New York and Philadelphia, were as mentally
detached, as universally at home, as touts at an
International Exhibition. If they were usually
recognized as Americans it was only because they
spoke French so well, and because Nick was too
fair to be "foreign," and too sharp-featured to be
English. But Charlie Strefford was English with
all the strength of an inveterate habit; and something in Susy was slowly waking to a sense of the
beauty of habit.

Lounging on the balcony, whither he had followed her without pausing to remove the stains of
travel, Strefford showed himself immensely interested in the last chapter of her history, greatly
pleased at its having been enacted under his roof,
and hugely and flippantly amused at the firmness
with which she refused to let him see Nick till the
latter's daily task was over.

"Writing? Rot! What's he writing? He's
breaking you in, my dear; that's what he's doing:
establishing an alibi. What'll you bet he's just
sitting there smoking and reading *Le Rire?* Let's
go and see."

But Susy was firm. "He's read me his first
chapter: it's wonderful. It's a philosophic romance—rather like *Marius,* you know."

"Oh, yes—I *do!*" said Strefford, with a laugh
that she thought idiotic.

She flushed up like a child. "You're stupid,
Streffy. You forget that Nick and I don't need
alibis. We've got rid of all that hyprocrisy by

agreeing that each will give the other a hand up when either of us wants a change. We've not married to spy and lie, and nag each other; we've formed a partnership for our mutual advantage."

"I see; that's capital. But how can you be sure that, when Nick wants a change, you'll consider it for his advantage to have one?"

It was the point that had always secretly tormented Susy; she often wondered if it equally tormented Nick.

"I hope I shall have enough common sense—" she began.

"Oh, of course: common sense is what you're both bound to base your argument on, whichever way you argue."

This flash of insight disconcerted her, and she said, a little irritably: "What should *you* do then, if you married?—Hush, Streffy! I forbid you to shout like that—all the gondolas are stopping to look!"

"How can I help it?" He rocked backward and forward in his chair. " 'If you marry,' she says: 'Streffy, what have you decided to do if you suddenly become a raving maniac?' "

"I said no such thing. If your uncle and your cousin died, you'd marry to-morrow; you know you would."

"Oh, now you're talking business." He folded his long arms and leaned over the balcony, looking down at the dusky ripples streaked with fire. "In that case I should say: 'Susan, my dear—Susan—

now that by the merciful intervention of Providence you have become Countess of Altringham in the peerage of Great Britain, and Baroness Dunsterville and d'Amblay in the peerages of Ireland and Scotland, I'll thank you to remember that you are a member of one of the most ancient houses in the United Kingdom—and not to get found out.' "

Susy laughed. "We know what those warnings mean! I pity my namesake."

He swung about and gave her a quick look out of his small ugly twinkling eyes. "Is there any other woman in the world named Susan?"

"I hope so, if the name's an essential. Even if Nick chucks me, don't count on *me* to carry out that programme. I've seen it in practice too often."

"Oh, well: as far as I know, everybody's in perfect health at Altringham." He fumbled in his pocket and drew out a fountain-pen, a handkerchief over which it had leaked, and a packet of dishevelled cigarettes. Lighting one, and restoring the other objects to his pocket, he continued calmly: "Tell me—how did you manage to smooth things over with the Gillows? Ursula was running amuck when I was in Newport last Summer; it was just when people were beginning to say that you were going to marry Nick. I was afraid she'd put a spoke in your wheel; and I hear she put a big cheque in your hand instead."

Susy was silent. From the first moment of

Strefford's appearance she had known that in the course of time he would put that question. He was as inquisitive as a monkey, and when he had made up his mind to find out anything it was useless to try to divert his attention. After a moment's hesitation she said: "I flirted with Fred. It was a bore—but he was very decent."

"He would be—poor Fred. And you got Ursula thoroughly frightened?"

"Well—enough. And then luckily that young Nerone Altineri turned up from Rome: he went over to New York to look for a job as an engineer, and Ursula made Fred put him in their iron works." She paused again, and then added abruptly: "Streffy! If you knew how I hate that kind of thing. I'd rather have Nick come in now and tell me frankly, as I know he would, that he's going off with—"

"With Coral Hicks?" Strefford suggested.

She laughed. "Poor Coral Hicks! What on earth made you think of the Hickses?"

"Because I caught a glimpse of them the other day at Capri. They're cruising about: they said they were coming in here."

"What a nuisance! I do hope they won't find us out. They were awfully kind to Nick when he went to India with them, and they're so simple-minded that they would expect him to be glad to see them."

Strefford aimed his cigarette-end at a tourist in a puggaree who was gazing up from his guidebook at the palace. "Ah," he murmured with satisfaction, seeing the shot take effect; then he added: "Coral Hicks is growing up rather pretty."

"Oh, Streff—you're dreaming! That lump of a girl with spectacles and thick ankles! Poor Mrs. Hicks used to say to Nick: 'When Mr. Hicks and I had Coral educated we presumed culture was in greater demand in Europe than it appears to be.'"

"Well, you'll see: that girl's education won't interfere with her, once she's started. So then: if Nick came in and told you he was going off—"

"I should be so thankful if it was with a fright like Coral! But you know," she added with a smile, "we've agreed that it's not to happen for a year."

VI

SUSY found Strefford, after his first burst of
nonsense, unusually kind and responsive. The
interest he showed in her future and Nick's
seemed to proceed not so much from his habitual
spirit of scientific curiosity as from simple friendliness. He was privileged to see Nick's first chapter, of which he formed so favourable an impression that he spoke sternly to Susy on the importance of respecting her husband's working hours;
and he even carried his general benevolence to the
length of showing a fatherly interest in Clarissa
Vanderlyn. He was always charming to children,
but fitfully and warily, with an eye on his independence, and on the possibility of being suddenly
bored by them; Susy had never seen him abandon
these precautions so completely as he did with
Clarissa.

"Poor little devil! Who looks after her when
you and Nick are off together? Do you mean to
tell me Ellie sacked the governess and went away
without having anyone to take her place?"

"I think she expected me to do it," said Susy
with a touch of asperity. There were moments
when her duty to Clarissa weighed on her somewhat heavily; whenever she went off alone with

Nick she was pursued by the vision of a little figure waving wistful farewells from the balcony.

"Ah, that's like Ellie: you might have known
she'd get an equivalent when she lent you all this.
But I don't believe she thought you'd be so conscientious about it."

Susy considered. "I don't suppose she did;
and perhaps I shouldn't have been, a year ago.
But you see"—she hesitated—"Nick's so awfully
good: it's made me look at a lot of things differently. . . ."

"Oh, hang Nick's goodness! It's happiness
that's done it, my dear. You're just one of the
people with whom it happens to agree."

Susy, leaning back, scrutinized between her
lashes his crooked ironic face.

"What is it that's agreeing with you, Streffy?
I've never seen you so human. You must be getting an outrageous price for the villa."

Strefford laughed and clapped his hand on his
breast-pocket. "I should be an ass not to: I've
got a wire here saying they must have it for another month at any price."

"What luck! I'm so glad. Who are they, by
the way?"

He drew himself up out of the long chair in
which he was disjointedly lounging, and looked
down at her with, a smile. "Another couple of
love-sick idiots like you and Nick. . . . I say, before I spend it all let's go out and buy something
ripping for Clarissa."

The days passed so quickly and radiantly that, but for her concern for Clarissa, Susy would hardly have been conscious of her hostess's protracted absence. Mrs. Vanderlyn had said: "Four weeks at the latest," and the four weeks were over, and she had neither arrived nor written to explain her non-appearance. She had, in fact, given no sign of life since her departure, save in the shape of a post-card which had reached Clarissa the day after the Lansings' arrival, and in which Mrs. Vanderlyn instructed her child to be awfully good, and not to forget to feed the mongoose. Susy noticed that this missive had been posted in Milan.

She communicated her apprehensions to Strefford. "I don't trust that green-eyed nurse. She's forever with the younger gondolier; and Clarissa's so awfully sharp. I don't see why Ellie hasn't come: she was due last Monday."

Her companion laughed, and something in the sound of his laugh suggested that he probably knew as much of Ellie's movements as she did, if not more. The sense of disgust which the subject always roused in her made her look away quickly from his tolerant smile. She would have given the world, at that moment, to have been free to tell Nick what she had learned on the night of their arrival, and then to have gone away with him, no matter where. But there was Clarissa—!

To fortify herself against the temptation, she resolutely fixed her thoughts on her husband. Of Nick's beatitude there could be no doubt. He

adored her, he revelled in Venice, he rejoiced in
his work; and concerning the quality of that work
her judgment was as confident as her heart. She
still doubted if he would ever earn a living by what
he wrote, but she no longer doubted that he would
write something remarkable. The mere fact that
he was engaged on a philosophic romance, and not
a mere novel, seemed the proof of an intrinsic
superiority. And if she had mistrusted her impartiality Strefford's approval would have reassured her. Among their friends Strefford passed
as an authority on such matters: in summing him
up his eulogists always added: "And you know
he writes." As a matter of fact, the paying public
had remained cold to his few published pages; but
he lived among the kind of people who confuse
taste with talent, and are impressed by the most
artless attempts at literary expression; and
though he affected to disdain their judgment, and
his own efforts, Susy knew he was not sorry to
have it said of him: "Oh, if only, Streffy had
chosen—!"

Strefford's approval of the philosophic romance convinced her that it had been worth while
staying in Venice for Nick's sake; and if only
Ellie would come back, and carry off Clarissa to
St. Moritz or Deauville, the disagreeable episode
on which their happiness was based would vanish
like a cloud, and leave them to complete enjoyment.

Ellie did not come; but the Mortimer Hickses

did, and Nick Lansing was assailed by the scruples
his wife had foreseen. Strefford, coming back one
evening from the Lido, reported having recognized
the huge outline of the *Ibis* among the pleasure
craft of the outer harbour; and the very next evening, as the guests of Palazzo Vanderlyn were
sipping their ices at Florian's, the Hickses loomed
up across the Piazza.

Susy pleaded in vain with her husband in defence of his privacy. "Remember you're here to
write, dearest; it's your duty not to let any one
interfere with that. Why shouldn't we tell them
we're just leaving?"

"Because it's no use: we're sure to be always
meeting them. And besides, I'll be hanged if I'm
going to shirk the Hickses. I spent five whole
months on the *Ibis,* and if they bored me occasionally, India didn't."

"We'll make them take us to Aquileia anyhow,"
said Strefford philosophically; and the next moment the Hickses were bearing down on the de-
fenceless trio.

They presented a formidable front, not only because of their mere physical bulk—Mr. and Mrs.
Hicks were equally and majestically three-dimen-
sional—but because they never moved abroad
without the escort of two private secretaries (one
for the foreign languages), Mr. Hicks's doctor, a
maiden lady known as Eldoradder Tooker, who
was Mrs. Hicks's cousin and stenographer, and
finally their daughter, Coral Hicks.

Coral Hicks, when Susy had last encountered the party, had been a fat spectacled school-girl, always lagging behind her parents, with a reluctant poodle in her wake. Now the poodle had gone, and his mistress led the procession. The fat school-girl had changed into a young lady of compact if not graceful outline; a long-handled eyeglass had replaced the spectacles, and through it, instead of a sullen glare, Miss Coral Hicks projected on the world a glance at once confident and critical. She looked so strong and so assured that Susy, taking her measure in a flash, saw that her position at the head of the procession was not fortuitous, and murmured inwardly: "Thank goodness she's not pretty too!"

If she was not pretty, she was well-dressed; and if she was overeducated, she seemed capable, as Strefford had suggested, of carrying off even this crowning disadvantage. At any rate, she was above disguising it; and before the whole party had been seated five minutes in front of a fresh supply of ices (with Eldorada and the secretaries at a table slightly in the background) she had taken up with Nick the question of exploration in Mesopotamia.

"Queer child, Coral," he said to Susy that night as they smoked a last cigarette on their balcony. "She told me this afternoon that she'd remembered lots of things she heard me say in India. I thought at the time that she cared only for caramels and picture-puzzles, but it seems she was listening to everything, and reading all the books she could lay her hands on; and she got so bitten with Oriental archæology that she took a course last year at Bryn Mawr. She means to go to Bagdad next spring, and back by the Persian plateau and Turkestan.''

Susy laughed luxuriously: she was sitting with her hand in Nick's, while the late moon—theirs again—rounded its orange-coloured glory above the belfry of San Giorgio.

''Poor Coral! How dreary—'' Susy murmured.

''Dreary? Why? A trip like that is about as well worth doing as anything I know.''

''Oh, I meant: dreary to do it without you or me,'' she laughed, getting up lazily to go indoors. A broad band of moonlight, dividing her room into two shadowy halves, lay on the painted Venetian bed with its folded-back sheet, its old damask coverlet and lace-edged pillows. She felt the warmth of Nick's enfolding arm and lifted her face to his.

The Hickses retained the most tender memory of Nick's sojourn on the *Ibis,* and Susy, moved by their artless pleasure in meeting him again, was glad he had not followed her advice and tried to elude them. She had always admired Strefford's ruthless talent for using and discarding the human material in his path, but now she began to hope that Nick would not remember her suggestion that he should mete out that measure to the Hickses. Even if it had been less pleasant to have a big

yacht at their door during the long golden days
and the nights of silver fire, the Hickses' admiration for Nick would have made Susy suffer them
gladly. She even began to be aware of a growing
liking for them, a liking inspired by the very
characteristics that would once have provoked her
disapproval. Susy had had plenty of training in
liking common people with big purses; in such
cases her stock of allowances and extenuations
was inexhaustible. But they had to be successful
common people; and the trouble was that the
Hickses, judged by her standards, were failures.
It was not only that they were ridiculous; so,
heaven knew, were many of their rivals. But the
Hickses were both ridiculous and unsuccessful.
They had consistently resisted the efforts of the
experienced advisers who had first descried them
on the horizon and tried to help them upward.
They were always taking up the wrong people,
giving the wrong kind of party, and spending millions on things that nobody who mattered cared
about. They all believed passionately in "movements" and "causes" and "ideals," and were always attended by the exponents of their latest be-
liefs, always asking you to hear lectures by haggard women in peplums, and having their portraits painted by wild people who never turned
out to be the fashion.

All this would formerly have increased Susy's
contempt; now she found herself liking the
Hickses most for their failings. She was touched

by their simple good faith, their isolation in the midst of all their queer apostles and parasites, their way of drifting about an alien and indifferent world in a compactly clinging group of which Eldorada Tooker, the doctor and the two secretaries formed the outer fringe, and by their view of themselves as a kind of collective re-incarnation of some past state of princely culture, symbolised for Mrs. Hicks in what she called "the court of the Renaissance." Eldorada, of course, was their chief prophetess; but even the intensely "bright" and modern young secretaries, Mr. Beck and Mr. Buttles, showed a touching tendency to share her view, and spoke of Mr. Hicks as "promoting art," in the spirit of Pandolfino celebrating the munificence of the Medicis.

"I'm getting really fond of the Hickses; I believe I should be nice to them even if they were staying at Danieli's," Susy said to Strefford.

"And even if *you* owned the yacht?" he answered; and for once his banter struck her as beside the point.

The *Ibis* carried them, during the endless June days, far and wide along the enchanted shores; they roamed among the Euganeans, they saw Aquileia and Pomposa and Ravenna. Their hosts would gladly have taken them farther, across the Adriatic and on into the golden network of the Aegean; but Susy resisted this infraction of Nick's rules, and he himself preferred to stick to his task. Only now he wrote in the early mornings, so that on most days they could set out before noon and steam back late to the low fringe of lights on the lagoon. His work continued to progress, and as page was added to page Susy obscurely but surely perceived that each one corresponded with a hidden secretion of energy, the gradual forming within him of something that might eventually alter both their lives. In what sense she could not conjecture: she merely felt that the fact of his having chosen a job and stuck to it, if only through a few rosy summer weeks, had already given him a new way of saying "Yes" and "No."

VII

OF some new ferment at work in him Nick
Lansing himself was equally aware. He was
a better judge of the book he was trying to write
than either Susy or Strefford; he knew its weak-
nesses, its treacheries, its tendency to slip through
his fingers just as he thought his grasp tightest;
but he knew also that at the very moment when
it seemed to have failed him it would suddenly be
back, beating its loud wings in his face.

He had no delusions as to its commercial value,
and had winced more than he triumphed when
Susy produced her allusion to *Marius*. His book
was to be called *The Pageant of Alexander*. His
imagination had been enchanted by the idea of
picturing the young conqueror's advance through
the fabulous landscapes of Asia: he liked writing
descriptions, and vaguely felt that under the guise
of fiction he could develop his theory of Oriental
influences in Western art at the expense of less
learning than if he had tried to put his ideas into
an essay. He knew enough of his subject to know
that he did not know enough to write about it; but
he consoled himself by remembering that *Wilhelm
Meister* has survived many weighty volumes on
æsthetics; and between his moments of self-dis-

trust he took himself at Susy's valuation, and found an unmixed joy in his task.

Never—no, never!—had he been so boundlessly, so confidently happy. His hack-work had given him the habit of application, and now habit wore the glow of inspiration. His previous literary ventures had been timid and tentative: if this one was growing and strengthening on his hands, it must be because the conditions were so different. He was at ease, he was secure, he was satisfied; and he had also, for the first time since his early youth, before his mother's death, the sense of having some one to look after, some one who was his own particular care, and to whom he was answerable for himself and his actions, as he had never felt himself answerable to the hurried and indifferent people among whom he had chosen to live.

Susy had the same standards as these people: she spoke their language, though she understood others, she required their pleasures if she did not revere their gods. But from the moment that she had become his property he had built up in himself a conception of her answering to some deepseated need of veneration. She was his, he had chosen her, she had taken her place in the long line of Lansing women who had been loved, honoured, and probably deceived, by bygone Lansing men. He didn't pretend to understand the logic of it; but the fact that she was his wife gave purpose and continuity to his scattered impulses, and a mysterious glow of consecration to his task.

Once or twice, in the first days of his marriage, he had asked himself with a slight shiver what would happen if Susy should begin to bore him. The thing had happened to him with other women as to whom his first emotions had not differed in intensity from those she inspired. The part he had played in his previous love-affairs might indeed have been summed up in the memorable line: "I am the hunter and the prey," for he had invariably ceased to be the first only to regard himself as the second. This experience had never ceased to cause him the liveliest pain, since his sympathy for his pursuer was only less keen than his commiseration for himself; but as he was always a little sorrier for himself, he had always ended by distancing the pursuer.

All these pre-natal experiences now seemed utterly inapplicable to the new man he had become. He could not imagine being bored by Susy—or trying to escape from her if he were. He could not think of her as an enemy, or even as an accomplice, since accomplices are potential enemies: she was some one with whom, by some unheard-of miracle, joys above the joys of friendship were to be tasted, but who, even through these fleeting ecstasies, remained simply and securely his friend.

These new feelings did not affect his general attitude toward life: they merely confirmed his faith in its ultimate "jolliness." Never had he more thoroughly enjoyed the things he had always enjoyed. A good dinner had never been as good

to him, a beautiful sunset as beautiful; he still
rejoiced in the fact that he appreciated both with
an equal acuity. He was as proud as ever of
Susy's cleverness and freedom from prejudice:
she couldn't be too "modern" for him now that
she was his. He shared to the full her passionate
enjoyment of the present, and all her feverish
eagerness to make it last. He knew when she was
thinking of ways of extending their golden opportunity, and he secretly thought with her, wondering what new means they could devise. He was
thankful that Ellie Vanderlyn was still absent, and
began to hope they might have the palace to themselves for the remainder of the summer. If they
did, he would have time to finish his book, and
Susy to lay up a little interest on their wedding
cheques; and thus their enchanted year might conceivably be prolonged to two.

Late as the season was, their presence and
Strefford's in Venice had already drawn thither
several wandering members of their set. It was
characteristic of these indifferent but agglutina-
tive people that they could never remain long
parted from each other without a dim sense of uneasiness. Lansing was familiar with the feeling.
He had known slight twinges of it himself, and
had often ministered to its qualms in others. It
was hardly stronger than the faint gnawing which
recalls the tea-hour to one who has lunched well
and is sure of dining as abundantly; but it gave a
purpose to the purposeless, and helped many hesi-

tating spirits over the annual difficulty of deciding
between Deauville and St. Moritz, Biarritz and
Capri.

Nick was not surprised to learn that it was becoming the fashion, that summer, to pop down to
Venice and take a look at the Lansings. Streffy
had set the example, and Streffy's example was
always followed. And then Susy's marriage was
still a subject of sympathetic speculation. People
knew the story of the wedding cheques, and were
interested in seeing how long they could be made
to last. It was going to be the thing, that year,
to help prolong the honey-moon by pressing houses
on the adventurous couple. Before June was over
a band of friends were basking with the Lansings
on the Lido.

Nick found himself unexpectedly disturbed by
their arrival. To avoid comment and banter he
put his book aside and forbade Susy to speak of
it, explaining to her that he needed an interval of
rest. His wife instantly and exaggeratedly
adopted this view, guarding him from the temptation to work as jealously as she had discouraged him from idling; and he was careful not to
let her find out that the change in his habits coincided with his having reached a difficult point in
his book. But though he was not sorry to stop
writing he found himself unexpectedly oppressed
by the weight of his leisure. For the first time
communal dawdling had lost its charm for him;
not because his fellow dawdlers were less con-

genial than of old, but because in the interval he had known something so immeasurably better. He had always felt himself to be the superior of his habitual associates, but now the advantage was too great: really, in a sense, it was hardly fair to them.

He had flattered himself that Susy would share this feeling; but he perceived with annoyance that the arrival of their friends heightened her animation. It was as if the inward glow which had given her a new beauty were now refracted upon her by the presence of the very people they had come to Venice to avoid.

Lansing was vaguely irritated; and when he asked her how she liked being with their old crowd again his irritation was increased by her answering with a laugh that she only hoped the poor dears didn't see too plainly how they bored her. The patent insincerity of the reply was a shock to Lansing. He knew that Susy was not really bored, and he understood that she had simply guessed his feelings and instinctively adopted them: that henceforth she was always going to think as he thought. To confirm this fear he said carelessly: "Oh, all the same, it's rather jolly knocking about with them again for a bit;" and she answered at once, and with equal conviction: "Yes, isn't it? The old darlings—all the same!"

A fear of the future again laid its cold touch on Lansing. Susy's independence and self-suf- ficiency had been among her chief attractions; if she were to turn into an echo their delicious duet ran the risk of becoming the dullest of monologues. He forgot that five minutes earlier he had resented her being glad to see their friends, and for a moment he found himself leaning dizzily over that insoluble riddle of the sentimental life: that to be differed with is exasperating, and to be agreed with monotonous.

Once more he began to wonder if he were not fundamentally unfitted for the married state; and was saved from despair only by remembering that Susy's subjection to his moods was not likely to last. But even then it never occurred to him to reflect that his apprehensions were superfluous, since their tie was avowedly a temporary one. Of the special understanding on which their marriage had been based not a trace remained in his thoughts of her; the idea that he or she might ever renounce each other for their mutual good had long since dwindled to the ghost of an old joke.

It was borne in on him, after a week or two of unbroken sociability, that of all his old friends it was the Mortimer Hickses who bored him the least. The Hickses had left the *Ibis* for an apartment in a vast dilapidated palace near the Canareggio. They had hired the apartment from a painter (one of their newest discoveries), and they put up philosophically with the absence of modern conveniences in order to secure the inestimable advantage of "atmosphere." In this privileged air they gathered about them their usual mixed company of quiet studious people and noisy exponents of new theories, themselves totally unconscious of the disparity between their different guests, and beamingly convinced that at last they were seated at the source of wisdom.

In old days Lansing would have got half an hour's amusement, followed by a long evening of boredom, from the sight of Mrs. Hicks, vast and jewelled, seated between a quiet-looking professor of archæology and a large-browed composer, or the high priest of a new dance-step, while Mr. Hicks, beaming above his vast white waistcoat, saw to it that the champagne flowed more abundantly than the talk, and the bright young secretaries industriously "kept up" with the dizzy cross-current of prophecy and erudition. But a change had come over Lansing. Hitherto it was in contrast to his own friends that the Hickses had seemed most insufferable; now it was as an escape from these same friends that they had become not only sympathetic but even interesting. It was something, after all, to be with people who did not regard Venice simply as affording exceptional opportunities for bathing and adultery, but who were reverently if confusedly aware that they were in the presence of something unique and ineffable, and determined to make the utmost of their privilege.

"After all," he said to himself one evening, as his eyes wandered, with somewhat of a convalescent's simple joy, from one to another of their large confiding faces, "after all, they've got a religion. . . ." The phrase struck him, in the moment of using it, as indicating a new element in his own state of mind, and as being, in fact, the key to his new feeling about the Hickses Their muddled ardour for great things was related to his own new view of the universe: the people who felt, however dimly, the wonder and weight of life must ever after be nearer to him than those to whom it was estimated solely by one's balance at the bank. He supposed, on reflexion, that that was what he meant when he thought of the Hickses as having "a religion" . . . .

A few days later, his well-being was unexpectedly disturbed by the arrival of Fred Gillow. Lansing had always felt a tolerant liking for Gillow, a large smiling silent young man with an intense and serious desire to miss nothing attainable by one of his fortune and standing. What use he made of his experiences, Lansing, who had always gone into his own modest adventures rather thoroughly, had never been able to guess; but he had always suspected the prodigal Fred of being no more than a well-disguised looker-on. Now for the first time he began to view him with another eye. The Gillows were, in fact, the one uneasy point in Nick's conscience. He and Susy, from the first, had talked of them less than of any other members of their group: they had tacitly avoided the name from the day on which Susy had come to Lansing's lodgings to say that Ursula Gillow had asked her to renounce him, till that other day, just before their marriage, when she had met him with the rapturous cry: "Here's our first wedding present! Such a thumping big cheque from Fred and Ursula!"

Plenty of sympathizing people were ready, Lansing knew, to tell him just what had happened in the interval between those two dates; but he had taken care not to ask. He had even affected an initiation so complete that the friends who burned to enlighten him were discouraged by his so obviously knowing more than they; and gradually he had worked himself around to their view, and had taken it for granted that he really did.

Now he perceived that he knew nothing at all, and that the "Hullo, old Fred!" with which Susy hailed Gillow's arrival might be either the usual tribal welcome—since they were all "old," and all nick-named, in their private jargon—or a greeting that concealed inscrutable depths of complicity.

Susy was visibly glad to see Gillow; but she was glad of everything just then, and so glad to show her gladness! The fact disarmed her husband and made him ashamed of his uneasiness. "You ought to have thought this all out sooner, or else you ought to chuck thinking of it at all," was the sound but ineffectual advice he gave himself on the day after Gillow's arrival; and immediately set to work to rethink the whole matter.

Fred Gillow showed no consciousness of disturbing any one's peace of mind. Day after day he sprawled for hours on the Lido sands, his arms folded under his head, listening to Streffy's nonsense and watching Susy between sleepy lids; but he betrayed no desire to see her alone, or to draw her into talk apart from the others. More than ever he seemed content to be the gratified spectator of a costly show got up for his private entertainment. It was not until he heard her, one morning, grumble a little at the increasing heat and the menace of mosquitoes, that he said, quite as if they had talked the matter over long before, and finally settled it: "The moor will be ready any time after the first of August."

Nick fancied that Susy coloured a little, and drew herself up more defiantly than usual as she sent a pebble skimming across the dying ripples at their feet.

"You'll be a lot cooler in Scotland," Fred added, with what, for him, was an unusual effort at explicitness.

"Oh, shall we?" she retorted gaily; and added with an air of mystery and importance, pivoting about on her high heels: "Nick's got work to do here. It will probably keep us all summer."

"Work? Rot! You'll die of the smells." Gillow stared perplexedly skyward from under his tilted hat-brim; and then brought out, as from the depth of a rankling grievance: "I thought it was all understood."

"Why," Nick asked his wife that night, as they

re-entered Ellie's cool drawing-room after a late dinner at the Lido, "did Gillow think it was understood that we were going to his moor in August?" He was conscious of the oddness of speaking of their friend by his surname, and reddened at his blunder.

Susy had let her lace cloak slide to her feet, and stood before him in the faintly-lit room, slim and shimmering-white through black transparencies.

She raised her eyebrows carelessly. "I told you long ago he'd asked us there for August."

"You didn't tell me you'd accepted."

She smiled as if he had said something as simple as Fred. "I accepted everything—from everybody!"

What could he answer? It was the very principle on which their bargain had been struck. And if he were to say: "Ah, but this is different, because I'm jealous of Gillow," what light would such an answer shed on his past? The time for being jealous—if so antiquated an attitude were on any ground defensible—would have been before his marriage, and before the acceptance of the bounties which had helped to make it possible. He wondered a little now that in those days such scruples had not troubled him. His inconsistency irritated him, and increased his irritation against Gillow. "I suppose he thinks he owns us!" he grumbled inwardly.

He had thrown himself into an armchair, and Susy, advancing across the shining arabesques of the floor, slid down at his feet, pressed her slender length against him, and whispered with lifted face and lips close to his: "We needn't ever go anywhere you don't want to." For once her submission was sweet, and folding her close he whispered back through his kiss: "Not there, then."

In her response to his embrace he felt the acquiescence of her whole happy self in whatever future he decided on, if only it gave them enough of such moments as this; and as they held each other fast in silence his doubts and distrust began to seem like a silly injustice.

"Let us stay here as long as ever Ellie will let us," he said, as if the shadowy walls and shining floors were a magic boundary, drawn about his happiness.

She murmured her assent and stood up, stretching her sleepy arm above her shoulders. "How dreadfully late it is. . . . Will you unhook me? . . . Oh, there's a telegram."

She picked it up from the table, and tearing it open stared a moment at the message. "It's from Ellie. She's coming to-morrow."

She turned to the window and strayed out onto the balcony. Nick followed her with enlacing arm. The canal below them lay in moonless shadow, barred with a few lingering lights. A last snatch of gondola-music came from far off, carried upward on a sultry gust.

"Dear old Ellie. All the same . . . I wish all this belonged to you and me," Susy sighed.

VIII

IT was not Mrs. Vanderlyn's fault if, after her
arrival, her palace seemed to belong any less
to the Lansings.

She arrived in a mood of such general benevolence that it was impossible for Susy, when they
finally found themselves alone, to make her view
even her own recent conduct in any but the most
benevolent light.

"I knew you'd be the veriest angel about it all,
darling, because I knew you'd understand me—
especially *now*," she declared, her slim hands in
Susy's, her big eyes (so like Clarissa's) resplen-
dent with past pleasures and future plans.

The expression of her confidence was unexpectedly distasteful to Susy Lansing, who had never
lent so cold an ear to such warm avowals. She
had always imagined that being happy one's self
made one—as Mrs. Vanderlyn appeared to assume
—more tolerant of the happiness of others, of
however doubtful elements composed; and she was
almost ashamed of responding so languidly to her
friend's outpourings. But she herself had no desire to confide her bliss to Ellie; and why should
not Ellie observe a similar reticence?

"It was all so perfect—you see, dearest, *I was meant to be happy,*" that lady continued, as if the possession of so unusual a characteristic singled her out for special privileges.

Susy, with a certain sharpness, responded that she had always supposed we all were.

"Oh, no, dearest: not governesses and mothers-in-law and companions, and that sort of people. They wouldn't know how if they tried. But you and I, darling—"

"Oh, I don't consider myself in any way exceptional," Susy intervened. She longed to add: "Not in *your* way, at any rate—" but a few minutes earlier Mrs. Vanderlyn had told her that the palace was at her disposal for the rest of the summer, and that she herself was only going to perch there—if they'd let her?—long enough to gather up her things and start for St. Moritz. The memory of this announcement had the effect of curbing Susy's irony, and of making her shift the conversation to the safer if scarcely less absorbing topic of the number of day and evening dresses required for a season at St. Moritz.

As she listened to Mrs. Vanderlyn—no less eloquent on this theme than on the other—Susy began to measure the gulf between her past and present. "This is the life I used to lead; these are the things I used to live for," she thought, as she stood before the outspread glories of Mrs. Vanderlyn's wardrobe. Not that she did not still care: she could not look at Ellie's laces and silks and furs without picturing herself in them, and wondering by what new miracle of management she could give herself the air of being dressed by the same consummate artists. But these had become minor interests: the past few months had given her a new perspective, and the thing that most puzzled and disconcerted her about Ellie was the fact that love and finery and bridge and dining-out were seemingly all on the same plane to her.

The inspection of the dresses lasted a long time, and was marked by many fluctuations of mood on the part of Mrs. Vanderlyn, who passed from comparative hopefulness to despair at the total inadequacy of her wardrobe. It wouldn't do to go to St. Moritz looking like a frump, and yet there was no time to get anything sent from Paris, and, whatever she did, she wasn't going to show herself in any dowdy re-arrangements done at home. But suddenly light broke on her, and she clasped her hands for joy. "Why, Nelson'll bring them—I'd forgotten all about Nelson! There'll be just time if I wire to him at once."

"Is Nelson going to join you at St. Moritz?" Susy asked, surprised.

"Heavens, no! He's coming here to pick up Clarissa and take her to some stuffy cure in Austria with his mother. It's too lucky: there's just time to telegraph him to bring my things. I didn't mean to wait for him; but it won't delay me more than a day or two."

Susy's heart sank. She was not much afraid of Ellie alone, but Ellie and Nelson together formed an incalculable menace. No one could tell what spark of truth might flash from their collision. Susy felt that she could deal with the two dangers separately and successively, but not together and simultaneously.

"But, Ellie, why should you wait for Nelson? I'm certain to find someone here who's going to St. Moritz and will take your things if he brings them. It's a pity to risk losing your rooms."

This argument appealed for a moment to Mrs. Vanderlyn. "That's true; they say all the hotels are jammed. You dear, you're always so practical!" She clasped Susy to her scented bosom. "And you know, darling, I'm sure you'll be glad to get rid of me—you and Nick! Oh, don't be hypocritical and say 'Nonsense!' You see, I understand . . . I used to think of you so often, you two . . . during those blessed weeks when *we* two were alone. . . ."

The sudden tears, brimming over Ellie's lovely eyes, and threatening to make the blue circles below them run into the adjoining carmine, filled Susy with compunction.

"Poor thing—oh, poor thing!" she thought; and hearing herself called by Nick, who was waiting to take her out for their usual sunset on the lagoon, she felt a wave of pity for the deluded creature who would never taste that highest of imaginable joys. "But all the same," Susy reflected, as she hurried down to her husband, "I'm glad I persuaded her not to wait for Nelson."

Some days had elapsed since Susy and Nick had had a sunset to themselves, and in the interval Susy had once again learned the superior quality of the sympathy that held them together. She now viewed all the rest of life as no more than a show: a jolly show which it would have been a thousand pities to miss, but which, if the need arose, they could get up and leave at any moment —provided that they left it together.

In the dusk, while their prow slid over inverted palaces, and through the scent of hidden gardens, she leaned against him and murmured, her mind returning to the recent scene with Ellie: "Nick, should you hate me dreadfully if I had no clothes?"

Her husband was kindling a cigarette, and the match lit up the grin with which he answered: "But, my dear, have I ever shown the slightest symptom—?"

"Oh, rubbish! When a woman says: 'No clothes,' she means: 'Not the right clothes.' "

He took a meditative puff. "Ah, you've been going over Ellie's finery with her."

"Yes: all those trunks and trunks full. And she finds she's got nothing for St. Moritz!"

"Of course," he murmured, drowsy with content, and manifesting but a languid interest in the subject of Mrs. Vanderlyn's wardrobe.

"Only fancy—she very nearly decided to stop

over for Nelson's arrival next week, so that he might bring her two or three more trunkfuls from Paris. But mercifully I've managed to persuade her that it would be foolish to wait.''

Susy felt a hardly perceptible shifting of her husband's lounging body, and was aware, through all her watchful tentacles, of a widening of his half-closed lids.

"You 'managed'—?" She fancied he paused on the word ironically. "But why?"

"Why—what?"

"Why on earth should you try to prevent Ellie's waiting for Nelson, if for once in her life she wants to?"

Susy, conscious of reddening suddenly, drew back as though the leap of her tell-tale heart might have penetrated the blue flannel shoulder against which she leaned.

"Really, dearest—!" she murmured; but with a sudden doggedness he renewed his "Why?"

"Because she's in such a fever to get to St. Moritz—and in such a funk lest the hotel shouldn't keep her rooms," Susy somewhat breathlessly produced.

"Ah—I see." Nick paused again. "You're a devoted friend, aren't you?"

"What an odd question! There's hardly any. one I've reason to be more devoted to than Ellie,'' his wife answered; and she felt his contrite clasp on her hand.

"Darling! No; nor I—. Or more grateful to
for leaving us alone in this heaven."

Dimness had fallen on the waters, and her lifted
lips met his bending ones.

Trailing late into dinner that evening, Ellie announced that, after all, she had decided it was
safest to wait for Nelson.

"I should simply worry myself ill if I weren't
sure of getting my things," she said, in the tone
of tender solicitude with which she always dis-
cussed her own difficulties. "After all, people
who deny themselves *everything* do get warped
and bitter, don't they?" she argued plaintively,
her lovely eyes wandering from one to the other
of her assembled friends.

Strefford remarked gravely that it was the com-
plaint which had fatally undermined his own
health; and in the laugh that followed the party
drifted into the great vaulted dining-room.

"Oh, I don't mind *your* laughing at me, Streffy
darling," his hostess retorted, pressing his arm
against her own; and Susy, receiving the shock
of their rapidly exchanged glance, said to herself,
with a sharp twinge of apprehension: "Of course
Streffy knows everything; he showed no surprise
at finding Ellie away when he arrived. And if
he knows, what's to prevent Nelson's finding
out?" For Strefford, in a mood of mischief, was
no more to be trusted than a malicious child.

Susy instantly resolved to risk speaking to him, if need be even betraying to him the secret of the letters. Only by revealing the depth of her own danger could she hope to secure his silence.

On the balcony, late in the evening, while the others were listening indoors to the low modulations of a young composer who had embroidered his fancies on Browning's "Toccata," Susy found her chance. Strefford, unsummoned, had followed her out, and stood silently smoking at her side.

"You see, Streff— oh, why should you and I make mysteries to each other?" she suddenly began.

"Why, indeed: but do we?"

Susy glanced back at the group around the piano. "About Ellie, I mean—and Nelson."

"Lord! Ellie and Nelson? You call *that* a mystery? I should as soon apply the term to one of the million-candle-power advertisements that adorn your native thoroughfares."

"Well, yes. But—" She stopped again. Had she not tacitly promised Ellie not to speak?

"My Susan, what's wrong?" Strefford asked.

"I don't know. . . ."

"Well, I do, then: you're afraid that, if Ellie and Nelson meet here, she'll blurt out something —injudicious."

"Oh, *she* won't!" Susy cried with conviction.

"Well, then—who will? I trust that superhuman child not to. And you and I and Nick——"

"Oh," she gasped, interrupting him, "that's just it. Nick doesn't know . . . doesn't even suspect. And if he did. . . ."

Strefford flung away his cigar and turned to scrutinize her. "I don't see—hanged if I do. What business is it of any of us, after all?"

That, of course, was the old view that cloaked connivance in an air of decency. But to Susy it no longer carried conviction, and she hesitated.

"If Nick should find out that I know. . . ."

"Good Lord—doesn't he know that you know? After all, I suppose it's not the first time—"

She remained silent.

"The first time you've received confidences—from married friends. Does Nick suppose you've lived even to your tender age without. . . Hang it, what's come over you, child?"

What had, indeed, that she could make clear to him? And yet more than ever she felt the need of having him securely on her side. Once his word was pledged, he was safe: otherwise there was no limit to his capacity for wilful harmfulness.

"Look here, Streff, you and I know that Ellie hasn't been away for a cure; and that if poor Clarissa was sworn to secrecy it was not because it 'worries father' to think that mother needs to take care of her health." She paused, hating herself for the ironic note she had tried to sound.

"Well—?" he questioned, from the depths of the chair into which he had sunk.

"Well, Nick doesn't . . . doesn't dream of it.

If he knew that we owed our summer here to . . .
to my knowing. . . ."

Strefford sat silent: she felt his astonished stare
through the darkness. "Jove!" he said at last,
with a low whistle. Susy bent over the balustrade, her heart thumping against the stone rail.

"*What of soul was left, I wonder—?*" the
young composer's voice shrilled through the open
windows.

Strefford sank into another silence, from which
he roused himself only as Susy turned back
toward the lighted threshold.

"Well, my dear, we'll see it through between
us; you and I—and Clarissa," he said with his
rasping laugh, rising to follow her. He caught
her hand and gave it a short pressure as they re-
entered the drawing-room, where Ellie was saying
plaintively to Fred Gillow: "I can never hear
that thing sung without wanting to cry like a
baby."

IX

MR. NELSON VANDERLYN, still in his travelling clothes, paused on the threshold of his own dining-room and surveyed the scene with pardonable satisfaction.

He was a short round man, with a grizzled head, small facetious eyes and a large and credulous smile.

At the luncheon table sat his wife, between Charlie Strefford and Nick Lansing. Next to Strefford, perched on her high chair, Clarissa throned in infant beauty, while Susy Lansing cut up a peach for her. Through wide orange awnings the sun slanted in upon the white-clad group.

"Well—well—well! So I've caught you at it!" cried the happy father, whose inveterate habit it was to address his wife and friends as if he had surprised them at an inopportune moment. Stealing up from behind, he lifted his daughter into the air, while a chorus of "Hullo, old Nelson," hailed his appearance.

It was two or three years since Nick Lansing had seen Mr. Vanderlyn, who was now the London representative of the big New York bank of Vanderlyn & Co., and had exchanged his sumptuous house in Fifth Avenue for another, more sumptuous still, in Mayfair; and the young man looked curiously and attentively at his host.

Mr. Vanderlyn had grown older and stouter, but his face still kept its look of somewhat worn optimism. He embraced his wife, greeted Susy affectionately, and distributed cordial hand-grasps to the two men.

"Hullo," he exclaimed, suddenly noticing a pearl and coral trinket hanging from Clarissa's neck. "Who's been giving my daughter jewellery, I'd like to know?"

"Oh, Streffy did—just think, father! Because I said I'd rather have it than a book, you know," Clarissa lucidly explained, her arms tight about her father's neck, her beaming eyes on Strefford.

Nelson Vanderlyn's own eyes took on the look of shrewdness which came into them whenever there was a question of material values.

"What, Streffy? Caught you at it, eh? Upon my soul—spoiling the brat like that! You'd no business to, my dear chap—a lovely baroque pearl—" he protested, with the half-apologetic tone of the rich man embarrassed by too costly a gift from an impecunious friend.

"Oh, hadn't I? Why? Because it's too good for Clarissa, or too expensive for me? Of course you daren't imply the first; and as for me—I've had a windfall, and am blowing it in on the ladies."

Strefford, Lansing had noticed, always used American slang when he was slightly at a loss, and wished to divert attention from the main point. But why was he embarrassed, whose attention did he wish to divert? It was plain that Vanderlyn's protest had been merely formal: like most of the wealthy, he had only the dimmest notion of what money represented to the poor. But it was unusual for Strefford to give any one a present, and especially an expensive one: perhaps that was what had fixed Vanderlyn's attention.

"A windfall?" he gaily repeated.

"Oh, a tiny one: I was offered a thumping rent for my little place at Como, and dashed over here to squander my millions with the rest of you," said Strefford imperturbably.

Vanderlyn's look immediately became interested and sympathetic. "What—the scene of the honey-moon?" He included Nick and Susy in his friendly smile.

"Just so: the reward of virtue. I say, give me a cigar, will you, old man? I left some awfully good ones at Como, worse luck—and I don't mind telling you that Ellie's no judge of tobacco, and that Nick's too far gone in bliss to care what he smokes," Strefford grumbled, stretching a hand toward his host's cigar-case.

"I *do* like jewellery best," Clarissa murmured, hugging her father.

Nelson Vanderlyn's first word to his wife had been that he had brought her all her toggery; and she had welcomed him with appropriate enthusiasm. In fact, to the lookers-on her joy at seeing him seemed rather too patently in proportion to her satisfaction at getting her clothes. But no such suspicion appeared to mar Mr. Vanderlyn's happiness in being, for once, and for nearly twenty-four hours, under the same roof with his wife and child. He did not conceal his regret at having promised his mother to join her the next day; and added, with a wistful glance at Ellie: "If only I'd known you meant to wait for me—!"

But being a man of duty, in domestic as well as business affairs, he did not even consider the possibility of disappointing the exacting old lady to whom he owed his being. "Mother cares for so few people," he used to say, not without a touch of filial pride in the parental exclusiveness, "that I have to be with her rather more than if she were more sociable"; and with smiling resignation he gave orders that Clarissa should be ready to start the next evening.

"And meanwhile," he concluded, "we'll have all the good time that's going."

The ladies of the party seemed united in the desire to further this resolve; and it was settled that as soon as Mr. Vanderlyn had despatched a hasty luncheon, his wife, Clarissa and Susy should carry him off for a tea-picnic at Torcello. They did not even suggest that Strefford or Nick should be of the party, or that any of the other young men of the group should be summoned; as Susy said, Nelson wanted to go off alone with his harem, and Lansing and Strefford were left to watch the departure of the happy Pasha ensconced between attentive beauties.

"Well—that's what you call being married!" Strefford commented, waving his battered Panama at Clarissa.

"Oh, no, I don't!" Lansing laughed.

"*He* does. But do you know—" Strefford paused and swung about on his companion—"do you know, when the Rude Awakening comes, I don't care to be there. I believe there'll be some crockery broken."

"Shouldn't wonder," Lansing answered indifferently. He wandered away to his own room, leaving Strefford to philosophize to his pipe.

Lansing had always known about poor old Nelson: who hadn't, except poor old Nelson? The case had once seemed amusing because so typical; now, it rather irritated Nick that Vanderlyn should be so complete an ass. But he would be off the next day, and so would Ellie, and then, for many enchanted weeks, the palace would once more be the property of Nick and Susy. Of all the people who came and went in it, they were the only ones who appreciated it, or knew how it was meant to be lived in; and that made it theirs in the only valid sense. In this light it became easy to regard the Vanderlyns as mere transient intruders.

Having relegated them to this convenient distance, Lansing shut himself up with his book. He had returned to it with fresh energy after his few weeks of holiday-making, and was determined to finish it quickly. He did not expect that it would bring in much money; but if it were moderately successful it might give him an opening in the reviews and magazines, and in that case he meant to abandon archæology for novels, since it was only as a purveyor of fiction that he could count on earning a living for himself and Susy.

Late in the afternoon he laid down his pen and wandered out of doors. He loved the increasing heat of the Venetian summer, the bruised peach-tints of worn house-fronts, the enamelling of sunlight on dark green canals, the smell of half-decayed fruits and flowers thickening the languid air. What visions he could build, if he dared, of being tucked away with Susy in the attic of some tumble-down palace, above a jade-green waterway, with a terrace overhanging a scrap of neglected garden—and cheques from the publishers dropping in at convenient intervals! Why should they not settle in Venice if he pulled it off?

He found himself before the church of the Scalzi, and pushing open the leathern door wandered up the nave under the whirl of rose-and-lemon angels in Tiepolo's great vault. It was not a church in which one was likely to run across sight-seers; but he presently remarked a young lady standing alone near the choir, and assiduously applying her field-glass to the celestial vortex, from which she occasionally glanced down at an open manual.

As Lansing's step sounded on the pavement, the young lady, turning, revealed herself as Miss Hicks.

"Ah—you like this too? It's several centuries out of your line, though, isn't it?" Nick asked as they shook hands.

She gazed at him gravely. "Why shouldn't one like things that are out of one's line?" she answered; and he agreed, with a laugh, that it was often an incentive.

She continued to fix her grave eyes on him, and after one or two remarks about the Tiepolos he perceived that she was feeling her way toward a subject of more personal interest.

"I'm glad to see you alone," she said at length, with an abruptness that might have seemed awkward had it not been so completely unconscious. She turned toward a cluster of straw chairs, and signed to Nick to seat himself beside her.

"I seldom do," she added, with the serious smile that made her heavy face almost handsome; and she went on, giving him no time to protest: "I wanted to speak to you—to explain about father's invitation to go with us to Persia and Turkestan."

"To explain?"

"Yes. You found the letter when you arrived here just after your marriage, didn't you? You must have thought it odd, our asking you just then; but we hadn't heard that you were married.''

"Oh, I guessed as much: it happened very quietly, and I was remiss about announcing it, even to old friends.''

Lansing frowned. His thoughts had wandered away to the evening when he had found Mrs. Hicks's letter in the mail awaiting him at Venice. The day was associated in his mind with the ridiculous and mortifying episode of the cigars— the expensive cigars that Susy had wanted to carry away from Strefford's villa. Their brief exchange of views on the subject had left the first blur on the perfect surface of his happiness, and he still felt an uncomfortable heat at the remembrance. For a few hours the prospect of life with Susy had seemed unendurable; and it was just at that moment that he had found the letter from Mrs. Hicks, with its almost irresistible invitation. If only her daughter had known how nearly he had accepted it!

"It was a dreadful temptation,'' he said, smiling.

"To go with us? Then why—?''

"Oh, everything's different now: I've got to stick to my writing.''

Miss Hicks still bent on him the same unblinking scrutiny. "Does that mean that you're going to give up your real work?''

"My real work—archæology?'' He smiled again to hide a twitch of regret. "Why, I'm afraid it hardly produces a living wage; and I've got to think of that.'' He coloured suddenly, as if suspecting that Miss Hicks might consider the avowal an opening for he hardly knew what ponderous offer of aid. The Hicks munificence was too uncalculating not to be occasionally oppressive. But looking at her again he saw that her eyes were full of tears.

"I thought it was your vocation," she said.

"So did I. But life comes along, and upsets things."

"Oh, I understand. There may be things—worth giving up all other things for."

"There *are!*" cried Nick with beaming emphasis.

He was conscious that Miss Hicks's eyes demanded of him even more than this sweeping affirmation.

"But your novel may fail," she said with her odd harshness.

"It may—it probably will," he agreed. "But if one stopped to consider such possibilities—"

"Don't you have to, with a wife?"

"Oh, my dear Coral—how old are you? Not twenty?" he questioned, laying a brotherly hand on hers.

She stared at him a moment, and sprang up clumsily from her chair. "I was never young . . . if that's what you mean. It's lucky, isn't it, that my parents gave me such a grand education?

Because, you see, art's a wonderful resource."
(She pronounced it *re*-source.)

He continued to look at her kindly. "You won't
need it—or any other—when you grow young, as
you will some day," he assured her.

"Do you mean, when I fall in love? But I *am*
in love— Oh, there's Eldorada and Mr. Beck!"
She broke off with a jerk, signalling with her field-
glass to the pair who had just appeared at the
farther end of the nave. "I told them that if
they'd meet me here to-day I'd try to make them
understand Tiepolo. Because, you see, at home
we've never really *have* understood Tiepolo;
and Mr. Beck and Eldorada are the only ones to
realize it. Mr. Buttles simply won't." She
turned to Lansing and held out her hand. "I *am*
in love," she repeated earnestly, "and that's the
reason why I find art such a *re*-source."

She restored her eye-glasses, opened her manual, and strode across the church to the expectant
neophytes.

Lansing, looking after her, wondered for half
a moment whether Mr. Beck were the object of
this apparently unrequited sentiment; then, with
a queer start of introspection, abruptly decided
that, no, he certainly was not. But then—but
then—. Well, there was no use in following up
such conjectures. . . . He turned homeward,
wondering if the picnickers had already reached
Palazzo Vanderlyn.

They got back only in time for a late dinner, full of chaff and laughter, and apparently still enchanted with each other's society. Nelson Vanerlyn beamed on his wife, sent his daughter off to bed with a kiss, and leaning back in his armchair before the fruit-and-flower-laden table, declared that he'd never spent a jollier day in his life. Susy seemed to come in for a full share of his approbation, and Lansing thought that Ellie was unusually demonstrative to her friend. Strefford, from his hostess's side, glanced across now and then at young Mrs. Lansing, and his glance seemed to Lansing a confidential comment on the Vanderlyn raptures. But then Strefford was always having private jokes with people or about them; and Lansing was irritated with himself for perpetually suspecting his best friends of vague complicities at his expense. "If I'm going to be jealous of Streffy now—!" he concluded with a grimace of self-derision.

Certainly Susy looked lovely enough to justify the most irrational pangs. As a girl she had been, for some people's taste, a trifle fine-drawn and sharp-edged; now, to her old lightness of line was added a shadowy bloom, a sort of star-reflecting depth. Her movements were slower, less angular; her mouth had a nestling droop, her lids seemed weighed down by their lashes; and then suddenly the old spirit would reveal itself through the new languor, like the tartness at the core of a sweet fruit. As her husband looked at her across the flowers and lights he laughed inwardly at the nothingness of all things else.

Vanderlyn and Clarissa left betimes the next morning; and Mrs. Vanderlyn, who was to start for St. Moritz in the afternoon, devoted her last hours to anxious conferences with her maid and Susy. Strefford, with Fred Gillow and the others, had gone for a swim at the Lido, and Lansing seized the opportunity to get back to his book.

The quietness of the great echoing place gave him a foretaste of the solitude to come. By mid-August all their party would be scattered: the Hickses off on a cruise to Crete and the Ægean, Fred Gillow on the way to his moor, Strefford to stay with friends in Capri till his annual visit to Northumberland in September. One by one the others would follow, and Lansing and Susy be left alone in the great sun-proof palace, alone under the star-laden skies, alone with the great orange moons—still theirs!—above the bell-tower of San Giorgio. The novel, in that blessed quiet, would unfold itself as harmoniously as his dreams.

He wrote on, forgetful of the passing hours, till the door opened and he heard a step behind him. The next moment two hands were clasped over his eyes, and the air was full of Mrs. Vanderlyn's last new scent.

"You dear thing—I'm just off, you know," she said. "Susy told me you were working, and I

forbade her to call you down. She and Streffy
are waiting to take me to the station, and I've run
up to say good-bye.''

"Ellie, dear!" Full of compunction, Lansing
pushed aside his writing and started up; but she
pressed him back into his seat.

"No, no! I should never forgive myself if I'd
interrupted you. I oughtn't to have come up;
Susy didn't want me to. But I had to tell you,
you dear. . . . I had to thank you. . . .''

In her dark travelling dress and hat, so discreetly conspicuous, so negligent and so studied,
with a veil masking her paint, and gloves hiding
her rings, she looked younger, simpler, more natural than he had ever seen her. Poor Ellie—such
a good fellow, after all!

"To thank me? For what? For being so
happy here?" he laughed, taking her hands.

She looked at him, laughed back, and flung her
arms about his neck.

"For helping *me* to be so happy elsewhere—
you and Susy, you two blessed darlings!" she
cried, with a kiss on his cheek.

Their eyes met for a second; then her arms
slipped slowly downward, dropping to her sides.
Lansing sat before her like a stone.

"Oh," she gasped, "why do you stare so?
Didn't you know . . . ?"

They heard Strefford's shrill voice on the
stairs. "Ellie, where the deuce are you? Susy's
in the gondola. You'll miss the train!"

Lansing stood up and caught Mrs. Vanderlyn by the wrist. "What do you mean? What are you talking about?"

"Oh, nothing. . . . But you were both such bricks about the letters. . . . And when Nelson was here, too. . . . Nick, don't hurt my wrist so! I must run!"

He dropped her hand and stood motionless, staring after her and listening to the click of her high heels as she fled across the room and along the echoing corridor.

When he turned back to the table he noticed that a small morocco case had fallen among his papers. In falling it had opened, and before him, on the pale velvet lining, lay a scarf-pin set with a perfect pearl. He picked the box up, and was about to hasten after Mrs. Vanderlyn—it was so like her to shed jewels on her path!—when he noticed his own initials on the cover.

He dropped the box as if it had been a hot coal, and sat for a long while gazing at the gold N. L., which seemed to have burnt itself into his flesh.

At last he roused himself and stood up.

X

WITH a sigh of relief Susy drew the pins from her hat and threw herself down on the lounge.

The ordeal she had dreaded was over, and Mr. and Mrs. Vanderlyn had safely gone their several ways. Poor Ellie was not noted for prudence, and when life smiled on her she was given to betraying her gratitude too openly; but thanks to Susy's vigilance (and, no doubt, to Strefford's tacit co-operation), the dreaded twenty-four hours were happily over. Nelson Vanderlyn had departed without a shadow on his brow, and though Ellie's, when she came down from bidding Nick good-bye, had seemed to Susy less serene than usual, she became her normal self as soon as it was discovered that the red morocco bag with her jewel-box was missing. Before it had been discovered in the depths of the gondola they had reached the station, and there was just time to thrust her into her "sleeper," from which she was seen to wave an unperturbed farewell to her friends.

"Well, my dear, we've seen it through," Strefford remarked with a deep breath as the St. Moritz express rolled away.

"Oh," Susy sighed in mute complicity; then, as if to cover her self-betrayal: "Poor darling, she does so like what she likes!"

"Yes—even if it's a rotten bounder," Strefford agreed.

"A rotten bounder? Why, I thought—"

"That it was still young Davenant? Lord, no —not for the last six months. Didn't she tell you—?"

Susy felt herself redden. "I didn't ask her—"

"Ask her? You mean you didn't let her!"

"I didn't let her. And I don't let you," Susy added sharply, as he helped her into the gondola.

"Oh, all right: I daresay you're right. It simplifies things," Strefford placidly acquiesced.

She made no answer, and in silence they glided homeward.

Now, in the quiet of her own room, Susy lay and pondered on the distance she had travelled during the last year. Strefford had read her mind with his usual penetration. It was true that there had been a time when she would have thought it perfectly natural that Ellie should tell her everything; that the name of young Davenant's successor should be confided to her as a matter of course. Apparently even Ellie had been obscurely aware of the change, for after a first attempt to force her confidences on Susy she had contented herself with vague expressions of gratitude, allusive smiles and sighs, and the pretty "surprise" of the sapphire bangle slipped onto her friend's wrist in the act of their farewell embrace.

The bangle was extremely handsome. Susy,

who had an auctioneer's eye for values, knew to a fraction the worth of those deep convex stones alternating with small emeralds and brilliants. She was glad to own the bracelet, and enchanted with the effect it produced on her slim wrist; yet, even while admiring it, and rejoicing that it was hers, she had already transmuted it into specie, and reckoned just how far it would go toward the paying of domestic necessities. For whatever came to her now interested her only as something more to be offered up to Nick.

The door opened and Nick came in. Dusk had fallen, and she could not see his face; but something in the jerk of the door-handle roused her ever-wakeful apprehension. She hurried toward him with outstretched wrist.

"Look, dearest — wasn't it too darling of Ellie?"

She pressed the button of the lamp that lit her dressing-table, and her husband's face started unfamiliarly out of the twilight. She slipped off the bracelet and held it up to him.

"Oh, I can go you one better," he said with a laugh; and pulling a morocco case from his pocket he flung it down among the scent-bottles.

Susy opened the case automatically, staring at the pearl because she was afraid to look again at Nick.

"Ellie—gave you this?" she asked at length.

"Yes. She gave me this." There was a pause. "Would you mind telling me," Lansing continued in the same dead-level tone, "exactly for what services we've both been so handsomely paid?"

"The pearl *is* beautiful," Susy murmured, to gain time, while her head spun round with unimaginable terrors.

"So are your sapphires; though, on closer examination, my services would appear to have been valued rather higher than yours. Would you be kind enough to tell me just what they were?"

Susy threw her head back and looked at him. "What on earth are you talking about, Nick? Why shouldn't Ellie have given us these things? Do you forget that it's like our giving her a pen-wiper or a button-hook? What is it you are trying to suggest?"

It had cost her a considerable effort to hold his eyes while she put the questions. Something had happened between him and Ellie, that was evident —one of those hideous unforeseeable blunders that may cause one's cleverest plans to crumble at a stroke; and again Susy shuddered at the frailty of her bliss. But her old training stood her in good stead. There had been more than one moment in her past when everything—somebody else's everything—had depended on her keeping a cool head and a clear glance. It would have been a wonder if now, when she felt her own everything at stake, she had not been able to put up as good a defence.

"What is it?" she repeated impatiently, as Lansing continued to remain silent.

"That's what I'm here to ask," he returned keeping his eyes as steady as she kept hers. "There's no reason on earth, as you say, why Ellie shouldn't give us presents—as expensive presents as she likes; and the pearl *is* a beauty. All I ask is: for what specific services were they given? For, allowing for all the absence of scruple that marks the intercourse of truly civilized people, you'll probably agree that there are limits; at least up to now there have been limits. . . ."

"I really don't know what you mean. I suppose Ellie wanted to show that she was grateful to us for looking after Clarissa."

"But she gave us all this in exchange for that, didn't she?" he suggested, with a sweep of the hand around the beautiful shadowy room. "A whole summer of it if we choose."

Susy smiled. "Apparently she didn't think that enough."

"What a doting mother! It shows the store she sets upon her child."

"Well, don't you set store upon Clarissa?"

"Clarissa is exquisite; but her mother didn't mention her in offering me this recompense."

Susy lifted her head again. "Whom *did* she mention?"

"Vanderlyn," said Lansing.

"Vanderlyn? Nelson?"

"Yes—and some letters . . . something about

letters. . . . What is it, my dear, that you and I have been hired to hide from Vanderlyn? Because I should like to know," Nick broke out savagely, "if we've been adequately paid."

Susy was silent: she needed time to reckon up her forces, and study her next move; and her brain was in such a whirl of fear that she could at last only retort: "What is it that Ellie said to you?"

Lansing laughed again. "That's just what you'd like to find out—isn't it?—in order to know the line to take in making your explanation."

The sneer had an effect that he could not have foreseen, and that Susy herself had not expected.

"Oh, don't—don't let us speak to each other like that!" she cried; and sinking down by the dressing-table she hid her face in her hands.

It seemed to her, now, that nothing mattered except that their love for each other, their faith in each other, should be saved from some unhealable hurt. She was willing to tell Nick everything—she wanted to tell him everything—if only she could be sure of reaching a responsive chord in him. But the scene of the cigars came back to her, and benumbed her. If only she could make him see that nothing was of any account as long as they continued to love each other!

His touch fell compassionately on her shoulder. "Poor child—don't," he said.

Their eyes met, but his expression checked the

smile breaking through her tears. "Don't you see," he continued, "that we've got to have this thing out?"

She continued to stare at him through a prism of tears. "I can't—while you stand up like that," she stammered, childishly.

She had cowered down again into a corner of the lounge; but Lansing did not seat himself at her side. He took a chair facing her, like a caller on the farther side of a stately tea-tray. "Will that do?" he asked with a stiff smile, as if to humour her.

"Nothing will do—as long as you're not you!"

"Not me?"

She shook her head wearily. "What's the use? You accept things theoretically—and then when they happen. . . ."

"What things? What *has* happened?"

A sudden impatience mastered her. What did he suppose, after all—? "But you know all about Ellie. We used to talk about her often enough in old times," she said.

"Ellie and young Davenant?"

"Young Davenant; or the others. . . ."

"Or the others. But what business was it of ours?"

"Ah, that's just what I think!" she cried, springing up with an explosion of relief. Lansing stood up also, but there was no answering light in his face.

"We're outside of all that; we've nothing to do with it, have we?" he pursued.

"Nothing whatever."

"Then what on earth is the meaning of Ellie's gratitude? Gratitude for what we've done about some letters—and about Vanderlyn?"

"Oh, not *you*," Susy cried, involuntarily.

"Not I? Then you?" He came close and took her by the wrist. "Answer me. Have you been mixed up in some dirty business of Ellie's?"

There was a pause. She found it impossible to speak, with that burning grasp on the wrist where the bangle had been. At length he let her go and moved away. "Answer," he repeated.

"I've told you it was my business and not yours."

He received this in silence; then he questioned: "You've been sending letters for her, I suppose? To whom?"

"Oh, why do you torment me? Nelson was not supposed to know that she'd been away. She left me the letters to post to him once a week. I found them here the night we arrived. . . . It was the price—for *this*. Oh, Nick, say it's been worth it —say at least that it's been worth it!" she implored him.

He stood motionless, unresponding. One hand drummed on the corner of her dressing-table, making the jewelled bangle dance.

"How many letters?"

"I don't know . . . four . . . five . . . What does it matter?"

"And once a week, for six weeks—?"

"Yes."

"And you took it all as a matter of course?"

"No: I hated it. But what could I do?"

"What could you do?"

"When our being together depended on it? Oh, Nick, how could you think I'd give you up?"

"Give me up?" he echoed.

"Well—doesn't our being together depend on —on what we can get out of people? And hasn't there always got to be some give-and-take? Did you ever in your life get anything for nothing?" she cried with sudden exasperation. "You've lived among these people as long as I have; I suppose it's not the first time—"

"By God, but it is," he exclaimed, flushing. "And that's the difference—the fundamental difference."

"The difference?"

"Between you and me. I've never in my life done people's dirty work for them—least of all for favours in return. I suppose you guessed it, or you wouldn't have hidden this beastly business from me."

The blood rose to Susy's temples also. Yes, she had guessed it; instinctively, from the day she had first visited him in his bare lodgings, she had been aware of his stricter standard. But how could she tell him that under his influence her standard had become stricter too, and that it was as much to hide her humiliation from herself as to escape his anger that she had held her tongue?

"You knew I wouldn't have stayed here another day if I'd known," he continued.

"Yes: and then where in the world should we have gone?"

"You mean that—in one way or another—what you call give-and-take is the price of our remaining together?"

"Well—isn't it?" she faltered.

"Then we'd better part, hadn't we?"

He spoke in a low tone, thoughtfully and deliberately, as if this had been the inevitable conclusion to which their passionate argument had led.

Susy made no answer. For a moment she ceased to be conscious of the causes of what had happened; the thing itself seemed to have smothered her under its ruins.

Nick wandered away from the dressing-table and stood gazing out of the window at the darkening canal flecked with lights. She looked at his back, and wondered what would happen if she were to go up to him and fling her arms about him. But even if her touch could have broken the spell, she was not sure she would have chosen that way of breaking it. Beneath her speechless anguish there burned the half-conscious sense of having been unfairly treated. When they had entered into their queer compact, Nick had known as well as she on what compromises and concessions the

life they were to live together must be based.
That he should have forgotten it seemed so unbelievable that she wondered, with a new leap of
fear, if he were using the wretched Ellie's indis-
cretion as a means of escape from a tie already
wearied of. Suddenly she raised her head with a
laugh.

"After all—you were right when you wanted
me to be your mistress."

He turned on her with an astonished stare.
"You—my mistress?"

Through all her pain she thrilled with pride at
the discovery that such a possibility had long
since become unthinkable to him. But she insisted. "That day at the Fulmers'—have you forgotten? When you said it would be sheer madness for us to marry."

Lansing stood leaning in the embrasure of the
window, his eyes fixed on the mosaic volutes of
the floor.

"I was right enough when I said it would be
sheer madness for us to marry," he rejoined at
length.

She sprang up trembling. "Well, that's easily
settled. Our compact—"

"Oh, that compact—" he interrupted her with
an impatient laugh.

"Aren't you asking me to carry it out now?"

"Because I said we'd better part?" He paused.
"But the compact—I'd almost forgotten it—was
to the effect, wasn't it, that we were to give each

other a helping hand if either of us had a better chance? The thing was absurd, of course; a mere joke; from my point of view, at least. I shall never want any better chance . . . any other chance. . . ."

"Oh, Nick, oh, Nick . . . but then. . . ." She was close to him, his face looming down through her tears; but he put her back.

"It would have been easy enough, wouldn't it," he rejoined, "if we'd been as detachable as all that? As it is, it's going to hurt horribly. But talking it over won't help. You were right just now when you asked how else we were going to live. We're born parasites, both, I suppose, or we'd have found out some way long ago. But I find there are things I might put up with for myself, at a pinch—and should, probably, in time—that I can't let you put up with for me . . . ever. . . . Those cigars at Como: do you suppose I didn't know it was for me? And this too? Well, it won't do . . . it won't do. . . ."

He stopped, as if his courage failed him; and she moaned out: "But your writing—if your book's a success. . . ."

"My poor Susy—that's all part of the humbug. We both know that my sort of writing will never pay. And what's the alternative—except more of the same kind of baseness? And getting more and more blunted to it? At least, till now, I've minded certain things; I don't want to go on till I find myself taking them for granted."

She reached out a timid hand. "But you needn't ever, dear . . . if you'd only leave it to me. . . ."

He drew back sharply. "That seems simple to you, I suppose? Well, men are different." He walked toward the dressing-table and glanced at the little enamelled clock which had been one of her wedding-presents.

"Time to dress, isn't it? Shall you mind if I leave you to dine with Streffy, and whoever else is coming? I'd rather like a long tramp, and no more talking just at present—except with myself."

He passed her by and walked rapidly out of the room. Susy stood motionless, unable to lift a detaining hand or to find a final word of appeal. On her disordered dressing-table Mrs. Vanderlyn's gifts glittered in the rosy lamp-light.

Yes: men were different, as he said.

XI

BUT there were necessary accommodations, there always had been; Nick in old times, had been the first to own it. . . . How they had laughed at the Perpendicular People, the people who went by on the other side (since you couldn't be a good Samaritan without stooping over and poking into heaps of you didn't know what)! And now Nick had suddenly become perpendicular. . . .

Susy, that evening, at the head of the dinner table, saw—in the breaks between her scudding thoughts—the nauseatingly familiar faces of the people she called her friends: Strefford, Fred Gillow, a giggling fool of a young Breckenridge, of their New York group, who had arrived that day, and Prince Nerone Altineri, Ursula's Prince, who, in Ursula's absence at a tiresome cure, had, quite simply and naturally, preferred to join her husband at Venice. Susy looked from one to the other of them, as if with newly-opened eyes, and wondered what life would be like with no faces but such as theirs to furnish it. . . .

Ah, Nick had become perpendicular! . . . 'After all, most people went through life making a given set of gestures, like dance-steps learned in advance. If your dancing manual told you at a given time to be perpendicular, you had to be, automatically—and that was Nick!

"But what on earth, Susy," Gillow's puzzled voice suddenly came to her as from immeasurable distances, "*are* you going to do in this beastly stifling hole for the rest of the summer?"

"Ask Nick, my dear fellow," Strefford answered for her; and: "By the way, where *is* Nick —if one may ask?" young Breckenridge interposed, glancing up to take belated note of his host's absence.

"Dining out," said Susy glibly. "People turned up: blighting bores that I wouldn't have dared to inflict on you." How easily the old familiar fibbing came to her!

"The kind to whom you say, 'Now *mind* you look me up'; and then spend the rest of your life dodging—like our good Hickses," Strefford amplified.

The Hickses—but, of course, Nick was with the Hickses! It went through Susy like a knife, and the dinner she had so lightly fibbed became a hateful truth. She said to herself feverishly: "I'll call him up there after dinner—and then he *will* feel silly"—but only to remember that the Hickses, in their mediæval setting, had of course sternly denied themselves a telephone.

The fact of Nick's temporary inaccessibility— since she was now convinced that he was really at the Hickses'—turned her distress to a mocking irritation. Ah, that was where he carried his principles, his standards, or whatever he called the new set of rules he had suddenly begun to apply to the old game! It was stupid of her not to have guessed it at once.

"Oh, the Hickses—Nick adores them, you know. He's going to marry Coral next," she laughed out, flashing the joke around the table with all her practised flippancy.

"Lord!" grasped Gillow, inarticulate: while the Prince displayed the unsurprised smile which Susy accused him of practising every morning with his Mueller exercises.

Suddenly Susy felt Strefford's eyes upon her.

"What's the matter with me? Too much rouge?" she asked, passing her arm in his as they left the table.

"No: too little. Look at yourself," he answered in a low tone.

"Oh, in these cadaverous old looking-glasses— everybody looks fished up from the canal!"

She jerked away from him to spin down the long floor of the *sala,* hands on hips, whistling a rag-time tune. The Prince and young Brecken-ridge caught her up, and she spun back with the latter, while Gillow—it was believed to be his sole accomplishment—snapped his fingers in simulation of bones, and shuffled after the couple on stamping feet.

Susy sank down on a sofa near the window, fanning herself with a floating scarf, and the men foraged for cigarettes, and rang for the gondoliers, who came in with trays of cooling drinks.

"Well, what next—this ain't all, is it?" Gillow

presently queried, from the divan where he lolled half-asleep with dripping brow. Fred Gillow, like Nature, abhorred a void, and it was inconceivable to him that every hour of man's rational existence should not furnish a motive for getting up and going somewhere else. Young Breckenridge, who took the same view, and the Prince, who earnestly desired to, reminded the company that somebody they knew was giving a dance that night at the Lido.

Strefford vetoed the Lido, on the ground that he'd just come back from there, and proposed that they should go out on foot for a change.

"Why not? What fun!" Susy was up in an instant. "Let's pay somebody a surprise visit— I don't know who! Streffy, Prince, can't you think of somebody who'd be particularly annoyed by our arrival?"

"Oh, the list's too long. Let's start, and choose our victim on the way," Strefford suggested.

Susy ran to her room for a light cloak, and without changing her high-heeled satin slippers went out with the four men. There was no moon —thank heaven there was no moon!—but the stars hung over them as close as fruit, and secret fragrances dropped on them from garden-walls. Susy's heart tightened with memories of Como.

They wandered on, laughing and dawdling, and yielding to the drifting whims of aimless people. Presently someone proposed taking a nearer look at the façade of San Giorgio Maggiore, and they hailed a gondola and were rowed out through the bobbing lanterns and twanging guitar-strings. When they landed again, Gillow, always acutely bored by scenery, and particularly resentful of midnight æsthetics, suggested a night club near at hand, which was said to be jolly. The Prince warmly supported this proposal; but on Susy's curt refusal they started their rambling again, circuitously threading the vague dark lanes and making for the Piazza and Florian's ices. Suddenly, at a *calle*-corner, unfamiliar and yet somehow known to her, Susy paused to stare about her with a laugh.

"But the Hickses—surely that's their palace? And the windows all lit up! They must be giving a party! Oh, do let's go up and surprise them!" The idea struck her as one of the drollest that she had ever originated, and she wondered that her companions should respond so languidly.

"I can't see anything very thrilling in surprising the Hickses," Gillow protested, defrauded of possible excitements; and Strefford added: "It would surprise *me* more than them if I went."

But Susy insisted feverishly: "You don't know. It may be awfully exciting! I have an idea that Coral's announcing her engagement—her engagement to Nick! Come, give me a hand, Streff—and you the other, Fred—" she began to hum the first bars of Donna Anna's entrance in *Don Giovanni*. "Pity I haven't got a black cloak and a mask. . . ."

"Oh, your face will do," said Strefford, laying his hand on her arm.

She drew back, flushing crimson. Breckenridge and the Prince had sprung on ahead, and Gillow, lumbering after them, was already halfway up the stairs.

"My face? My face? What's the matter with my face? Do you know any reason why I shouldn't go to the Hickses to-night?" Susy broke out in sudden wrath.

"None whatever; except that if you do it will bore me to death," Strefford returned, with serenity.

"Oh, in that case—!"

"No; come on. I hear those fools banging on the door already." He caught her by the hand, and they started up the stairway. But on the first landing she paused, twisted her hand out of his, and without a word, without a conscious thought, dashed down the long flight, across the great resounding vestibule and out into the darkness of the *calle*.

Strefford caught up with her, and they stood a moment silent in the night.

"Susy—what the devil's the matter?"

"The matter? Can't you see? That I'm tired, that I've got a splitting headache—that you bore me to death, one and all of you!" She turned and laid a deprecating hand on his arm. "Streffy, old dear, don't mind me: but for God's sake find a gondola and send me home."

"Alone?"

"Alone."

It was never any concern of Streff's if people wanted to do things he did not understand, and she knew that she could count on his obedience. They walked on in silence to the next canal, and he picked up a passing gondola and put her in it.

"Now go and amuse yourself," she called after him, as the boat shot under the nearest bridge. Anything, anything, to be alone, away from the folly and futility that would be all she had left if Nick were to drop out of her life. . . .

"But perhaps he has dropped already—dropped for good," she thought as she set her foot on the Vanderlyn threshold.

The short summer night was already growing transparent: a new-born breeze stirred the soiled surface of the water and sent it lapping freshly against the old palace doorways. Nearly two o'clock! Nick had no doubt come back long ago. Susy hurried up the stairs, reassured by the mere thought of his nearness. She knew that when their eyes and their lips met it would be impossible for anything to keep them apart.

The gondolier dozing on the landing roused himself to receive her, and to proffer two envelopes. The upper one was a telegram for Strefford: she threw it down again and paused under the lantern hanging from the painted vault, the other envelope in her hand. The address it bore was in Nick's writing.

"When did the signore leave this for me? Has he gone out again?"

Gone out again? But the signore had not come in since dinner: of that the gondolier was positive, as he had been on duty all the evening. A boy had brought the letter—an unknown boy: he had left it without waiting. It must have been about half an hour after the signora had herself gone out with her guests.

Susy, hardly hearing him, fled on to her own room, and there, beside the very lamp which, two months before, had illuminated Ellie Vanderlyn's fatal letter, she opened Nick's.

"Don't think me hard on you, dear; but I've got to work this thing out by myself. The sooner the better—don't you agree? So I'm taking the express to Milan presently. You'll get a proper letter in a day or two. I wish I could think, now, of something to say that would show you I'm not a brute—but I can't. N. L."

There was not much of the night left in which to sleep, even had a semblance of sleep been achievable. The letter fell from Susy's hands, and she crept out onto the balcony and cowered there, her forehead pressed against the balustrade, the dawn-wind stirring in her thin laces. Through her closed eyelids and the tightly-clenched fingers pressed against them, she felt the penetration of the growing light, the relentless advance of another day—a day without purpose and without meaning—a day without Nick.

At length she dropped her hands, and staring from dry lids saw a rim of fire above the roofs across the Grand Canal. She sprang up, ran back into her room, and dragging the heavy curtains shut across the windows, stumbled over in the darkness to the lounge and fell among its pillows —face downward—groping, delving for a deeper night. . . .

She started up, stiff and aching, to see a golden wedge of sun on the floor at her feet. She had slept, then—was it possible?—it must be eight or nine o'clock already! She had slept—slept like a drunkard—with that letter on the table at her elbow! Ah, now she remembered — she had dreamed that the letter was a dream! But there, inexorably, it lay; and she picked it up, and slowly, painfully re-read it. Then she tore it into shreds, hunted for a match, and kneeling before the empty hearth, as though she were accomplishing some funeral rite, she burnt every shred of it to ashes. Nick would thank her for that some day!

After a bath and a hurried toilet she began to be aware of feeling younger and more hopeful. After all, Nick had merely said that he was going away for "a day or two." And the letter was not cruel: there were tender things in it, showing through the curt words. She smiled at herself a little stiffly in the glass, put a dash of red on her colourless lips, and rang for the maid.

"Coffee, Giovanna, please; and will you tell Mr. Strefford that I should like to see him presently."

If Nick really kept to his intention of staying away for a few days she must trump up some explanation of his absence; but her mind refused to work, and the only thing she could think of was to take Strefford into her confidence. She knew that he could be trusted in a real difficulty; his impish malice transformed itself into a resourceful ingenuity when his friends required it.

The maid stood looking at her with a puzzled gaze, and Susy somewhat sharply repeated her order. "But don't wake him on purpose," she added, foreseeing the probable effect on Strefford's temper.

"But, signora, the gentleman is already out."

"Already out?" Strefford, who could hardly be routed from his bed before luncheon-time! "Is it so late?" Susy cried, incredulous.

"After nine. And the gentleman took the eight o'clock train for England. Gervaso said he had received a telegram. He left word that he would write to the signora."

The door closed upon the maid, and Susy continued to gaze at her painted image in the glass, as if she had been trying to outstare an importunate stranger. There was no one left for her to take counsel of, then—no one but poor Fred Gillow! She made a grimace at the idea. . . . But what on earth could have summoned Strefford back to England?

XII

NICK LANSING, in the Milan express, was roused by the same bar of sunshine lying across his knees. He yawned, looked with disgust at his stolidly sleeping neighbours, and wondered why he had decided to go to Milan, and what on earth he should do when he got there. The difficulty about trenchant decisions was°that the next morning they generally left one facing a void. . . .

When the train drew into the station at Milan, he scrambled out, got some coffee, and having drunk it decided to continue his journey to Genoa. The state of being carried passively onward postponed action and dulled thought; and after twelve hours of furious mental activity that was exactly what he wanted.

He fell into a doze again, waking now and then to haggard intervals of more thinking, and then dropping off to the clank and rattle of the train. Inside his head, in his waking intervals, the same clanking and grinding of wheels and chains went on unremittingly. He had done all his lucid thinking within an hour of leaving the Palazzo Vanderlyn the night before; since then, his brain had simply continued to revolve indefatigably about the same old problem. His cup of coffee, instead

of clearing his thoughts, had merely accelerated
their pace.

At Genoa he wandered about in the hot streets,
bought a cheap suit-case and some underclothes,
and then went down to the port in search of a little
hotel he remembered there. An hour later he was
sitting in the coffee-room, smoking and glancing
vacantly over the papers while he waited for dinner, when he became aware of being timidly but
intently examined by a small round-faced gentleman with eyeglasses who sat alone at the adjoining table.

"Hullo—Buttles!" Lansing exclaimed, recog-
nising with surprise the recalcitrant secretary
who had resisted Miss Hicks's endeavour to con-
vert him to Tiepolo.

Mr. Buttles, blushing to the roots of his scant
hair, half rose and bowed ceremoniously.

Nick Lansing's first feeling was of annoyance
at being disturbed in his solitary broodings; his
next, of relief at having to postpone them even to
converse with Mr. Buttles.

"No idea you were here: is the yacht in harbour?" he asked, remembering that the *Ibis* must
be just about to spread her wings.

Mr. Buttles, at salute behind his chair, signed
a mute negation: for the moment he seemed too
embarrassed to speak.

"Ah—you're here as an advance guard? I remember now—I saw Miss Hicks in Venice the
day before yesterday," Lansing continued, dazed

at the thought that hardly forty-eight hours had passed since his encounter with Coral in the Scalzi.

Mr. Buttles, instead of speaking, had tentatively approached his table. "May I take this seat for a moment, Mr. Lansing? Thank you. No, I am not here as an advance guard—though I believe the *Ibis* is due some time to-morrow." He cleared his throat, wiped his eyeglasses on a silk handkerchief, replaced them on his nose, and went on solemnly: "Perhaps, to clear up any possible misunderstanding, I ought to say that I am no longer in the employ of Mr. Hicks."

Lansing glanced at him sympathetically. It was clear that he suffered horribly in imparting this information, though his compact face did not lend itself to any dramatic display of emotion.

"Really?" Nick smiled, and then ventured: "I hope it's not owing to conscientious objections to Tiepolo?"

Mr. Buttles's blush became a smouldering agony. "Ah, Miss Hicks mentioned to you . . . told you . . . ? No, Mr. Lansing. I am principled against the effete art of Tiepolo, and of all his contemporaries, I confess; but if Miss Hicks chooses to surrender herself momentarily to the unwholesome spell of the Italian decadence it is not for me to protest or to criticize. Her intellectual and æsthetic range so far exceeds my humble capacity that it would be ridiculous, unbecoming. . . ."

He broke off, and once more wiped a faint moisture from his eyeglasses. It was evident that he was suffering from a distress which he longed and yet dreaded to communicate. But Nick made no farther effort to bridge the gulf of his own preoccupations; and Mr. Buttles, after an expectant pause, went on: "If you see me here to-day it is only because, after a somewhat abrupt departure, I find myself unable to take leave of our friends without a last look at the *Ibis*—the scene of so many stimulating hours. But I must beg you," he added earnestly, "should you see Miss Hicks —or any other member of the party—to make no allusion to my presence in Genoa. I wish," said Mr. Buttles with simplicity, "to preserve the strictest incognito."

Lansing glanced at him kindly. "Oh, but —isn't that a little unfriendly?"

"No other course is possible, Mr. Lansing," said the ex-secretary, "and I commit myself to your discretion. The truth is, if I am here it is not to look once more at the *Ibis,* but at Miss Hicks: once only. You will understand me, and appreciate what I am suffering."

He bowed again, and trotted away on his small, tightly-booted feet; pausing on the threshold to say: "From the first it was hopeless," before he disappeared through the glass doors.

A gleam of commiseration flashed through Nick's mind: there was something quaintly poignant in the sight of the brisk and efficient Mr.

Buttles reduced to a limp image of unrequited
passion. And what a painful surprise to the
Hickses to be thus suddenly deprived of the secretary who possessed "the foreign languages"!
Mr. Beck kept the accounts and settled with the
hotel-keepers; but it was Mr. Buttles's loftier task
to entertain in their own tongues the unknown
geniuses who flocked about the Hickses, and Nick
could imagine how disconcerting his departure
must be on the eve of their Grecian cruise—which
Mrs. Hicks would certainly call an Odyssey.

The next moment the vision of Coral's hopeless
suitor had faded, and Nick was once more spin-
ning around on the wheel of his own woes. The
night before, when he had sent his note to Susy,
from a little restaurant close to Palazzo Vanderlyn that they often patronized, he had done so
with the firm intention of going away for a day
or two in order to collect his wits and think over
the situation. But after his letter had been entrusted to the landlord's little son, who was a particular friend of Susy's, Nick had decided to await
the lad's return. The messenger had not been
bidden to ask for an answer; but Nick, knowing
the friendly and inquisitive Italian mind, was almost sure that the boy, in the hope of catching
a glimpse of Susy, would linger about while the
letter was carried up. And he pictured the maid
knocking at his wife's darkened room, and Susy
dashing some powder on her tear-stained face
before she turned on the light—poor foolish child!

The boy had returned rather sooner than Nick expected, and he had brought no answer, but merely the statement that the signora was out: that everybody was out.

"Everybody?"

"The signora and the four gentlemen who were dining at the palace. They all went out together on foot soon after dinner. There was no one to whom I could give the note but the gondolier on the landing, for the signora had said she would be very late, and had sent the maid to bed; and the maid had, of course, gone out immediately with her *innamorato*."

"Ah—" said Nick, slipping his reward into the boy's hand, and walking out of the restaurant.

Susy had gone out—gone out with their usual band, as she did every night in these sultry summer weeks, gone out after her talk with Nick, as if nothing had happened, as if his whole world and hers had not crashed in ruins at their feet. Ah, poor Susy! After all, she had merely obeyed the instinct of self-preservation, the old hard habit of keeping up, going ahead and hiding her troubles; unless indeed the habit had already engendered indifference, and it had become as easy for her as for most of her friends to pass from drama to dancing, from sorrow to the cinema. What of soul was left, he wondered—?

His train did not start till midnight, and after leaving the restaurant Nick tramped the sultry by-ways till his tired legs brought him to a stand-

still under the vine-covered pergola of a gondolier's wine-shop at a landing close to the Piaz-
zetta. There he could absorb cooling drinks until
it was time to go to the station.

It was after eleven, and he was beginning to
look about for a boat, when a black prow pushed
up to the steps, and with much chaff and laughter
a party of young people in evening dress jumped
out. Nick, from under the darkness of the vine,
saw that there was only one lady among them,
and it did not need the lamp above the landing to
reveal her identity. Susy, bareheaded and laughing, a light scarf slipping from her bare shoulders, a cigarette between her fingers, took Strefford's arm and turned in the direction of Florian's, with Gillow, the Prince and young Breckenridge in her wake. . . .

Nick had relived this rapid scene hundreds of
times during his hours in the train and his aimless
trampings through the streets of Genoa. In that
squirrel-wheel of a world of his and Susy's you
had to keep going or drop out—and Susy, it was
evident, had chosen to keep going. Under the
lamp-flare on the landing he had had a good look
at her face, and had seen that the mask of paint
and powder was carefully enough adjusted to hide
any ravages the scene between them might have
left. He even fancied that she had dropped a
little atropine into her eyes. . . .

There was no time to spare if he meant to

catch the midnight train, and no gondola in sight
but that which his wife had just left. He sprang
into it, and bade the gondolier carry him to the
station. The cushions, as he leaned back, gave
out a breath of her scent; and in the glare of electric light at the station he saw at his feet a rose
which had fallen from her dress. He ground his
heel into it as he got out.

There it was, then; that was the last picture
he was to have of her. For he knew now that he
was not going back; at least not to take up their
life together. He supposed he should have to see
her once, to talk things over, settle something for
their future. He had been sincere in saying that
he bore her no ill-will; only he could never go
back into that slough again. If he did, he knew
he would inevitably be drawn under, slipping
downward from concession to concession. . . .

The noises of a hot summer night in the port
of Genoa would have kept the most care-free from
slumber; but though Nick lay awake he did not
notice them, for the tumult in his brain was more
deafening. Dawn brought a negative relief, and
out of sheer weariness he dropped into a heavy
sleep. When he woke it was nearly noon, and
from his window he saw the well-known outline
of the *Ibis* standing up dark against the glitter
of the harbour. He had no fear of meeting her
owners, who had doubtless long since landed and
betaken themselves to cooler and more fashion-

able regions: oddly enough, the fact seemed to ac-
centuate his loneliness, his sense of having no one
on earth to turn to. He dressed, and wandered
out disconsolately to pick up a cup of coffee in
some shady corner.

As he drank his coffee his thoughts gradually
cleared. It became obvious to him that he had behaved like a madman or a petulant child—he preferred to think it was like a madman. If he and
Susy were to separate there was no reason why
it should not be done decently and quietly, as such
transactions were habitually managed among
people of their kind. It seemed grotesque to in-
troduce melodrama into their little world of un-
ruffled Sybarites, and he felt inclined, now, to
smile at the incongruity of his gesture. . . . But
suddenly his eyes filled with tears. The future
without Susy was unbearable, inconceivable.
Why, after all, should they separate? At the
question, her soft face seemed close to his, and
that slight lift of the upper lip that made her
smile so exquisite. Well—he would go back.
But not with any pretence of going to talk things
over, come to an agreement, wind up their joint
life like a business association. No—if he went
back he would go without conditions, for good,
forever. . . .

Only, what about the future? What about the
not far-distant day when the wedding cheques
would have been spent, and Granny's pearls sold,
and nothing left except unconcealed and uncondi-

tional dependence on rich friends, the rôle of the acknowledged hangers-on? Was there no other possible solution, no new way of ordering their lives? No—there was none: he could not picture Susy out of her setting of luxury and leisure, could not picture either of them living such a life as the Nat Fulmers, for instance! He remembered the shabby untidy bungalow in New Hampshire, the slatternly servants, uneatable food and ubiquitous children. How could he ask Susy to share such a life with him? If he did, she would probably have the sense to refuse. Their alliance had been based on a moment's midsummer madness; now the score must be paid. . . .

He decided to write. If they were to part he could not trust himself to see her. He called a waiter, asked for pen and paper, and pushed aside a pile of unread newspapers on the corner of the table where his coffee had been served. As he did so, his eye lit on a *Daily Mail* of two days before. As a pretext for postponing his letter, he took up the paper and glanced down the first page. He read:

"Tragic Yachting Accident in the Solent. The Earl of Altringham and his son Viscount d'Amblay drowned in midnight collision. Both bodies recovered."

He read on. He grasped the fact that the disaster had happened the night before he had left

Venice—and that, as the result of a fog in the
Solent, their old friend Strefford was now Earl
of Altringham, and possessor of one of the largest
private fortunes in England. It was vertiginous
to think of their old impecunious Streff as the
hero of such an adventure. And what irony in
that double turn of the wheel which, in one day,
had plunged him, Nick Lansing, into nether-
most misery, while it tossed the other to the
stars!

With an intenser precision he saw again Susy's
descent from the gondola at the *calle* steps, the
sound of her laughter and of Strefford's chaff,
the way she had caught his arm and clung to it,
sweeping the other men on in her train. Strefford—Susy and Strefford! . . . More than once,
Nick had noticed the softer inflections of his
friend's voice when he spoke to Susy, the brooding look in his lazy eyes when they rested on her.
In the security of his wedded bliss Nick had made
light of those signs. The only real jealousy he
had felt had been of Fred Gillow, because of his
unlimited power to satisfy a woman's whims.
Yet Nick knew that such material advantages
would never again suffice for Susy. With Strefford it was different. She had delighted in his
society while he was notoriously ineligible; might
not she find him irresistible now?

The forgotten terms of their bridal compact
came back to Nick: the absurd agreement on
which he and Susy had solemnly pledged their

faith. But was it so absurd, after all? It had
been Susy's suggestion (not his, thank God!);
and perhaps in making it she had been more
serious than he imagined. Perhaps, even if their
rupture had not occurred, Strefford's sudden
honours might have caused her to ask for her
freedom. . . .

Money, luxury, fashion, pleasure: those were
the four cornerstones of her existence. He had
always known it—she herself had always acknowledged it, even in their last dreadful talk together; and once he had gloried in her frankness.
How could he ever have imagined that, to have
her fill of these things, she would not in time stoop
lower than she had yet stooped? Perhaps in giving her up to Strefford he might be saving her.
At any rate, the taste of the past was now so bitter to him that he was moved to thank whatever
gods there were for pushing that mortuary paragraph under his eye. . . .

"Susy, dear [he wrote], the fates seem to have
taken our future in hand, and spared us the
trouble of unravelling it. If I have sometimes
been selfish enough to forget the conditions on
which you agreed to marry me, they have come
back to me during these two days of solitude.
You've given me the best a man can have, and
nothing else will ever be worth much to me. But
since I haven't the ability to provide you with

what you want, I recognize that I've no right to stand in your way. We must owe no more Venetian palaces to underhand services. I see by the newspapers that Streff can now give you as many palaces as you want. Let him have the chance— I fancy he'll jump at it, and he's the best man in sight. I wish I were in his shoes.

"I'll write again in a day or two, when I've collected my wits, and can give you an address. NICK."

He added a line on the subject of their modest funds, put the letter into an envelope, and addressed it to Mrs. Nicholas Lansing. As he did so, he reflected that it was the first time he had ever written his wife's married name.

"Well—by God, no other woman shall have it after her," he vowed, as he groped in his pocketbook for a stamp.

He stood up with a stretch of weariness—the heat was stifling!—and put the letter in his pocket.

"I'll post it myself, it's safer," he thought; "and then what in the name of goodness shall I do next, I wonder?" He jammed his hat down on his head and walked out into the sun-blaze.

As he was turning away from the square by the general Post Office, a white parasol waved from a passing cab, and Coral Hicks leaned forward with outstretched hand.

"I knew I'd find you," she triumphed. "I've been driving up and down in this broiling sun for hours, shopping and watching for you at the same time."

He stared at her blankly, too bewildered even to wonder how she knew he was in Genoa; and she continued, with the kind of shy imperiousness that always made him feel, in her presence, like a member of an orchestra under a masterful *bâton;* "Now please get right into this carriage, and don't keep me roasting here another minute." To the cab-driver she called out: *"Al porto."*

Nick Lansing sank down beside her. As he did so he noticed a heap of bundles at her feet, and felt that he had simply added one more to the number. He supposed that she was taking her spoils to the *Ibis,* and that he would be carried up to the deck-house to be displayed with the others. Well, it would all help to pass the day—and by night he would have reached some kind of a decision about his future.

On the third day after Nick's departure the post brought to the Palazzo Vanderlyn three letters for Mrs. Lansing.

The first to arrive was a word from Strefford, scribbled in the train and posted at Turin. In it he briefly said that he had been called home by the dreadful accident of which Susy had probably

read in the daily papers. He added that he would
write again from England, and then—in a blotted
postscript—: "I wanted uncommonly badly to
see you for good-bye, but the hour was impossible.
Regards to Nick. Do write me just a word to Altringham."

The other two letters, which came together in
the afternoon, were both from Genoa. Susy
scanned the addresses and fell upon the one in
her husband's writing. Her hand trembled so
much that for a moment she could not open the
envelope. When she had done so, she devoured
the letter in a flash, and then sat and brooded over
the outspread page as it lay on her knee. It
might mean so many things—she could read into
it so many harrowing alternatives of indifference
and despair, of irony and tenderness! Was he
suffering tortures when he wrote it, or seeking
only to inflict them upon her? Or did the words
represent his actual feelings, no more and no less,
and did he really intend her to understand that
he considered it his duty to abide by the letter
of their preposterous compact? He had left her
in wrath and indignation, yet, as a closer scrutiny
revealed, there was not a word of reproach in his
brief lines. Perhaps that was why, in the last
issue, they seemed so cold to her. . . She shivered
and turned to the other envelope.

The large stilted characters, though half-fa-
miliar, called up no definite image. She opened

the envelope and discovered a post-card of the
Ibis, canvas spread, bounding over a rippled sea.
On the back was written:

"So awfully dear of you to lend us Mr. Lansing
for a little cruise. You may count on our taking
the best of care of him. COBAL."

PART II

XIII

WHEN Violet Melrose had said to Susy Branch, the winter before in New York: "But why on earth don't you and Nick go to my little place at Versailles for the honeymoon? I'm off to China, and you could have it to yourselves all summer," the offer had been tempting enough to make the lovers waver.

It was such an artless ingenuous little house, so full of the demoralizing simplicity of great wealth, that it seemed to Susy just the kind of place in which to take the first steps in renunciation. But Nick had objected that Paris, at that time of year, would be swarming with acquaintances who would hunt them down at all hours; and Susy's own experience had led her to remark that there was nothing the very rich enjoyed more than taking pot-luck with the very poor. They therefore gave Strefford's villa the preference, with an inward proviso (on Susy's part) that Violet's house might very conveniently serve their purpose at another season.

These thoughts were in her mind as she drove up to Mrs. Melrose's door on a rainy afternoon late in August, her boxes piled high on the roof of the cab she had taken at the station. She had travelled straight through from Venice, stopping in Milan just long enough to pick up a reply to the telegram she had despatched to the perfect house-keeper whose permanent presence enabled Mrs. Melrose to say: "Oh, when I'm sick of everything I just rush off without warning to my little shanty at Versailles, and live there all alone on scrambled eggs."

The perfect house-keeper had replied to Susy's enquiry: "Am sure Mrs. Melrose most happy"; and Susy, without further thought, had jumped into a Versailles train, and now stood in the thin rain before the sphinx-guarded threshold of the pavilion.

The revolving year had brought around the season at which Mrs. Melrose's house might be convenient: no visitors were to be feared at Versailles at the end of August, and though Susy's reasons for seeking solitude were so remote from those she had once prefigured, they were none the less cogent. To be alone—alone! After those first exposed days when, in the persistent presence of Fred Gillow and his satellites, and in the mocking radiance of late summer on the lagoons, she had turned and turned about in her agony like a trapped animal in a cramping cage, to be alone had seemed the only respite, the one craving: to be alone somewhere in a setting as unlike as possible to the sensual splendours of Venice, under skies as unlike its azure roof. If she could have chosen she would have crawled away into a dingy inn in a rainy northern town, where she had never been and no one knew her. Failing that unobtainable luxury, here she was on the threshold of an empty house, in a deserted place, under lowering skies. She had shaken off Fred Gillow, sulkily departing for his moor (where she had half-promised to join him in September); the Prince, young Breckenridge, and the few remaining survivors of the Venetian group, had dispersed in the direction of the Engadine or Biarritz; and now she could at least collect her wits, take stock of herself, and prepare the countenance with which she was to face the next stage in her career. Thank God it was raining at Versailles!

The door opened, she heard voices in the drawing-room, and a slender languishing figure appeared on the threshold.

"Darling!" Violet Melrose cried in an embrace, drawing her into the dusky perfumed room.

"But I thought you were in China!" Susy stammered.

"In China . . . in China?" Mrs. Melrose stared with dreamy eyes, and Susy remembered her drifting disorganised life, a life more planless, more inexplicable than that of any of the other ephemeral beings blown about upon the same winds of pleasure.

"Well, Madam, I thought so myself till I got a wire from Mrs. Melrose last evening," remarked the perfect house-keeper, following with Susy's hand-bag.

Mrs. Melrose clutched her cavernous temples in her attenuated hands. "Of course, of course! I *had* meant to go to China—no, India. . . . But I've discovered a genius . . . and Genius, you know. . . ." Unable to complete her thought, she sank down upon a pillowy divan, stretched out an arm, cried: "Fulmer! Fulmer!" and, while Susy Lansing stood in the middle of the room with widening eyes, a man emerged from the more deeply cushioned and scented twilight of some inner apartment, and she saw with surprise Nat Fulmer, the good Nat Fulmer of the New Hampshire bungalow and the ubiquitous progeny, standing before her in lordly ease, his hands in his pockets, a cigarette between his lips, his feet solidly planted in the insidious depths of one of Violet Melrose's white leopard skins.

"Susy!" he shouted with open arms; and Mrs. Melrose murmured: "You didn't know, then? You hadn't heard of his masterpieces?"

In spite of herself, Susy burst into a laugh. "Is Nat your genius?"

Mrs. Melrose looked at her reproachfully.

Fulmer laughed. "No; I'm Grace's. But Mrs. Melrose has been our Providence, and. . . ."

"Providence?" his hostess interrupted. "Don't talk as if you were at a prayer-meeting! He had an exhibition in New York . . . it was the most fabulous success. He's come abroad to make studies for the decoration of my music-room in New York. Ursula Gillow has given him her

garden-house at Roslyn to do. And Mrs. Bockheimer's ball-room—oh, Fulmer, where *are* the
cartoons?'' She sprang up, tossed about some
fashion-papers heaped on a lacquer table, and
sank back exhausted by the effort. ''I'd got as
far as Brindisi. I've travelled day and night to
be here to meet him,'' she declared. ''But, you
darling,'' and she held out a caressing hand
to Susy, ''I'm forgetting to ask if you've had
tea?''

An hour later, over the tea-table, Susy already
felt herself mysteriously reabsorbed into what
had so long been her native element. Ellie Vanderlyn had brought a breath of it to Venice; but
Susy was then nourished on another air, the air
of Nick's presence and personality; now that she
was abandoned, left again to her own devices, she
felt herself suddenly at the mercy of the influences
from which she thought she had escaped.

In the queer social whirligig from which she
had so lately fled, it seemed natural enough that a
shake of the box should have tossed Nat Fulmer
into celebrity, and sent Violet Melrose chasing
back from the ends of the earth to bask in his success. Susy knew that Mrs. Melrose belonged to
the class of moral parasites; for in that strange
world the parts were sometimes reversed, and the
wealthy preyed upon the pauper. Wherever there
was a reputation to batten on, there poor Violet
appeared, a harmless vampire in pearls who
sought only to feed on the notoriety which all her

millions could not create for her.   Any one less
versed than Susy in the shallow mysteries of her
little world would have seen in Violet Melrose a
baleful enchantress, in Nat Fulmer her helpless
victim. Susy knew better. Violet, poor Violet,
was not even that. The insignificant Ellie Vanderlyn, with her brief trivial passions, her artless
mixture of amorous and social interests, was a
woman with a purpose, a creature who fulfilled
herself; but Violet was only a drifting interroga-
tion.

And what of Fulmer? Mustering with new eyes
his short sturdily-built figure, his nondescript
bearded face, and the eyes that dreamed and wandered, and then suddenly sank into you like claws,
Susy seemed to have found the key to all his years
of dogged toil, his indifference to neglect, indifference to poverty, indifference to the needs of his
growing family. . . . Yes: for the first time she
saw that he looked commonplace enough to be a
genius—*was* a genius, perhaps, even though it
was Violet Melrose who affirmed it! Susy looked
steadily at Fulmer, their eyes met, and he smiled
at her faintly through his beard.

"Yes, I did discover him—I *did*," Mrs. Melrose
was insisting, from the depths of the black velvet
divan in which she lay sunk like a wan Nereid in
a midnight sea. "You mustn't believe a word
that Ursula Gillow tells you about having pounced
on his 'Spring Snow Storm' in a dark corner of
the American Artists' exhibition—*skied,* if you

please! They *skied* him less than a year ago! And naturally Ursula never in her life looked higher than the first line at a picture-show. And now she actually pretends . . . oh, for pity's sake don't say it doesn't matter, Fulmer! Your saying that just encourages her, and makes people think she *did*. When, in reality, any one who saw me at the exhibition on varnishing-day. . . . Who? Well, Eddy Breckenridge, for instance. He was in Egypt, you say? Perhaps he was! As if one could remember the people about one, when suddenly one comes upon a great work of art, as St. Paul did—didn't he?—and the scales fell from his eyes. Well . . . that's exactly what happened to me that day . . . and Ursula, everybody knows, was down at Roslyn at the time, and didn't come up for the opening of the exhibition at all. And Fulmer sits there and laughs, and says it doesn't matter, and that he'll paint another picture any day for me to discover!"

Susy had rung the door-bell with a hand trembling with eagerness—eagerness to be alone, to be quiet, to stare her situation in the face, and collect herself before she came out again among her kind. She had stood on the door-step, cowering among her bags, counting the instants till a step sounded and the door-knob turned, letting her in from the searching glare of the outer world. . . . And now she had sat for an hour in Violet's drawing-room, in the very house where her honey-moon might have been spent; and no one had asked her where she had come from, or why she was alone, or what was the key to the tragedy written on her shrinking face. . . .

That was the way of the world they lived in. Nobody questioned, nobody wondered any more —because nobody had time to remember. The old risk of prying curiosity, of malicious gossip, was virtually over: one was left with one's drama, one's disaster, on one's hands, because there was nobody to stop and notice the little shrouded object one was carrying. As Susy watched the two people before her, each so frankly unaffected by her presence, Violet Melrose so engrossed in her feverish pursuit of notoriety, Fulmer so plunged in the golden sea of his success, she felt like a ghost making inaudible and imperceptible appeals to the grosser senses of the living.

"If I wanted to be alone," she thought, "I'm alone enough, in all conscience." There was a deathly chill in such security. She turned to Fulmer.

"And Grace?"

He beamed back without sign of embarrassment. "Oh, she's here, naturally—we're in Paris, kids and all. In a *pension*, where we can polish up the lingo. But I hardly ever lay eyes on her, because she's as deep in music as I am in paint; it was as big a chance for her as for me, you see, and she's making the most of it, fiddling and listening to the fiddlers. Well, it's a considerable change from

New Hampshire.'' He looked at her dreamily, as if making an intense effort to detach himself from his dream, and situate her in the fading past. ''Remember the bungalow? And Nick—ah, how's Nick?'' he brought out triumphantly.

''Oh, yes—darling Nick?'' Mrs. Melrose chimed in; and Susy, her head erect, her cheeks aflame, declared with resonance: ''Most awfully well—splendidly!''

''He's not here, though?'' from Fulmer.

''No. He's off travelling—cruising.''

Mrs. Melrose's attention was faintly roused. ''With anybody interesting?''

''No; you wouldn't know them. People we met. . . .'' She did not have to continue, for her hostess's gaze had again strayed.

''And you've come for your clothes, I suppose, darling? Don't listen to people who say that skirts are to be wider. I've discovered a new woman—a Genius—and she absolutely *swathes* you. . . . Her name's my secret; but we'll go to her together.''

Susy rose from her engulphing armchair. ''Do you mind if I go up to my room? I'm rather tired —coming straight through.''

''Of course, dear. I think there are some people coming to dinner . . . Mrs. Match will tell you. She has such a memory . . . Fulmer, where on *earth* are those cartoons of the music-room?''

Their voices pursued Susy upstairs, as, in Mrs.

Match's perpendicular wake, she mounted to the white-panelled room with its gay linen hangings and the low bed heaped with more cushions.

"If we'd come here," she thought, "everything might have been different." And she shuddered at the sumptuous memories of the Palazzo Vanderlyn, and the great painted bedroom where she had met her doom.

Mrs. Match, hoping she would find everything, and mentioning that dinner was not till nine, shut her softly in among her terrors.

"Find everything?" Susy echoed the phrase. Oh, yes, she would always find everything: every time the door shut on her now, and the sound of voices ceased, her memories would be there waiting for her, every one of them, waiting quietly, patiently, obstinately, like poor people in a doctor's office, the people who are always last to be attended to, but whom nothing will discourage or drive away, people to whom time is nothing, fatigue nothing, hunger nothing, other engagements nothing: who just wait. . . . Thank heaven, after all, that she had not found the house empty, if, whenever she returned to her room, she was to meet her memories there!

It was just a week since Nick had left her. During that week, crammed with people, questions, packing, explaining, evading, she had believed that in solitude lay her salvation. Now she understood that there was nothing she was so unprepared for, so unfitted for. When, in all her life,

had she ever been alone? And how was she to
bear it now, with all these ravening memories
besetting her?

Dinner not till nine? What on earth was she to
do till nine o'clock? She knelt before her boxes,
and feverishly began to unpack. . . .

Gradually, imperceptibly, the subtle influences
of her old life were stealing into her. As she
pulled out her tossed and crumpled dresses she
remembered Violet's emphatic warning: "Don't
believe the people who tell you that skirts are going to be wider." Were hers, perhaps, too wide
as it was? She looked at her limp raiment, piling
itself up on bed and sofa, and understood that,
according to Violet's standards, and that of all
her set, those dresses, which Nick had thought so
original and exquisite, were already commonplace
and dowdy, fit only to be passed on to poor relations or given to one's maid. And Susy would
have to go on wearing them till they fell to bits—
or else. . . . Well, or else begin the old life again
in some new form. . . .

She laughed aloud at the turn of her thoughts.
Dresses? How little they had mattered a few
short weeks ago! And now, perhaps, they would
again be one of the foremost considerations in her
life. How could it be otherwise, if she were to
return again to her old dependence on Ellie Vanderlyn, Ursula Gillow, Violet Melrose? And beyond that, only the Bockheimers and their kind
awaited her. . . .

A knock on the door—what a relief! It was
Mrs. Match again, with a telegram. To whom had
Susy given her new address? With a throbbing
heart she tore open the envelope and read:

"Shall be in Paris Friday for twenty-four
hours where can I see you write Nouveau Luxe."

Ah, yes—she remembered now: she had written
to Strefford! And this was his answer: he was
coming. She dropped into a chair, and tried to
think. What on earth had she said in her letter?
It had been mainly, of course, one of condolence;
but now she remembered having added, in a pre-
cipitate postscript: "I can't give your message to
Nick, for he's gone off with the Hickses—I don't
know where, or for how long. It's all right, of
course: it was in our bargain."

She had not meant to put in that last phrase;
but as she sealed her letter to Strefford her eye
had fallen on Nick's missive, which lay beside it.
Nothing in her husband's brief lines had embit-
tered her as much as the allusion to Strefford. It
seemed to imply that Nick's own plans were made,
that his own future was secure, and that he could
therefore freely and handsomely take thought for
hers, and give her a pointer in the right direction.
Sudden rage had possessed her at the thought:
where she had at first read jealousy she now saw
only a cold providence, and in a blur of tears she
had scrawled her postscript to Strefford. She remembered that she had not even asked him to

keep her secret. Well—after all, what would it matter if people should already know that Nick had left her? Their parting could not long remain a mystery, and the fact that it was known might help her to keep up a pretence of indifference.

"It was in the bargain—in the bargain," rang through her brain as she re-read Strefford's telegram. She understood that he had snatched the time for this hasty trip solely in the hope of seeing her, and her eyes filled. The more bitterly she thought of Nick the more this proof of Strefford's friendship moved her.

The clock, to her relief, reminded her that it was time to dress for dinner. She would go down presently, chat with Violet and Fulmer, and with Violet's other guests, who would probably be odd and amusing, and too much out of her world to embarrass her by awkward questions. She would sit at a softly-lit table, breathe delicate scents, eat exquisite food (trust Mrs. Match!), and be gradually drawn again under the spell of her old associations. Anything, anything but to be alone. . . .

She dressed with even more than her habitual care, reddened her lips attentively, brushed the faintest bloom of pink over her drawn cheeks, and went down—to meet Mrs. Match coming up with a tray.

"Oh, Madam, I thought you were too tired. . . . I was bringing it up to you myself—just a little morsel of chicken."

Susy, glancing past her, saw, through the open door, that the lamps were not lit in the drawing-room.

"Oh, no, I'm not tired, thank you. I thought Mrs. Melrose expected friends at dinner?"

"Friends at dinner—*to-night?*" Mrs. Match heaved a despairing sigh. Sometimes, the sigh seemed to say, her mistress put too great a strain upon her. "Why, Mrs. Melrose and Mr. Fulmer were engaged to dine in Paris. They left an hour ago. Mrs. Melrose told me she'd told you," the house-keeper wailed.

Susy kept her little fixed smile. "I must have misunderstood. In that case . . . well, yes, if it's no trouble, I believe I *will* have my tray up-stairs."

Slowly she turned, and followed the house-keeper up into the dread solitude she had just left.

XIV

THE next day a lot of people turned up unannounced for luncheon. They were not of the far-fetched and the exotic, in whom Mrs. Melrose now specialized, but merely commonplace fashionable people belonging to Susy's own group, people familiar with the amusing romance of her penniless marriage, and to whom she had to explain (though none of them really listened to the explanation) that Nick was not with her just now, but had gone off cruising . . . cruising in the Ægean with friends . . . getting up material for his book (this detail had occurred to her in the night).

It was the kind of encounter she had most dreaded; but it proved, after all, easy enough to go through compared with those endless hours of turning to and fro, the night before, in the cage of her lonely room. Anything, anything, but to be alone. . . .

Gradually, from the force of habit, she found herself actually in tune with the talk of the luncheon table, interested in the references to absent friends, the light allusions to last year's loves and quarrels, scandals and absurdities. The women, in their pale summer dresses, were so graceful, indolent and sure of themselves, the men so easy and good-humoured! Perhaps, after all, Susy reflected, it was the world she was meant for, since the other, the brief Paradise of her dreams, had already shut its golden doors upon her. And then, as they sat on the terrace after luncheon, looking across at the yellow tree-tops of the park, one of the women said something—made just an allusion—that Susy would have let pass unnoticed in the old days, but that now filled her with a sudden deep disgust. . . . She stood up and wandered away, away from them all through the fading garden.

Two days later Susy and Strefford sat on the terrace of the Tuileries above the Seine. She had asked him to meet her there, with the desire to avoid the crowded halls and drawing-room of the Nouveau Luxe where, even at that supposedly "dead" season, people one knew were always drifting to and fro; and they sat on a bench in the pale sunlight, the discoloured leaves heaped at their feet, and no one to share their solitude but a lame working-man and a haggard woman who were lunching together mournfully at the other end of the majestic vista.

Strefford, in his new mourning, looked unnaturally prosperous and well-valeted; but his ugly untidy features remained as undisciplined, his smile as whimsical, as of old. He had been on cool though friendly terms with the pompous uncle and the poor sickly cousin whose joint disappearance had so abruptly transformed his future; and it was his way to understate his feelings rather than to pretend more than he felt. Nevertheless, beneath his habitual bantering tone Susy discerned a change. The disaster had shocked him profoundly; already, in his brief sojourn among his people and among the great possessions so tragically acquired, old instincts had awakened, forgotten associations had spoken in him. Susy listened to him wistfully, silenced by her imaginative perception of the distance that these things had put between them.

"It was horrible . . . seeing them both there together, laid out in that hideous Pugin chapel at Altringham . . . the poor boy especially . . I suppose that's really what's cutting me up now," he murmured, almost apologetically.

"Oh, it's more than that—more than you know," she insisted; but he jerked back: "Now, my dear, don't be edifying, please," and fumbled for a cigarette in the pocket which was already beginning to bulge with his miscellaneous properties.

"And now about you—for that's what I came for," he continued, turning to her with one of his sudden movements. "I couldn't make head or tail of your letter."

She paused a moment to steady her voice. "Couldn't you? I suppose you'd forgotten my bargain with Nick. *He* hadn't—and he's asked me to fulfil it."

Strefford stared. "What—that nonsense about your setting each other free if either of you had the chance to make a good match?"

She signed "Yes."

"And he's actually asked you—?"

"Well: practically. He's gone off with the Hickses. Before going he wrote me that we'd better both consider ourselves free. And Coral sent me a post-card to say that she would take the best of care of him."

Strefford mused, his eyes upon his cigarette. "'But what the deuce led up to all this? It can't have happened like that, out of a clear sky."

Susy flushed, hesitated, looked away. She had meant to tell Strefford the whole story; it had been one of her chief reasons for wishing to see him again, and half-unconsciously, perhaps, she had hoped, in his laxer atmosphere, to recover something of her shattered self-esteem. But now she suddenly felt the impossibility of confessing to anyone the depths to which Nick's wife had stooped. She fancied that her companion guessed the nature of her hesitation.

"Don't tell me anything you don't want to, you know, my dear."

"No; I *do* want to; only it's difficult. You see —we had so very little money. . . ."

"Yes?"

"And Nick—who was thinking of his book, and of all sorts of big things, fine things—didn't realise . . . left it all to me . . . to manage. . . ."

She stumbled over the word, remembering how
Nick had always winced at it. But Strefford did
not seem to notice her, and she hurried on, unfold-
ing in short awkward sentences the avowal of
their pecuniary difficulties, and of Nick's inability
to understand that, to keep on with the kind of
life they were leading, one had to put up with
things . . . accept favours. . . .

"Borrow money, you mean?"

"Well—yes; and all the rest." No—decidedly
she could not reveal to Strefford the episode of
Ellie's letters. "Nick suddenly felt, I suppose,
that he couldn't stand it," she continued; "and
instead of asking me to try—to try to live differently, go off somewhere with him and live like
work-people, in two rooms, without a servant, as
I was ready to do; well, instead he wrote me that
it had all been a mistake from the beginning, that
we couldn't keep it up, and had better recognize
the fact; and he went off on the Hickses' yacht.
The last evening that you were in Venice—the
day he didn't come back to dinner—he had gone
off to Genoa to meet them. I suppose he intends
to marry Coral."

Strefford received this in silence. "Well—it
was your bargain, wasn't it?" he said at length.

"Yes; but—"

"Exactly: I always told you so. You weren't
ready to have him go yet—that's all."

She flushed to the forehead. "Oh, Streff—is it
really all?"

"A question of time? If you doubt it, I'd like to see you try, for a while, in those two rooms without a servant; and then let me hear from you. Why, my dear, it's only a question of time in a palace, with a steam-yacht lying off the door-step, and a flock of motors in the garage; look around you and see. And did you ever imagine that you and Nick, of all people, were going to escape the common doom, and survive like Mr. and Mrs. Tithonus, while all about you the eternal passions were crumbling to pieces, and your native Divorce-states piling up their revenues?"

She sat with bent head, the weight of the long years to come pressing like a leaden load on her shoulders.

"But I'm so young . . . life's so long. What does last, then?"

"Ah, you're too young to believe me, if I were to tell you; though you're intelligent enough to understand."

"What does, then?"

"Why, the hold of the things we all think we could do without. Habits—they outstand the Pyramids. Comforts, luxuries, the atmosphere of ease . . . above all, the power to get away from dulness and monotony, from constraints and uglinesses. You chose that power, instinctively, before you were even grown up; and so did Nick. And the only difference between you is that he's had the sense to see sooner than you that those *are* the things that last, the prime necessities."

"I don't believe it!"

"Of course you don't: at your age one doesn't reason one's materialism. And besides you're mortally hurt that Nick has found out sooner than you, and hasn't disguised his discovery under any hypocritical phrases."

"But surely there are people—"

"Yes—saints and geniuses and heroes: all the fanatics! To which of their categories do you suppose we soft people belong? And the heroes and the geniuses—haven't they their enormous frailties and their giant appetites? And how should we escape being the victims of our little ones?"

She sat for a while without speaking. "But, Streff, how can you say such things, when I know you care: care for me, for instance?"

"Care?" He put his hand on hers. "But, my dear, it's just the fugitiveness of mortal caring that makes it so exquisite! It's because we *know* we can't hold fast to it, or to each other, or to anything. . . ."

"Yes . . . yes . . . but hush, please! Oh, don't say it!" She stood up, the tears in her throat, and he rose also.

"Come along, then; where do we lunch?" he said with a smile, slipping his hand through her arm.

"Oh, I don't know. Nowhere. I think I'm going back to Versailles."

"Because I've disgusted you so deeply? Just

my luck—when I came over to ask you to marry me!''

She laughed, but he had become suddenly grave. ''Upon my soul, I did.''

''Dear Streff! As if—now—''

''Oh, not now—I know. I'm aware that even with your accelerated divorce methods—''

''It's not that. I told you it was no use, Streff —I told you long ago, in Venice.''

He shrugged ironically. ''It's not Streff who's asking you now. Streff was not a marrying man: he was only trifling with you. The present offer comes from an elderly peer of independent means. Think it over, my dear: as many days out as you like, and five footmen kept. There's not the least hurry, of course; but I rather think Nick himself would advise it.''

She flushed to the temples, remembering that Nick had; and the remembrance made Strefford's sneering philosophy seem less unbearable. Why should she not lunch with him, after all? In the first days of his mourning he had come to Paris expressly to see her, and to offer her one of the oldest names and one of the greatest fortunes in England. She thought of Ursula Gillow, Ellie Vanderlyn, Violet Melrose, of their condescending kindnesses, their last year's dresses, their Christmas cheques, and all the careless bounties that were so easy to bestow and so hard to accept. ''I should rather enjoy paying them back,'' something in her maliciously murmured.

She did not mean to marry Strefford—she had not even got as far as contemplating the possibility of a divorce—but it was undeniable that this sudden prospect of wealth and freedom was like fresh air in her lungs. She laughed again, but now without bitterness.

"Very good, then; we'll lunch together. But it's Streff I want to' lunch with to-day."

"Ah, well," her companion agreed, "I rather think that for a *tête-à-tête* he's better company."

During their repast in a little restaurant over the Seine, where she insisted on the cheapest dishes because she was lunching with "Streff," he became again his old whimsical companionable self. Once or twice she tried to turn the talk to his altered future, and the obligations and interests that lay before him; but he shrugged away from the subject, questioning her instead about the motley company at Violet Melrose's, and fitting a droll or malicious anecdote to each of the people she named.

It was not till they had finished their coffee, and she was glancing at her watch with a vague notion of taking the next train, that he asked abruptly: "But what are you going to do? You can't stay forever at Violet's."

"Oh, no!" she cried with a shiver.

"Well, then—you've got some plan, I suppose?"

"Have I?" she wondered, jerked back into grim

reality from the soothing interlude of their hour together.

"You can't drift indefinitely, can you? Unless you mean to go back to the old sort of life once for all."

She reddened and her eyes filled. "I can't do that, Streff—I know I can't!"

"Then what—?"

She hesitated, and brought out with lowered head: "Nick said he would write again—in a few days. I must wait—"

"Oh, naturally. Don't do anything in a hurry." Strefford also glanced at his watch. *"Garçon, l'addition!* I'm taking the train back to-night, and I've a lot of things left to do. But look here, my dear—when you come to a decision one way or the other let me know, will you? Oh, I don't mean in the matter I've most at heart; we'll consider that closed for the present. But at least I can be of use in other ways—hang it, you know, I can even lend you money. There's a new sensation for our jaded palates!"

"Oh, Streff . . . Streff!" she could only falter; and he pressed on gaily: "Try it, now do try it —I assure you there'll be no interest to pay, and no conditions attached. And promise to let me know when you've decided anything."

She looked into his humorously puckered eyes, answering their friendly smile with hers.

"I promise!" she said.

XV

THAT hour with Strefford had altered her whole perspective. Instead of possible dependence, an enforced return to the old life of connivances and concessions, she saw before her —whenever she chose to take them—freedom, power and dignity. Dignity! It was odd what weight that word had come to have for her. She had dimly felt its significance, felt the need of its presence in her inmost soul, even in the young thoughtless days when she had seemed to sacrifice so little to the austere divinities. And since she had been Nick Lansing's wife she had consciously acknowledged it, had suffered and agonized when she fell beneath its standard. Yes: to marry Strefford would give her that sense of self-respect which, in such a world as theirs, only wealth and position could ensure. If she had not the mental or moral training to attain independence in any other way, was she to blame for seeking it on such terms?

Of course there was always the chance that Nick would come back, would find life without her as intolerable as she was finding it without him. If that happened—ah, if that happened! Then she would cease to strain her eyes into the future,

would seize upon the present moment and plunge
into it to the very bottom of oblivion. Nothing
on earth would matter then—money or freedom
or pride, or her precious moral dignity, if only
she were in Nick's arms again!

But there was Nick's icy letter, there was Coral
Hicks's insolent post-card, to show how little
chance there was of such a solution. Susy understood that, even before the discovery of her transaction with Ellie Vanderlyn, Nick had secretly
wearied, if not of his wife, at least of the life that
their marriage compelled him to lead. His passion was not strong enough—had never been
strong enough—to outweigh his prejudices, scruples, principles, or whatever one chose to call
them. Susy's dignity might go up like tinder in
the blaze of her love; but his was made of a less
combustible substance. She had felt, in their last
talk together, that she had forever destroyed the
inner harmony between them.

Well—there it was, and the fault was doubtless
neither hers nor his, but that of the world they
had grown up in, of their own moral contempt
for it and physical dependence on it, of his half-
talents and her half-principles, of the something
in them both that was not stout enough to resist
nor yet pliant enough to yield. She stared at the
fact on the journey back to Versailles, and all
that sleepless night in her room; and the next
morning, when the housemaid came in with her
breakfast tray, she felt the factitious energy that

comes from having decided, however half-heartedly, on a definite course.

She had said to herself: "If there's no letter from Nick this time next week I'll write to Streff—" and the week had passed, and there was no letter.

It was now three weeks since he had left her, and she had had no word but his note from Genoa. She had concluded that, foreseeing the probability of her leaving Venice, he would write to her in care of their Paris bank. But though she had immediately notified the bank of her change of address no communication from Nick had reached her; and she smiled with a touch of bitterness at the difficulty he was doubtless finding in the composition of the promised letter. Her own scrap-basket, for the first days, had been heaped with the fragments of the letters she had begun; and she told herself that, since they both found it so hard to write, it was probably because they had nothing left to say to each other.

Meanwhile the days at Mrs. Melrose's drifted by as they had been wont to drift when, under the roofs of the rich, Susy Branch had marked time between one episode and the next of her precarious existence. Her experience of such sojourns was varied enough to make her acutely conscious of their effect on her temporary hosts; and in the present case she knew that Violet was hardly aware of her presence. But if no more than tolerated she was at least not felt to be an

inconvenience; when your hostess forgot about
you it proved that at least you were not in her
way.

Violet, as usual, was perpetually on the wing,
for her profound indolence expressed itself in a
disordered activity. Nat Fulmer had returned to
Paris; but Susy guessed that his benefactress was
still constantly in his company, and that when
Mrs. Melrose was whirled away in her noiseless
motor it was generally toward the scene of some
new encounter between Fulmer and the arts. On
these occasions she sometimes offered to carry
Susy to Paris, and they devoted several long
and hectic mornings to the dress-makers, where
Susy felt herself gradually succumbing to the familiar spell of heaped-up finery. It seemed impossible, as furs and laces and brocades were
tossed aside, brought back, and at last carelessly
selected from, that anything but the whim of the
moment need count in deciding whether one
should take all or none, or that any woman could
be worth looking at who did not possess the
means to make her choice regardless of cost.

Once alone, and in the street again, the evil
fumes would evaporate, and daylight re-enter
Susy's soul; yet she felt that the old poison was
slowly insinuating itself into her system. To dis-
pel it she decided one day to look up Grace Fulmer. She was curious to know how the happy-
go-lucky companion of Fulmer's evil days was
bearing the weight of his prosperity, and she

vaguely felt that it would be refreshing to see some one who had never been afraid of poverty.

The airless *pension* sitting-room, where she waited while a reluctant maid-servant screamed about the house for Mrs. Fulmer, did not have the hoped-for effect. It was one thing for Grace to put up with such quarters when she shared them with Fulmer; but to live there while he basked in the lingering radiance of Versailles, or rolled from *château* to picture gallery in Mrs. Melrose's motor, showed a courage that Susy felt unable to emulate.

"My dear! I knew you'd look me up," Grace's joyous voice rang down the stairway; and in another moment she was clasping Susy to her tumbled person.

"Nat couldn't remember if he'd given you our address, though he promised me he would, the last time he was here." She held Susy at arms' length, beaming upon her with blinking short-sighted eyes: the same old dishevelled Grace, so careless of her neglected beauty and her squandered youth, so amused and absent-minded and improvident, that the boisterous air of the New Hampshire bungalow seemed to enter with her into the little air-tight *salon*.

While she poured out the tale of Nat's sudden celebrity, and its unexpected consequences, Susy marvelled and dreamed. Was the secret of his triumph perhaps due to those long hard unrewarded years, the steadfast scorn of popularity,

the indifference to every kind of material ease in
which his wife had so gaily abetted him? Had it
been bought at the cost of her own freshness and
her own talent, of the children's "advantages," of
everything except the closeness of the tie between
husband and wife? Well—it was worth the price,
no doubt; but what if, now that honours and prosperity had come, the tie were snapped, and Grace
were left alone among the ruins?

There was nothing in her tone or words to suggest such a possibility. Susy noticed that her ill-
assorted raiment was costlier in quality and more
professional in cut than the home-made garments
which had draped her growing bulk at the bungalow: it was clear that she was trying to dress up
to Nat's new situation. But, above all, she was
rejoicing in it, filling her hungry lungs with the
strong air of his success. It had evidently not
occurred to her as yet that those who consent to
share the bread of adversity may want the whole
cake of prosperity for themselves.

"My dear, it's too wonderful! He's told me to
take as many concert and opera tickets as I like;
he lets me take all the children with me. The big
concerts don't begin till later; but of course the
Opera is always going. And there are little things
—there's music in Paris at all seasons. And
later it's just possible we may get to Munich for
a week—oh, Susy!" Her hands clasped, her eyes
brimming, she drank the new wine of life almost
sacramentally.

"Do you remember, Susy, when you and Nick came to stay at the bungalow? Nat said you'd be horrified by our primitiveness—but I knew better! And I was right, wasn't I? Seeing us so happy made you and Nick decide to follow our example, didn't it?" She glowed with the remembrance. "And now, what are your plans? Is Nick's book nearly done? I suppose you'll have to live very economically till he finds a publisher. And the baby, darling—when is *that* to be? If you're coming home soon I could let you have a lot of the children's little old things."

"You're always so dear, Grace. But we haven't any special plans as yet—not even for a baby. And I wish you'd tell me all of yours instead."

Mrs. Fulmer asked nothing better: Susy perceived that, so far, the greater part of her European experience had consisted in talking about what it was to be. "Well, you see, Nat is so taken up all day with sight-seeing and galleries and meeting important people that he hasn't had time to go about with us; and as so few theatres are open, and there's so little music, I've taken the opportunity to catch up with my mending. Junie helps me with it now—she's our eldest, you remember? She's grown into a big girl since you saw her. And later, perhaps, we're to travel. And the most wonderful thing of all—next to Nat's recognition, I mean—is not having to contrive and skimp, and give up something every single minute. Just think—Nat has even made special arrangements here in the *pension,* so that the children all have second helpings to everything. And when I go up to bed I can think of my music, instead of lying awake calculating and wondering how I can make things come out at the end of the month. Oh, Susy, that's simply *heaven!*"

Susy's heart contracted. She had come to her friend to be taught again the lesson of indifference to material things, and instead she was hearing from Grace Fulmer's lips the long-repressed avowal of their tyranny. After all, that battle with poverty on the New Hampshire hillside had not been the easy smiling business that Grace and Nat had made it appear. And yet . . . and yet. . . .

Susy stood up abruptly, and straightened the expensive hat which hung irresponsibly over Grace's left ear.

"What's wrong with it? Junie helped me choose it, and she generally knows," Mrs. Fulmer wailed with helpless hands.

"It's the way you wear it, dearest—and the bow is rather top-heavy. Let me have it a minute, please." Susy lifted the hat from her friend's head and began to manipulate its trimming. "This is the way Maria Guy or Suzanne would do it. . . . And now go on about Nat. . . ."

She listened musingly while Grace poured forth the tale of her husband's triumph, of the notices

in the papers, the demand for his work, the fine
ladies' battles over their priority in discovering
him, and the multiplied orders that had resulted
from their rivalry.

"Of course they're simply furious with each
other—Mrs. Melrose and Mrs. Gillow especially
—because each one pretends to have been the first
to notice his 'Spring Snow-Storm,' and in reality
it wasn't either of them, but only poor Bill Has-
lett, an art-critic we've known for years, who
chanced on the picture, and rushed off to tell a
dealer who was looking for a new painter to
push." Grace suddenly raised her soft myopic
eyes to Susy's face. "But, do you know, the
funny thing is that I believe Nat is beginning to
forget this, and to believe that it *was* Mrs. Melrose who stopped short in front of his picture on
the opening day, and screamed out: 'This is
genius!' It seems funny he should care so much,
when I've always known he had genius—and *he*
has known it too. But they're all so kind to him;
and Mrs. Melrose especially. And I suppose it
makes a thing sound new to hear it said in a new
voice."

Susy looked at her meditatively. "And how
should you feel if Nat liked too much to hear Mrs.
Melrose say it? Too much, I mean, to care any
longer what you felt or thought?"

Her friend's worn face flushed quickly, and then
paled: Susy almost repented the question. But
Mrs. Fulmer met it with a tranquil dignity. "You

haven't been married long enough, dear, to understand . . . how people like Nat and me feel about such things . . . or how trifling they seem, in the balance . . . the balance of one's memories."

Susy stood up again, and flung her arms about her friend. "Oh, Grace," she laughed with wet eyes, "how can you be as wise as that, and yet not have sense enough to buy a decent hat?" She gave Mrs. Fulmer a quick embrace and hurried away. She had learned her lesson after all; but it was not exactly the one she had come to seek.

The week she had allowed herself had passed, and still there was no word from Nick. She allowed herself yet another day, and that too went by without a letter. She then decided on a step from which her pride had hitherto recoiled; she would call at the bank and ask for Nick's address. She called, embarrassed and hesitating; and was told, after enquiries in the post-office department, that Mr. Nicholas Lansing had given no address since that of the Palazzo Vanderlyn, three months previously. She went back to Versailles that afternoon with the definite intention of writing to Strefford unless the next morning's post brought a letter.

The next morning brought nothing from Nick, but a scribbled message from Mrs. Melrose: would Susy, as soon as possible, come into her room for a word? Susy jumped up, hurried through her bath, and knocked at her hostess's

door. In the immense low bed that faced the rich
umbrage of the park Mrs. Melrose lay smoking
cigarettes and glancing over her letters. She
looked up with her vague smile, and said dreamily: "Susy darling, have you any particular plans
—for the next few months, I mean?"

Susy coloured: she knew the intonation of old,
and fancied she understood what it implied.

"Plans, dearest? Any number . . . I'm tearing myself away the day after to-morrow . . . to
the Gillows' moor, very probably," she hastened
to announce.

Instead of the relief she had expected to read
on Mrs. Melrose's dramatic countenance she discovered there the blankest disappointment.

"Oh, really? That's too bad. Is it absolutely,
settled—?"

"As far as I'm concerned," said Susy crisply.

The other sighed. "I'm too sorry. You see,
dear, I'd meant to ask you to stay on here quietly,
and look after the Fulmer children. Fulmer and
I are going to Spain next week—I want to be with
him when he makes his studies, receives his first
impressions; such a marvellous experience, to be
there when he and Velasquez meet!" She broke
off, lost in prospective ecstasy. "And, you see,
as Grace Fulmer insists on coming with us—"

"Ah, I see."

"Well, there are the five children—such a problem," sighed the benefactress. "If you *were* at
a loose end, you know, dear, while Nick's away

with his friends, I could really make it worth your while. . . ."

"So awfully good of you, Violet; only I'm not, as it happens."

Oh the relief of being able to say that, gaily, firmly and even truthfully! Take charge of the Fulmer children, indeed! Susy remembered how Nick and she had fled from them that autumn afternoon in New Hampshire. The offer gave her a salutary glimpse of the way in which, as the years passed, and she lost her freshness and novelty, she would more and more be used as a convenience, a stop-gap, writer of notes, runner of errands, nursery governess or companion. She called to mind several elderly women of her acquaintance, pensioners of her own group, who still wore its livery, struck its attitudes and chattered its jargon, but had long since been ruthlessly relegated to these slave-ant offices. Never in the world would she join their numbers.

Mrs. Melrose's face fell, and she looked at Susy with the plaintive bewilderment of the wielder of millions to whom everything that cannot be bought is imperceptible.

"But I can't see why you can't change your plans," she murmured with a soft persistency.

"Ah, well, you know"—Susy paused on a slow inward smile—"they're not mine only, as it happens."

Mrs. Melrose's brow clouded. The unforeseen

complication of Mrs. Fulmer's presence on the
journey had evidently tried her nerves, and this
new obstacle to her arrangements shook her faith
in the divine order of things.

"Your plans are not yours only? But surely
you won't let Ursula Gillow dictate to you? . . .
There's my jade pendant; the one you said you
liked the other day. . . . The Fulmers won't go
with me, you understand, unless they're satisfied
about the children; the whole plan will fall
through. Susy darling, you were always too un-
selfish; I hate to see you sacrificed to Ursula."

Susy's smile lingered. Time was when she
might have been glad to add the jade pendant to
the collection already enriched by Ellie Vanderlyn's sapphires; more recently, she would have resented the offer as an insult to her newly-found
principles. But already the mere fact that she
might henceforth, if she chose, be utterly out of
reach of such bribes, enabled her to look down on
them with tolerance. Oh, the blessed moral freedom that wealth conferred! She recalled Mrs.
Fulmer's uncontrollable cry: "The most wonderful thing of all is not having to contrive and
skimp, and give up something every single minute!" Yes; it was only on such terms that one
could call one's soul one's own. The sense of it
gave Susy the grace to answer amicably: "If I
could possibly help you out, Violet, I shouldn't
want a present to persuade me. And, as you say,

there's no reason why I should sacrifice myself to Ursula—or to anybody else. Only, as it happens"
—she paused and took the plunge—"I'm going to England because I've promised to see a friend."

That night she wrote to Strefford.

XVI

STRETCHED out under an awning on the deck of the *Ibis* Nick Lansing looked up for a moment at the vanishing cliffs of Malta and then plunged again into his book.

He had had nearly three weeks of drug-taking on the *Ibis*. The drugs he had absorbed were of two kinds: visions of fleeing landscapes, looming up from the blue sea to vanish into it again, and visions of study absorbed from the volumes piled up day and night at his elbow. For the first time in months he was in reach of a real library, just the kind of scholarly yet miscellaneous library that his restless and impatient spirit craved. He was aware that the books he read, like the fugitive scenes on which he gazed, were merely a form of anæsthetic: he swallowed them with the careless greed of the sufferer who seeks only to still pain and deaden memory. But they were beginning to produce in him a moral languor that was not disagreeable, that, indeed, compared with the fierce pain of the first days, was almost pleasurable. It was exactly the kind of drug that he needed.

There is probably no point on which the average man has more definite views than on the uselessness of writing a letter that is hard to write. In the line he had sent to Susy from Genoa Nick had told her that she would hear from him again in a few days; but when the few days had passed, and he began to consider setting himself to the task, he found fifty reasons for postponing it.

Had there been any practical questions to write about it would have been different; he could not have borne for twenty-four hours the idea that she was in uncertainty as to money. But that had all been settled long ago. From the first she had had the administering of their modest fortune. On their marriage Nick's own meagre income, paid in, none too regularly, by the agent who had managed for years the dwindling family properties, had been transferred to her: it was the only wedding present he could make. And the wedding cheques had of course all been deposited in her name. There were therefore no "business" reasons for communicating with her; and when it came to reasons of another order, the mere thought of them benumbed him.

For the first few days he reproached himself for his inertia; then he began to seek reasons for justifying it. After all, for both their sakes a waiting policy might be the wisest he could pursue. He had left Susy because he could not tolerate the conditions on which he had discovered their life together to be based; and he had told her so. What more was there to say?

Nothing was changed in their respective situations; if they came together it could be only to resume the same life; and that, as the days went by, seemed to him more and more impossible. He had not yet reached the point of facing a definite separation; but whenever his thoughts travelled back over their past life he recoiled from any attempt to return to it. As long as this state of mind continued there seemed nothing to add to the letter he had already written, except indeed the statement that he was cruising with the Hickses. And he saw no pressing reason for communicating that.

To the Hickses he had given no hint of his situation. When Coral Hicks, a fortnight earlier, had picked him up in the broiling streets of Genoa, and carried him off to the *Ibis,* he had thought only of a cool dinner and perhaps a moonlight sail. Then, in reply to their friendly urging, he had confessed that he had not been well—had indeed gone off hurriedly for a few days' change of air—and that left him without defence against the immediate proposal that he should take his change of air on the *Ibis*. They were just off to Corsica and Sardinia, and from there to Sicily: he could rejoin the railway at Naples, and be back at Venice in ten days.

Ten days of respite—the temptation was irresistible. And he really liked the kind uncomplicated Hickses. A wholesome honesty and simplicity breathed through all their opulence, as if the rich trappings of their present life still exhaled the fragrance of their native prairies. The mere fact of being with such people was like a

purifying bath. When the yacht touched at
Naples he agreed—since they were so awfully kind
—to go on to Sicily. And when the chief steward,
going ashore at Naples for the last time before
they got up steam, said: "Any letters for the post,
sir?" he answered, as he had answered at each
previous halt: "No, thank you: none."

Now they were heading for Rhodes and Crete—
Crete, where he had never been, where he had so
often longed to go. In spite of the lateness of the
season the weather was still miraculously fine: the
short waves danced ahead under a sky without a
cloud, and the strong bows of the *Ibis* hardly
swayed as she flew forward over the flying crests.

Only his hosts and their daughter were on the
yacht—of course with Eldorada Tooker and Mr.
Beck in attendance. An eminent archæologist,
who was to have joined them at Naples, had telegraphed an excuse at the last moment; and Nick
noticed that, while Mrs. Hicks was perpetually
apologizing for the great man's absence, Coral
merely smiled and said nothing.

As a matter of fact, Mr. and Mrs. Hicks were
never as pleasant as when one had them to one's
self. In company, Mr. Hicks ran the risk of ap-
pearing over-hospitable, and Mrs. Hicks confused
dates and names in the desire to embrace all culture in her conversation. But alone with Nick,
their old travelling-companion, they shone out in
their native simplicity, and Mr. Hicks talked
soundly of investments, and Mrs. Hicks recalled

her early married days in Apex City, when, on being brought home to her new house in Aeschylus Avenue, her first thought had been: "How on earth shall I get all those windows washed?"

The loss of Mr. Buttles had been as serious to them as Nick had supposed: Mr. Beck could never hope to replace him. Apart from his mysterious gift of languages, and his almost superhuman faculty for knowing how to address letters to eminent people, and in what terms to conclude them, he had a smattering of archæology and general culture on which Mrs. Hicks had learned to depend—her own memory being, alas, so inadequate to the range of her interests.

Her daughter might perhaps have helped her; but it was not Miss Hicks's way to mother her parents. She was exceedingly kind to them, but left them, as it were, to bring themselves up as best they could, while she pursued her own course of self-development. A sombre zeal for knowledge filled the mind of this strange girl: she appeared interested only in fresh opportunities of adding to her store of facts. They were illuminated by little imagination and less poetry; but, carefully catalogued and neatly sorted in her large cool brain, they were always as accessible as the volumes in an up-to-date public library.

To Nick there was something reposeful in this lucid intellectual curiosity. He wanted above all things to get away from sentiment, from seduction, from the moods and impulses and flashing

contradictions that were Susy. Susy was not a
great reader: her store of facts was small, and she
had grown up among people who dreaded ideas as
much as if they had been a contagious disease.
But, in the early days especially, when Nick had
put a book in her hand, or read a poem to her, her
swift intelligence had instantly shed a new light
on the subject, and, penetrating to its depths, had
extracted from them whatever belonged to her.
What a pity that this exquisite insight, this intui-
tive discrimination, should for the most part have
been spent upon reading the thoughts of vulgar
people, and extracting a profit from them—should
have been wasted, since her childhood, on all the
hideous intricacies of "managing"!

And visible beauty—how she cared for that too!
He had not guessed it, or rather he had not been
sure of it, till the day when, on their way through
Paris, he had taken her to the Louvre, and they
had stood before the little Crucifixion of Man-
tegna. He had not been looking at the picture, or
watching to see what impression it produced on
Susy. His own momentary mood was for Correg-
gio and Fragonard, the laughter of the Music Lesson and the bold pagan joys of the Antiope;
and then he had missed her from his side, and
when he came to where she stood, forgetting him,
forgetting everything, had seen the glare of that
tragic sky in her face, her trembling lip, the tears
on her lashes. That was Susy. . . .

Closing his book he stole a glance at Coral

Hicks's profile, thrown back against the cushions of the deck-chair at his side. There was something harsh and bracing in her blunt primitive build, in the projection of the black eyebrows that nearly met over her thick straight nose, and the faint barely visible black down on her upper lip. Some miracle of will-power, combined with all the artifices that wealth can buy, had turned the fat sallow girl he remembered into this commanding young woman, almost handsome—at times indisputably handsome—in her big authoritative way. Watching the arrogant lines of her profile against the blue sea, he remembered, with a thrill that was sweet to his vanity, how twice—under the dome of the Scalzi and in the streets of Genoa—he had seen those same lines soften at his approach, turn womanly, pleading and almost humble. That was Coral. . . .

Suddenly she said, without turning toward him: "You've had no letters since you've been on board."

He looked at her, surprised. "No—thank the Lord!" he laughed.

"And you haven't written one either," she continued in her hard statistical tone.

"No," he again agreed, with the same laugh.

"That means that you really *are* free—"

"Free?"

He saw the cheek nearest him redden. "Really off on a holiday, I mean; not tied down."

After a pause he rejoined: "No, I'm not particularly tied down."

"And your book?"

"Oh, my book—" He stopped and considered. He had thrust *The Pageant of Alexander* into his hand-bag on the night of his flight from Venice; but since then he had never looked at it. Too many memories and illusions were pressed between its pages; and he knew just at what page he had felt Ellie Vanderlyn bending over him from behind, caught a whiff of her scent, and heard her breathless "I *had* to thank you!"

"My book's hung up," he said impatiently, annoyed with Miss Hicks's lack of tact. *There* was a girl who never put out feelers. . . .

"Yes; I thought it was," she went on quietly, and he gave her a startled glance. What the devil else did she think, he wondered? He had never supposed her capable of getting far enough out of her own thick carapace of self-sufficiency to penetrate into any one else's feelings.

"The truth is," he continued, embarrassed, "I suppose I dug away at it rather too continuously; that's probably why I felt the need of a change. You see I'm only a beginner."

She still continued her relentless questioning. "But later—you'll go on with it, of course?"

"Oh, I don't know." He paused, glanced down the glittering deck, and then out across the glittering water. "I've been dreaming dreams, you see. I rather think I shall have to drop the book altogether, and try to look out for a job that will pay. To indulge in my kind of literature one must first have an assured income."

He was instantly annoyed with himself for having spoken. Hitherto in his relations with the Hickses he had carefully avoided the least allusion that might make him feel the heavy hand of their beneficence. But the idle procrastinating weeks had weakened him and he had yielded to the need of putting into words his vague intentions. To do so would perhaps help to make them more definite.

To his relief Miss Hicks made no immediate reply; and when she spoke it was in a softer voice, and with an unwonted hesitation.

"It seems a shame that with gifts like yours you shouldn't find some kind of employment that would leave you leisure enough to do your real work. . . ."

He shrugged ironically. "Yes—there are a goodish number of us hunting for that particular kind of employment."

Her tone became more business-like. "I know it's hard to find—almost impossible. But would you take it, I wonder, if it were offered to you—?"

She turned her head slightly, and their eyes met. For an instant blank terror loomed upon him; but before he had time to face it she continued, in the same untroubled voice: "Mr. Buttles's place.

I mean. My parents must absolutely have some one they can count on. You know what an easy place it is. . . . I think you would find the salary satisfactory.''

Nick drew a deep breath of relief. For a moment her eyes had looked as they had in the Scalzi —and he liked the girl too much not to shrink from re-awakening that look. But Mr. Buttles's place: why not?

''Poor Buttles!'' he murmured, to gain time.

''Oh,'' she said, ''you won't find the same reasons as he did for throwing up the job. He was the martyr of his artistic convictions.''

He glanced at her sideways, wondering. After all she did not know of his meeting with Mr. Buttles in Genoa, nor of the latter's confidences; perhaps she did not even know of Mr. Buttles's hopeless passion. At any rate her face remained calm.

''Why not consider it—at least just for a few months? Till after our expedition to Mesopotamia?'' she pressed on, a little breathlessly.

''You're awfully kind: but I don't know—''

She stood up with one of her abrupt movements. ''You needn't, all at once. Take time—think it over. Father wanted me to ask you,'' she appended.

He felt the inadequacy of his response. ''It tempts me awfully, of course. But I must wait, at any rate—wait for letters. The fact is I shall have to wire from Rhodes to have them sent. I had chucked everything, even letters, for a few weeks."

"Ah, you *are* tired," she murmured, giving him a last downward glance as she turned away.

From Rhodes Nick Lansing telegraphed to his Paris bank to send his letters to Candia; but when the *Ibis* reached Candia, and the mail was brought on board, the thick envelope handed to him contained no letter from Susy.

Why should it, since he had not yet written to her?

He had not written, no: but in sending his address to the bank he knew he had given her the opportunity of reaching him if she wished to. And she had made no sign.

Late that afternoon, when they returned to the yacht from their first expedition, a packet of newspapers lay on the deck-house table. Nick picked up one of the London journals, and his eye ran absently down the list of social events.

He read:

"Among the visitors expected next week at Ruan Castle (let for the season to Mr. Frederick J. Gillow of New York) are Prince Altineri of Rome, the Earl of Altringham and Mrs. Nicholas Lansing, who arrived in London last week from Paris."

Nick threw down the paper. It was just a month since he had left the Palazzo Vanderlyn and flung himself into the night express for Milan. A whole month—and Susy had not written. Only a month—and Susy and Strefford were already together!

XVII

S USY had decided to wait for Strefford in London.

The new Lord Altringham was with his family in the north, and though she found a telegram on arriving, saying that he would join her in town the following week, she had still an interval of several days to fill.

London was a desert; the rain fell without ceasing, and alone in the shabby family hotel which, even out of season, was the best she could afford, she sat at last face to face with herself.

From the moment when Violet Melrose had failed to carry out her plan for the Fulmer children her interest in Susy had visibly waned. Often before, in the old days, Susy Branch had felt the same abrupt change of temperature in the manner of the hostess of the moment; and often—how often!—had yielded, and performed the required service, rather than risk the consequences of estrangement. To that, at least, thank heaven, she need never stoop again.

But as she hurriedly packed her trunks at Versailles, scraped together an adequate tip for Mrs. Match, and bade good-bye to Violet (grown suddenly fond and demonstrative as she saw her

visitor safely headed for the station)—as Susy
went through the old familiar mummery of the
enforced leave-taking, there rose in her so deep a
disgust for the life of makeshifts and accommodations, that if at that moment Nick had reappeared and held out his arms to her, she was not
sure she would have had the courage to return to
them.

In her London solitude the thirst for independence grew fiercer. Independence with ease, of
course. Oh, her hateful useless love of beauty
. . . the curse it had always been to her, the blessing it might have been if only she had had the
material means to gratify and to express it! And
instead, it only gave her a morbid loathing of that
hideous hotel bedroom drowned in yellow rain-
light, of the smell of soot and cabbage through
the window, the blistered wall-paper, the dusty
wax bouquets under glass globes, and the electric
lighting so contrived that as you turned on the
feeble globe hanging from the middle of the ceiling
the feebler one beside the bed went out!

What a sham world she and Nick had lived in
during their few months together! What right
had either of them to those exquisite settings of
the life of leisure: the long white house hidden in
camellias and cypresses above the lake, or the
great rooms on the Giudecca with the shimmer of
the canal always playing over their frescoed ceilings? Yet she had come to imagine that these
places really belonged to them, that they would al-

ways go on living, fondly and irreproachably, in
the frame of other people's wealth. . . . That,
again, was the curse of her love of beauty, the way
she always took to it as if it belonged to her!

Well, the awakening was bound to come, and it
was perhaps better that it should have come so
soon. At any rate there was no use in letting her
thoughts wander back to that shattered fool's
paradise of theirs. Only, as she sat there and
reckoned up the days till Strefford arrived, what
else in the world was there to think of?

Her future and his?

But she knew that future by heart already! She
had not spent her life among the rich and fashionable without having learned every detail of the
trappings of a rich and fashionable marriage.
She had calculated long ago just how many din-
ner-dresses, how many tea-gowns and how much
lacy *lingerie* would go to make up the outfit of
the future Countess of Altringham. She had even
decided to which dress-maker she would go for her
chinchilla cloak—for she meant to have one, and
down to her feet, and softer and more voluminous
and more extravagantly sumptuous than Violet's
or Ursula's . . . not to speak of silver foxes and
sables . . . nor yet of the Altringham jewels.

She knew all this by heart; had always known
it. It all belonged to the make-up of the life of
elegance: there was nothing new about it. What
had been new to her was just that short interval
with Nick—a life unreal indeed in its setting, but

so real in its essentials: the one reality she had ever known. As she looked back on it she saw how much it had given her besides the golden flush of her happiness, the sudden flowering of sensuous joy in heart and body. Yes—there had been the flowering too, in pain like birth-pangs, of something graver, stronger, fuller of future power, something she had hardly heeded in her first light rapture, but that always came back and possessed her stilled soul when the rapture sank: the deep disquieting sense of something that Nick and love had taught her, but that reached out even beyond love and beyond Nick.

Her nerves were racked by the ceaseless swish-swish of the rain on the dirty panes and the smell of cabbage and coal that came in under the door when she shut the window. This nauseating fore-taste of the luncheon she must presently go down to was more than she could bear. It brought with it a vision of the dank coffee-room below, the sooty Smyrna rug, the rain on the sky-light, the listless waitresses handing about food that tasted as if it had been rained on too. There was really no reason why she should let such material miseries add to her depression. . . .

She sprang up, put on her hat and jacket, and calling for a taxi drove to the London branch of the Nouveau Luxe hotel. It was just one o'clock and she was sure to pick up a luncheon, for though London was empty that great establishment was not. It never was. Along those sultry velvet-car-

peted halls, in that great flowered and scented dining-room, there was always a come-and-go of rich
aimless people, the busy people who, having nothing to do, perpetually pursue their inexorable
task from one end of the earth to the other.

Oh, the monotony of those faces—the faces one
always knew, whether one knew the people they,
belonged to or not! A fresh disgust seized her at
the sight of them: she wavered, and then turned
and fled. But on the threshold a still more familiar figure met her: that of a lady in exaggerated pearls and sables, descending from an exaggerated motor, like the motors in magazine advertisements, the huge arks in which jewelled
beauties and slender youths pause to gaze at snow-
peaks from an Alpine summit.

It was Ursula Gillow—dear old Ursula, on her
way to Scotland—and she and Susy fell on each
other's necks. It appeared that Ursula, detained
till the next evening by a dress-maker's delay, was
also out of a job and killing time, and the two were
soon smiling at each other over the exquisite preliminaries of a luncheon which the head-waiter
had authoritatively asked Mrs. Gillow to "leave
to him, as usual."

Ursula was in a good humour. It did not often
happen; but when it did her benevolence knew no
bounds.

Like Mrs. Melrose, like all her tribe in fact, she
was too much absorbed in her own affairs to give
more than a passing thought to any one else's; but

she was delighted at the meeting with Susy, as her wandering kind always were when they ran across fellow-wanderers, unless the meeting happened to interfere with choicer pleasures. Not to be alone was the urgent thing; and Ursula, who had been forty-eight hours alone in London, at once exacted from her friend a promise that they should spend the rest of the day together. But once the bargain struck her mind turned again to her own affairs, and she poured out her confidences to Susy over a succession of dishes that manifested the head-waiter's understanding of the case.

Ursula's confidences were always the same, though they were usually about a different person. She demolished and rebuilt her sentimental life with the same frequency and impetuosity as that with which she changed her dress-makers, did over her drawing-rooms, ordered new motors, altered the mounting of her jewels, and generally renewed the setting of her life. Susy knew in advance what the tale would be; but to listen to it over perfect coffee, an amber-scented cigarette at her lips, was pleasanter than consuming cold mutton alone in a mouldy coffee-room. The contrast was so soothing that she even began to take a languid interest in her friend's narrative.

After luncheon they got into the motor together and began a systematic round of the West End shops: furriers, jewellers and dealers in old furniture. Nothing could be more unlike Violet Melrose's long hesitating sessions before the things

she thought she wanted till the moment came to
decide. Ursula pounced on silver foxes and old
lacquer as promptly and decisively as on the objects of her surplus sentimentality: she knew at
once what she wanted, and valued it more after
it was hers.

"And now—I wonder if you couldn't help me
choose a grand piano?" she suggested, as the last
antiquarian bowed them out.

"A piano?"

"Yes: for Ruan. I'm sending one down for
Grace·Fulmer. She's coming to stay . . . did I
tell you? I want people to hear her. I want her
to get engagements in London. My dear, she's a
Genius."

"A Genius—Grace?" Susy gasped. "I thought
it was Nat. . . ."

"Nat—Nat Fulmer?" Ursula laughed deris-
ively. "Ah, of course—you've been staying with
that silly Violet! The poor thing is off her head
about Nat—it's really pitiful. Of course he has
talent: *I* saw that long before Violet had ever
heard of him. Why, on the opening day of
the American Artists' exhibition, last winter, I
stopped short before his 'Spring Snow-Storm'
(which nobody else had noticed till that moment),
and said to the Prince, who was with me: 'The man
has *talent*.' But genius—why, it's his wife who has
genius! Have you never heard Grace play the violin?
Poor Violet, as usual, is off on the wrong tack.
I've given Fulmer my garden-house to do—no

doubt Violet told you—because I wanted to help him. But Grace is *my* discovery, and I'm determined to make her known, and to have every one understand that *she* is the genius of the two. I've told her she simply must come to Ruan, and bring the best accompanyist she can find. You know poor Nerone is dreadfully bored by sport, though of course he goes out with the guns. And if one didn't have a little art in the evening. . . . Oh, Susy, do you mean to tell me you don't know how to choose a piano? I thought you were so fond of music!"

"I am fond of it; but without knowing anything about it—in the way we're all of us fond of the worth-while things in our stupid set," she added to herself—since it was obviously useless to impart such reflections to Ursula.

"But are you sure Grace is coming?" she questioned aloud.

"Quite sure. Why shouldn't she I wired to her yesterday. I'm giving her a thousand dollars and all her expenses."

It was not till they were having tea in a Piccadilly tea-room that Mrs. Gillow began to manifest some interest in her companion's plans. The thought of losing Susy became suddenly intolerable to her. The Prince, who did not see why he should be expected to linger in London out of season, was already at Ruan, and Ursula could not face the evening and the whole of the next day by herself.

"But what are you doing in town, darling? I
don't remember if I've asked you," she said, resting her firm elbows on the tea-table while she took
a light from Susy's cigarette.

Susy hesitated. She had foreseen that the time
must soon come when she should have to give
some account of herself; and why should she not
begin by telling Ursula?

But telling her what?

Her silence appeared to strike Mrs. Gillow as
a reproach, and she continued with compunction:
"And Nick? Nick's with you? How is he? I
thought you and he still were in Venice with Ellie
Vanderlyn."

"We were, for a few weeks." She steadied her
voice. "It was delightful. But now we're both
on our own again—for a while."

Mrs. Gillow scrutinized her more searchingly.
"Oh, you're alone here, then; quite alone?"

"Yes: Nick's cruising with some friends in the
Mediterranean."

Ursula's shallow gaze deepened singularly.
"But, Susy darling, then if you're alone—and out
of a job, just for the moment?"

Susy smiled. "Well, I'm not sure."

"Oh, but if you *are*, darling, and you would
come to Ruan! I know Fred asked you—didn't
he? And he told me that both you and Nick had
refused. He was awfully huffed at your not coming; but I suppose that was because Nick had
other plans. We couldn't have him *now*, because

there's no room for another gun; but since he's not here, and you're free, why you know, dearest, don't you, how we'd love to have you? Fred would be too glad—too outrageously glad—but you don't much mind Fred's love-making, do you? And you'd be such a help to me—if *that's* any argument! With that big house full of men, and people flocking over every night to dine, and Fred caring only for sport, and Nerone simply loathing it and ridiculing it, and not a minute to myself to try to keep him in a good humour. . . . Oh, Susy darling, don't say no, but let me telephone at once for a place in the train to-morrow night!''

Susy leaned back, letting the ash lengthen on her cigarette. How familiar, how hatefully familiar, was that old appeal! Ursula felt the pressing need of someone to flirt with Fred for a few weeks . . . and here was the very person she needed. Susy shivered at the thought. She had never really meant to go to Ruan. She had simply used the moor as a pretext when Violet Melrose had gently put her out of doors. Rather than do what Ursula asked she would borrow a few hundred pounds of Strefford, as he had suggested, and then look about for some temporary occupation until—

Until she became Lady Altringham? Well, perhaps. At any rate, she was not going back to slave for Ursula.

She shook her head with a faint smile. ''I'm so

sorry, Ursula: of course I want awfully to oblige
you—"

Mrs. Gillow's gaze grew reproachful. "I
should have supposed you would," she murmured.
Susy, meeting her eyes, looked into them down a
long vista of favours bestowed, and perceived
that Ursula was not the woman to forget on which
side the obligation lay between them.

Susy hesitated: she remembered the weeks of
ecstasy she had owed to the Gillows' wedding
cheque, and it hurt her to appear ungrateful.

"If I could, Ursula . . . but really . . . I'm
not free at the moment." She paused, and then
took an abrupt decision. "The fact is, I'm waiting here to see Strefford."

"Strefford?   Lord Altringham?"   Ursula
stared. "Ah, yes—I remember. You and he
used to be great friends, didn't you?" Her rov-
ing attention deepened. . . . But if Susy were
waiting to see Lord Altringham—one of the richest men in England? Suddenly Ursula opened
her gold-meshed bag and snatched a miniature
diary from it.

"But wait a moment—yes, it *is* next week! I
knew it was next week he's coming to Ruan! But,
you darling, that makes everything all right.
You'll send him a wire at once, and come with
me to-morrow, and meet him there instead of in
this nasty sloppy desert. . . . Oh, Susy, if you
knew how hard life is for me in Scotland between

the Prince and Fred you couldn't possibly say no!"

Susy still wavered; but, after all, if Strefford were really bound for Ruan, why not see him there, agreeably and at leisure, instead of spending a dreary day with him in roaming the wet London streets, or screaming at him through the rattle of a restaurant orchestra? She knew he would not be likely to postpone his visit to Ruan in order to linger in London with her: such concessions had never been his way, and were less than ever likely to be, now that he could do so thoroughly and completely as he pleased.

For the first time she fully understood how different his destiny had become. Now of course all his days and hours were mapped out in advance: invitations assailed him, opportunities pressed on him, he had only to choose. . . . And the women! She had never before thought of the women. All the girls in England would be wanting to marry him, not to mention her own enterprising compatriots. And there were the married women, who were even more to be feared. Streff might, for the time, escape marriage; though she could guess the power of persuasion, family pressure, all the converging traditional influences he had so often ridiculed, yet, as she knew, had never completely thrown off. . . . Yes, those quiet invisible women at Altringham—his uncle's widow, his mother, the spinster sisters—it was not impossible that, with tact and patience—and the stupid-

est women could be tactful and patient on such
occasions—they might eventually persuade him
that it was his duty, they might put just the right
young loveliness in his way. . . . But meanwhile,
now, at once, there were the married women. Ah,
they wouldn't wait, *they* were doubtless laying
their traps already! Susy winced at the
thought. She knew too much about the way the
trick was done, had followed, too often, all the
sinuosities of such approaches. Not that they were
very sinuous nowadays: more often there was
just a swoop and a pounce when the time came;
but she knew all the arts and the wiles that led
up to it. She knew them, oh, how she knew them
—though with Streff, thank heaven, she had never
been called upon to exercise them! His love was
there for the asking: would she not be a fool to
refuse it?

Perhaps; though on that point her mind still
wavered. But at any rate she saw that, decidedly,
it would be better to yield to Ursula's pressure;
better to meet him at Ruan, in a congenial setting,
where she would have time to get her bearings,
observe what dangers threatened him, and make
up her mind whether, after all, it was to be her
mission to save him from the other women. . . .

"Well, if you like, then, Ursula. . . ."

"Oh, you angel, you! I'm so glad! We'll go
to the nearest post office, and send off the wire
ourselves."

As they got into the motor Mrs. Gillow seized Susy's arm with a pleading pressure. "And you *will* let Fred make love to you a little, won't you, darling?"

XVIII

"**B**UT I can't think," said Ellie Vanderlyn earnestly, "why you don't announce your engagement before waiting for your divorce. People are beginning to do it, I assure you—it's so much safer!"

Mrs. Vanderlyn, on the way back from St. Moritz to England, had paused in Paris to renew the depleted wardrobe which, only two months earlier, had filled so many trunks to bursting. Other ladies, flocking there from all points of the globe for the same purpose, disputed with her the Louis XVI suites of the Nouveau Luxe, the pink-candled tables in the restaurant, the hours for trying-on at the dress-makers'; and just because they were so many, and all feverishly fighting to get the same things at the same time, they were all excited, happy and at ease. It was the most momentous period of the year: the height of the "dress-makers' season."

Mrs. Vanderlyn had run across Susy Lansing at one of the Rue de la Paix openings, where rows of ladies wan with heat and emotion sat for hours in rapt attention while spectral apparitions in incredible raiment tottered endlessly past them on aching feet.

Distracted from the regal splendours of a chinchilla cloak by the sense that another lady was also examining it, Mrs. Vanderlyn turned in surprise at sight of Susy, whose head was critically bent above the fur.

"Susy! I'd no idea you were here! I saw in the papers that you were with the Gillows." The customary embraces followed; then Mrs. Vanderlyn, her eyes pursuing the matchless cloak as it disappeared down a vista of receding *mannequins,* interrogated sharply: "Are you shopping for Ursula? If you mean to order that cloak for *her* I'd rather know."

Susy smiled, and paused a moment before answering. During the pause she took in all the exquisite details of Ellie Vanderlyn's perpetually youthful person, from the plumed crown of her head to the perfect arch of her patent-leather shoes. At last she said quietly: "No—to-day I'm shopping for myself."

"Yourself? Yourself?" Mrs. Vanderlyn echoed with a stare of incredulity.

"Yes; just for a change," Susy serenely acknowledged.

"But the cloak—I meant the chinchilla cloak . . . the one with the ermine lining. . . ."

"Yes; it *is* awfully good, isn't it? But I mean to look elsewhere before I decide."

Ah, how often she had heard her friends use that phrase; and how amusing it was, now, to see Ellie's amazement as she heard it tossed off in her own tone of contemptuous satiety! Susy was becoming more and more dependent on such diversions; without them her days, crowded as they were, would nevertheless have dragged by heavily. But it still amused her to go to the big dressmakers', watch the *mannequins* sweep by, and be seen by her friends superciliously examining all the most expensive dresses in the procession. She knew the rumour was abroad that she and Nick were to be divorced, and that Lord Altringham was "devoted" to her. She neither confirmed nor denied the report: she just let herself be luxuriously carried forward on its easy tide. But although it was now three months since Nick had left the Palazzo Vanderlyn she had not yet written to him—nor he to her.

Meanwhile, in spite of all that she packed into them, the days passed more and more slowly, and the excitements she had counted on no longer excited her. Strefford was hers: she knew that he would marry her as soon as she was free. They had been together at Ruan for ten days, and after that she had motored south with him, stopping on the way to see Altringham, from which, at the moment, his mourning relatives were absent.

At Altringham they had parted; and after one or two more visits in England she had come back to Paris, where he was now about to join her. After her few hours at Altringham she had understood that he would wait for her as long as was necessary: the fear of the "other women" had ceased to trouble her. But, perhaps for that very reason, the future seemed less exciting than she had expected. Sometimes she thought it was the sight of that great house which had overwhelmed her: it was too vast, too venerable, too like a huge monument built of ancient territorial traditions and obligations. Perhaps it had been lived in for too long by too many serious-minded and conscientious women: somehow she could not picture it invaded by bridge and debts and adultery. And yet that was what would have to be, of course . . . she could hardly picture either Strefford or herself continuing there the life of heavy county responsibilities, dull parties, laborious duties, weekly church-going, and presiding over local committees. . . . What a pity they couldn't sell it and have a little house on the Thames!

Nevertheless she was not sorry to let it be known that Altringham was hers when she chose to take it. At times she wondered whether Nick knew . . . whether rumours had reached him. If they had, he had only his own letter to thank for it. He had told her what course to pursue; and she was pursuing it.

For a moment the meeting with Ellie Vanderlyn had been a shock to her; she had hoped never to see Ellie again. But now that they were actually face to face Susy perceived how dulled her sensibilities were. In a few moments she had grown used to Ellie, as she was growing used to everybody and to everything in the old life she had

returned to. What was the use of making such
a fuss about things? She and Mrs. Vanderlyn
left the dress-maker's together, and after an absorbing session at a new milliner's were now taking tea in Ellie's drawing-room at the Nouveau
Luxe.

Ellie, with her spoiled child's persistency, had
come back to the question of the chinchilla cloak.
It was the only one she had seen that she fancied
in the very least, and as she hadn't a decent fur
garment left to her name she was naturally in
somewhat of a hurry . . . but, of course, if Susy
had been choosing that model for a friend. . . .

Susy, leaning back aginst her cushions, examined through half-closed lids Mrs. Vanderlyn's
small delicately-restored countenance, which wore
the same expression of childish eagerness as when
she discoursed of the young Davenant of the moment. Once again Susy remarked that, in Ellie's
agitated existence, every interest appeared to be
on exactly the same plane.

"The poor shivering dear," she answered
laughing, "of course it shall have its nice warm
winter cloak, and I'll choose another one instead."

"Oh, you darling, you! If you would! Of
course, whoever you were ordering it for need
never know. . . ."

"Ah, you can't comfort yourself with that, I'm
afraid. I've already told you that I was ordering it for myself." Susy paused to savour to the

full Ellie's look of blank bewilderment; then her
amusement was checked by an indefinable change
in her friend's expression.

"Oh, dearest—seriously? I didn't know there
was someone. . . ."

Susy flushed to the forehead. A horror of humiliation overwhelmed her. That Ellie should
dare to think that of her—that anyone should
dare to!

"Someone buying chinchilla cloaks for me?
Thanks!" she flared out. "I suppose I ought to
be glad that the idea didn't immediately occur to
you. At least there was a decent interval of
doubt. . . ." She stood up, laughing again, and
began to wander about the room. In the mirror
above the mantel she caught sight of her flushed
angry face, and of Mrs. Vanderlyn's disconcerted
stare. She turned toward her friend.

"I suppose everybody else will think it if you
do; so perhaps I'd better explain." She paused,
and drew a quick breath. "Nick and I mean to
part—have parted, in fact. He's decided that
the whole thing was a mistake. He will probably
marry again soon—and so shall I."

She flung the avowal out breathlessly, in her
nervous dread of letting Ellie Vanderlyn think
for an instant longer that any other explanation
was conceivable. She had not meant to be so
explicit; but once the words were spoken she was
not altogether sorry. Of course people would
soon begin to wonder why she was again straying

about the world alone; and since it was by Nick's choice, why should she not say so? Remembering the burning anguish of those last hours in Venice she asked herself what possible consideration she owed to the man who had so humbled her.

Ellie Vanderlyn glanced at her in astonishment. "You? You and Nick—are going to part?" A light appeared to dawn on her. "Ah—then that's why he sent me back my pin, I suppose?"

"Your pin?" Susy wondered, not at once remembering.

"The poor little scarf-pin I gave him before I left Venice. He sent it back almost at once, with the oddest note—just: 'I haven't earned it, really.' I couldn't think why he didn't care for the pin. But now I suppose it was because you and he had quarrelled; though really, even so, I can't see why he should bear *me* a grudge. . . ."

Susy's quick blood surged up. Nick had sent back the pin—the fatal pin! And she, Susy, had kept the bracelet—locked it up out of sight, shrunk away from the little packet whenever her hand touched it in packing or unpacking—but never thought of returning it, no, not once! Which of the two, she wondered, had been right? Was it not an indirect slight to her that Nick should fling back the gift to poor uncomprehending Ellie? Or was it not rather another proof of his finer moral sensitiveness? . . . And how could one tell, in their bewildering world?

"It was not because we've quarrelled; we haven't quarrelled," she said slowly, moved by the sudden desire to defend her privacy and Nick's, to screen from every eye their last bitter hour together. "We've simply decided that our experiment was impossible—for two paupers."

"Ah, well—of course we all felt that at the time. And now somebody else wants to marry you? And it's your *trousseau* you were choosing that cloak for?" Ellie cried in incredulous rapture; then she flung her arms about Susy's shrinking shoulders. "You lucky lucky girl! You clever clever darling! But who on earth can he be?"

And it was then that Susy, for the first time, had pronounced the name of Lord Altringham.

"Streff—Streff? Our dear old Streff? You mean to say he wants to *marry* you?" As the news took possession of her mind Ellie became dithyrambic. "But, my dearest, what a miracle of luck! Of course I always knew he was awfully gone on you: Fred Davenant used to say so, I remember . . . and even Nelson, who's so stupid about such things, noticed it in Venice. . . . But then it was so different. No one could possibly have thought of marrying him then; whereas now of course every woman is trying for him. Oh, Susy, whatever you do, don't miss your chance! You can't conceive of the wicked plotting and intriguing there will be to get him—on all sides, and even where one least suspects it. You don't know what horrors women will do—and even girls!'' A shudder ran through her at the thought, and she caught Susy's wrists in vehement fingers. "But I can't think, my dear, why you don't announce your engagement at once. People are beginning to do it, I assure you—it's so much safer!''

Susy looked at her, wondering. Not a word of sympathy for the ruin of her brief bliss, not even a gleam of curiosity as to its cause! No doubt Ellie Vanderlyn, like all Susy's other friends, had long since ''discounted'' the brevity of her dream, and perhaps planned a sequel to it before she herself had seen the glory fading. She and Nick had spent the greater part of their few weeks together under Ellie Vanderlyn's roof; but to Ellie, obviously, the fact meant no more than her own escapade, at the same moment, with young Davenant's supplanter—the ''bounder'' whom Strefford had never named. Her one thought for her friend was that Susy should at last secure her prize—her incredible prize. And therein at any rate Ellie showed the kind of cold disinterestedness that raised her above the smiling perfidy of the majority of her kind. At least her advice was sincere; and perhaps it was wise. Why should Susy not let every one know that she meant to marry Strefford as soon as the ''formalities'' were fulfilled?

She did not immediately answer Mrs. Vanderlyn's question; and the latter, repeating it, added impatiently: "I don't understand you; if Nick agrees—"

"Oh, he agrees," said Susy.

"Then what more do you want? Oh, Susy, if you'd only follow my example!"

"Your example?" Susy paused, weighed the word, was struck by something embarrassed, arch yet half-apologetic in her friend's expression. "Your example?" she repeated. "Why, Ellie, what on earth do you mean? Not that you're going to part from poor Nelson?"

Mrs. Vanderlyn met her reproachful gaze with a crystalline glance. "I don't want to, heaven knows—poor dear Nelson! I assure you I simply *hate* it. He's always such an angel to Clarissa . . . and then we're used to each other. But what in the world am I to do? Algie's so rich, so appallingly rich, that I have to be perpetually on the watch to keep other women away from him— and it's too exhausting. . . ."

"Algie?"

Mrs. Vanderlyn's lovely eyebrows rose. "Algie: Algie Bockheimer. Didn't you know? I think he said you've dined with his parents. Nobody else in the world is as rich as the Bockheimers; and Algie's their only child. Yes, it was with him . . . with him I was so dreadfully happy last spring . . . and now I'm in mortal terror of losing him. And I do assure you there's no other way of keeping them, when they're as hideously rich as that!"

Susy rose to her feet. A little shudder ran over her. She remembered, now, having seen Algie Bockheimer at one of his parents' first entertainments, in their newly-inaugurated marble halls in Fifth Avenue. She recalled his too faultless clothes and his small glossy furtive countenance. She looked at Ellie Vanderlyn with sudden scorn.

"I think you're abominable," she exclaimed.

The other's perfect little face collapsed. "A-bo-mi-nable? A-bo-mi-nable? Susy!"

"Yes . . . with Nelson . . . and Clarissa . . . and your past together . . . and all the money you can possibly want . . . and *that* man! Abominable."

Ellie stood up trembling: she was not used to scenes, and they disarranged her thoughts as much as her complexion.

"You're very cruel, Susy—so cruel and dreadful that I hardly know how to answer you," she stammered. "But you simply don't know what you're talking about. *As if anybody ever had all the money they wanted!*" She wiped her dark-rimmed eyes with a cautious handkerchief, glanced at herself in the mirror, and added magnanimously: "But I shall try to forget what you've said."

XIX

JUST such a revolt as she had felt as a girl, such a disgusted recoil from the standards and ideals of everybody about her as had flung her into her mad marriage with Nick, now flamed in Susy Lansing's bosom.

How could she ever go back into that world again? How echo its appraisals of life and bow down to its judgments? Alas, it was only by marrying according to its standards that she could escape such subjection. Perhaps the same thought had actuated Nick: perhaps he had understood sooner than she that to attain moral freedom. they must both be above material cares. Perhaps. . .

Her talk with Ellie Vanderlyn had left Susy so oppressed and humiliated that she almost shrank from her meeting with Altringham the next day. She knew that he was coming to Paris for his final answer; he would wait as long as was necessary if only she would consent to take immediate steps for a divorce. She was staying at a modest hotel in the Faubourg St. Germain, and had once more refused his suggestion that they should lunch at the Nouveau Luxe, or at some fashionable restaurant of the Boulevards. As before, she insisted on going to an out-of-the-way place near the Luxembourg, where the prices were moderate enough for her own purse.

"I can't understand," Strefford objected, as they turned from her hotel door toward this obscure retreat, "why you insist on giving me bad food, and depriving me of the satisfaction of being seen with you. Why must we be so dreadfully clandestine? Don't people know by this time that we're to be married?"

Susy winced a little: she wondered if the word would always sound so unnatural on his lips.

"No," she said, with a laugh, "they simply think, for the present, that you're giving me pearls and chinchilla cloaks."

He wrinkled his brows good-humouredly. "Well, so I would, with joy—at this particular minute. Don't you think perhaps you'd better take advantage of it? I don't wish to insist—but I foresee that I'm much too rich not to become stingy."

She gave a slight shrug. "At present there's nothing I loathe more than pearls and chinchilla . . . or anything else in the world that's expensive and enviable. . . ."

Suddenly she broke off, colouring with the consciousness that she had said exactly the kind of thing that all the women who were trying for him (except the very cleverest) would be sure to say; and that he would certainly suspect her of attempting the conventional comedy of disinterestedness, than which nothing was less likely to deceive or to flatter him.

His twinkling eyes played curiously over her face, and she went on, meeting them with a smile: "But don't imagine, all the same, that if I should . . . decide . . . it would be altogether for your *beaux yeux.* . . ."

He laughed, she thought, rather drily. "No," he said, "I don't suppose that's ever likely to happen to me again."

"Oh, Streff—" she faltered with compunction. It was odd—once upon a time she had known exactly what to say to the man of the moment, whoever he was, and whatever kind of talk he required; she had even, in the difficult days before her marriage, reeled off glibly enough the sort of lime-light sentimentality that plunged poor Fred Gillow into such speechless beatitude. But since then she had spoken the language of real love, looked with its eyes, embraced with its hands; and now the other trumpery art had failed her, and she was conscious of bungling and groping like a beginner under Strefford's ironic scrutiny.

They had reached their obscure destination and he opened the door and glanced in.

"It's jammed—not a table. And stifling! Where shall we go? Perhaps they could give us a room to ourselves—" he suggested.

She assented, and they were led up a cork-screw staircase to a squat-ceilinged closet lit by the arched top of a high window, the lower panes of

which served for the floor below. Strefford
opened the window, and Susy, throwing her cloak
on the divan, leaned on the balcony while he ordered luncheon.

On the whole she was glad they were to be alone.
Just because she felt so sure of Strefford it
seemed ungenerous to keep him longer in suspense. The moment had come when they must
have a decisive talk, and in the crowded rooms
below it would have been impossible.

Strefford, when the waiter had brought the
first course and left them to themselves, made no
effort to revert to personal matters. He turned
instead to the topic always most congenial to him:
the humours and ironies of the human comedy, as
presented by his own particular group. His malicious commentary on life had always amused
Susy because of the shrewd flashes of philosophy
he shed on the social antics they had so often
watched together. He was in fact the one person
she knew (excepting Nick) who was in the show
and yet outside of it; and she was surprised, as
the talk proceeded, to find herself so little interested in his scraps of gossip, and so little amused
by his comments on them.

With an inward shrug of discouragement she
said to herself that probably nothing would ever
really amuse her again; then, as she listened, she
began to understand that her disappointment
arose from the fact that Strefford, in reality,
could not live without these people whom he saw

through and satirized, and that the rather commonplace scandals he narrated interested him as
much as his own racy considerations on them;
and she was filled with terror at the thought that
the inmost core of the richly-decorated life of the
Countess of Altringham would be just as poor
and low-ceilinged a place as the little room in
which he and she now sat, elbow to elbow yet so
unapproachably apart.

If Strefford could not live without these people,
neither could she and Nick; but for reasons how
different!   And if his opportunities had been
theirs, what a world they would have created for
themselves!   Such imaginings were vain, and she
shrank back from them into the present.   After
all, as Lady Altringham she would have the power
to create that world which she and Nick had
dreamed . . . only she must create it alone.   Well,
that was probably the law of things.   All human
happiness was thus conditioned and circumscribed, and hers, no doubt, must always be of the
lonely kind, since material things did not suffice
for it, even though it depended on them as Grace
Fulmer's, for instance, never had.   Yet even
Grace Fulmer had succumbed to Ursula's offer,
and had arrived at Ruan the day before Susy left,
instead of going to Spain with her husband and
Violet Melrose.   But then Grace was making the
sacrifice for her children, and somehow one had
the feeling that in giving up her liberty she was

not surrendering a tittle of herself. All the difference was there. . . .

"How I do bore you!" Susy heard Strefford exclaim. She became aware that she had not been listening: stray echoes of names of places and people—Violet Melrose, Ursula, Prince Altineri, others of their group and persuasion—had vainly knocked at her barricaded brain; what had he been telling her about them? She turned to him and their eyes met; his were full of a melancholy irony.

"Susy, old girl, what's wrong?"

She pulled herself together. "I was thinking, Streff, just now—when I said I hated the very sound of pearls and chinchilla—how impossible it was that you should believe me; in fact, what a blunder I'd made in saying it."

He smiled. "Because it was what so many other women might be likely to say—so awfully unoriginal, in fact?"

She laughed for sheer joy at his insight. "It's going to be easier than I imagined," she thought. Aloud she rejoined: "Oh, Streff—how you're always going to find me out! Where on earth shall I ever hide from you?"

"Where?" He echoed her laugh, laying his hand lightly on hers. "In my heart, I'm afraid."

In spite of the laugh his accent shook her: something about it took all the mockery from his retort, checked on her lips the: "What? A valentine!" and made her suddenly feel that, if he were

afraid, so was she. Yet she was touched also,
and wondered half exultingly if any other woman
had ever caught that particular deep inflexion of
his shrill voice. She had never liked him as much
as at that moment; and she said to herself, with
an odd sense of detachment, as if she had been
rather breathlessly observing the vacillations of
someone whom she longed to persuade but dared
not: "Now—*now,* if he speaks, I shall say yes!"

He did not speak; but abruptly, and as start-
lingly to her as if she had just dropped from a
sphere whose inhabitants had other methods of
expressing their sympathy, he slipped his arm
around her and bent his keen ugly melting face
to hers. . . .

It was the lightest touch—in an instant she was
free again. But something within her gasped and
resisted long after his arm and his lips were gone,
and he was proceeding, with a too-studied ease,
to light a cigarette and sweeten his coffee.

He had kissed her. . . . Well, naturally: why
not? It was not the first time she had been kissed.
It was true that one didn't habitually associate
Streff with such demonstrations; but she had not
that excuse for surprise, for even in Venice she
had begun to notice that he looked at her differently, and avoided her hand when he used to seek
it.

No—she ought not to have been surprised; nor
ought a kiss to have been so disturbing. Such in-
cidents had punctuated the career of Susy

Branch: there had been, in particular, in far-off discarded times, Fred Gillow's large but artless embraces. Well—nothing of that kind had seemed of any more account than the flick of a leaf in a woodland walk. It had all been merely epidermal, ephemeral, part of the trivial accepted "business" of the social comedy. But this kiss of Strefford's was what Nick's had been, under the New Hampshire pines, on the day that had decided their fate. It was a kiss with a future in it: like a ring slipped upon her soul. And now, in the dreadful pause that followed—while Strefford fidgeted with his cigarette-case and rattled the spoon in his cup—Susy remembered what she had seen through the circle of Nick's kiss: that blue illimitable distance which was at once the landscape at their feet and the future in their souls. . . .

Perhaps that was what Strefford's sharply narrowed eyes were seeing now, that same illimitable distance that she had lost forever—perhaps he was saying to himself, as she had said to herself when her lips left Nick's: "Each time we kiss we shall see it all again. . . ." Whereas all she herself had felt was the gasping recoil from Strefford's touch, and an intenser vision of the sordid room in which he and she sat, and of their two selves, more distant from each other than if their embrace had been a sudden thrusting apart. . . .

The moment prolonged itself, and they sat

numb. How long had it lasted? How long ago
was it that she had thought: "It's going to be
easier than I imagined"? Suddenly she felt
Strefford's queer smile upon her, and saw in
his eyes a look, not of reproach or disappointment, but of deep and anxious comprehension.
Instead of being angry or hurt, he had seen, he
had understood, he was sorry for her!

Impulsively she slipped her hand into his, and
they sat silent for another moment. Then he
stood up and took her cloak from the divan.
"Shall we go now? I've got cards for the private
view of the Reynolds exhibition at the Petit
Palais. There are some portraits from Altringham. It might amuse you."

In the taxi she had time, through their light
rattle of talk, to readjust herself and drop back
into her usual feeling of friendly ease with him.
He had been extraordinarily considerate, for anyone who always so undisguisedly sought his own
satisfaction above all things; and if his consider-
ateness were just an indirect way of seeking that
satisfaction now, well, that proved how much he
cared for her, how necessary to his happiness she
had become. The sense of power was undeniably
pleasant; pleasanter still was the feeling that
someone really needed her, that the happiness of
the man at her side depended on her yes or no.
She abandoned herself to the feeling, forgetting
the abysmal interval of his caress, or at least saying to herself that in time she would forget it,

that really there was nothing to make a fuss about in being kissed by anyone she liked as much as Streff. . . .

She had guessed at once why he was taking her to see the Reynoldses. Fashionable and artistic Paris had recently discovered English eighteenth century art. The principal collections of England had yielded up their best examples of the great portrait painter's work, and the private view at the Petit Palais was to be the social event of the afternoon. Everybody—Strefford's everybody and Susy's—was sure to be there; and these, as she knew, were the occasions that revived Strefford's intermittent interest in art. He really liked picture shows as much as the races, if one could be sure of seeing as many people there. With Nick how different it would have been! Nick hated openings and varnishing days, and worldly æsthetics in general; he would have waited till the tide of fashion had ebbed, and slipped off with Susy to see the pictures some morning when they were sure to have the place to themselves.

But Susy divined that there was another reason for Strefford's suggestion. She had never yet shown herself with him publicly, among their own group of people: now he had determined that she should do so, and she knew why. She had humbled his pride; he had understood, and forgiven her. But she still continued to treat him as she had always treated the Strefford of old, Charlie Strefford, dear old negligible impecuni-

ous Streff; and he wanted to show her, ever so
casually and adroitly, that the man who had asked
her to marry him was no longer Strefford, but
Lord Altringham.

At the very threshold, his Ambassador's greeting marked the difference: it was followed, wherever they turned, by ejaculations of welcome from
the rulers of the world they moved in. Everybody rich enough or titled enough, or clever
enough or stupid enough, to have forced a way
into the social citadel, was there, waving and flag-
flying from the battlements; and to all of them
Lord Altringham had become a marked figure.
During their slow progress through the dense
mass of important people who made the approach
to the pictures so well worth fighting for, he never
left Susy's side, or failed to make her feel herself
a part of his triumphal advance. She heard her
name mentioned: "Lansing—a Mrs. Lansing—an
American ... Susy Lansing? Yes, of course. ...
You remember her? At Newport? At St.
Moritz? Exactly. ... Divorced already? They
say so ... Susy darling! I'd no idea you were
here ... and Lord Altringham! You've forgotten me, I know, Lord Altringham. ... Yes, last
year, in Cairo ... or at Newport ... or in Scotland .. Susy, dearest, when will you bring Lord
Altringham to dine? Any night that you and he
are free I'll arrange to be. ..."

"You and he": they were "you and he" already!

"Ah, there's one of them—of my great-grand-mothers," Strefford explained, giving a last push that drew him and Susy to the front rank, before a tall isolated portrait which, by sheer majesty of presentment, sat in its great carved golden frame as on a throne above the other pictures.

Susy read on the scroll beneath it: "The Honble Diana Lefanu, fifteenth Countess of Altringham"—and heard Strefford say: "Do you remember? It hangs where you noticed the empty space above the mantel-piece, in the Vandyke room. They say Reynolds stipulated that it should be put with the Vandykes."

She had never before heard him speak of his possessions, whether ancestral or merely material, in just that full and satisfied tone of voice: the rich man's voice. She saw that he was already feeling the influence of his surroundings, that he was glad the portrait of a Countess of Altringham should occupy the central place in the principal room of the exhibition, that the crowd about it should be denser there than before any of the other pictures, and that he should be standing there with Susy, letting her feel, and letting all the people about them guess, that the day she chose she could wear the same name as his pictured ancestress.

On the way back to her hotel, Strefford made no farther allusion to their future; they chatted like old comrades in their respective corners of the taxi. But as the carriage stopped at her door he said: "I must go back to England the day after to-morrow, worse luck! Why not dine with me to-night at the Nouveau Luxe? I've got to have the Ambassador and Lady Ascot, with their youngest girl and my old Dunes aunt, the Dowager Duchess, who's over here hiding from her creditors; but I'll try to get two or three amusing men to leaven the lump. We might go on to a *boîte* afterward, if you're bored. Unless the dancing amuses you more. . . ."

She understood that he had decided to hasten his departure rather than linger on in uncertainty; she also remembered having heard the Ascots' youngest daughter, Lady Joan Senechal, spoken of as one of the prettiest girls of the season; and she recalled the almost exaggerated warmth of the Ambassador's greeting at the private view.

"Of course I'll come, Streff dear!" she cried, with an effort at gaiety that sounded successful to her own strained ears, and reflected itself in the sudden lighting up of his face.

She waved a good-bye from the step, saying to herself, as she looked after him: "He'll drive me home to-night, and I shall say 'yes'; and then he'll kiss me again. But the next time it won't be nearly as disagreeable."

She turned into the hotel, glanced automatically at the empty pigeon-hole for letters under her key-hook, and mounted the stairs following the same train of images. "Yes, I shall say 'yes' to-night," she repeated firmly, her hand on the door of her room. "That is, unless, they've brought up a letter. . . ." She never re-entered the hotel without imagining that the letter she had not found below had already been brought up.

Opening the door, she turned on the light and sprang to the table on which her correspondence sometimes awaited her.

There was no letter; but the morning papers, still unread, lay at hand, and glancing listlessly down the column which chronicles the doings of society, she read:

"After an extended cruise in the Ægean and the Black Sea on their steam-yacht *Ibis,* Mr. and Mrs. Mortimer Hicks and their daughter are established at the Nouveau Luxe in Rome. They have lately had the honour of entertaining at dinner the Reigning Prince of Teutoburger-Waldhain and his mother the Princess Dowager, with their suite. Among those invited to meet their Serene Highnesses were the French and Spanish Ambassadors, the Duchesse de Vichy, Prince and Princess Bagnidilucca, Lady Penelope Pantiles—" Susy's eye flew impatiently on over the long list of titles—"and Mr. Nicholas Lansing of New York, who has been cruising with Mr. and Mrs. Hicks on the *Ibis* for the last few months."

XX

THE Mortimer Hickses were in Rome; not, as they would in former times have been, in one of the antiquated hostelries of the Piazza di Spagna or the Porta del Popolo, where of old they had so gaily defied fever and nourished themselves on local colour; but spread out, with all the ostentation of philistine millionaires, under the *piano nobile* ceilings of one of the high-perched "Palaces," where, as Mrs. Hicks shamelessly declared, they could "rely on the plumbing," and "have the privilege of over-looking the Queen Mother's Gardens."

It was that speech, uttered with beaming aplomb at a dinner-table surrounded by the cosmopolitan nobility of the Eternal City, that had suddenly revealed to Lansing the profound change in the Hicks point of view.

As he looked back over the four monuths since he had so unexpectedly joined the *Ibis* at Genoa, he saw that the change, at first insidious and unperceived, dated from the ill-fated day when the Hickses had run across a Reigning Prince on his travels.

Hitherto they had been proof against such perils: both Mr. and Mrs. Hicks had often de-

clared that the aristocracy of the intellect was the
only one which attracted them. But in this case
the Prince possessed an intellect, in addition to his
few square miles of territory, and to one of the
most beautiful Field Marshal's uniforms that had
ever encased a royal warrior. The Prince was
not a warrior, however; he was stooping, pacific
and spectacled, and his possession of the uniform
had been revealed to Mrs. Hicks only by the gift
of a full-length photograph in a Bond Street
frame, with *Anastasius* written slantingly across
its legs. The Prince—and herein lay the Hickses'
undoing—the Prince was an archæologist: an
earnest anxious enquiring and scrupulous archæologist. Delicate health (so his suite hinted)
banished him for a part of each year from his
cold and foggy principality; and in the company of his mother, the active and enthusiastic
Dowager Princess, he wandered from one Mediterranean shore to another, now assisting at the
exhumation of Ptolemaic mummies, now at the
excavation of Delphic temples or of North Afri-
can basilicas. The beginning of winter usually
brought the Prince and his mother to Rome or
Nice, unless indeed they were summoned by
family duties to Berlin, Vienna or Madrid; for
an extended connection with the principal royal
houses of Europe compelled them, as the Princess
Mother said, to be always burying or marrying
a cousin. At other moments they were seldom
seen in the glacial atmosphere of courts, prefer-

ring to royal palaces those of the other, and more
modern type, in one of which the Hickses were
now lodged.

Yes: the Prince and his mother (they gaily
avowed it) revelled in Palace Hotels; and, being
unable to afford the luxury of inhabiting them,
they liked, as often as possible, to be invited to
dine there by their friends—"or even to tea, my
dear," the Princess laughingly avowed, "for I'm
so awfully fond of buttered scones; and Anastasius gives me so little to eat in the desert."

The encounter with these ambulant Highnesses
had been fatal—Lansing now perceived it—to
Mrs. Hicks's principles. She had known a great
many archæologists, but never one as agreeable
as the Prince, and above all never one who had left
a throne to camp in the desert and delve in Libyan
tombs. And it seemed to her infinitely pathetic
that these two gifted beings, who grumbled when
they had to go to "marry a cousin" at the Palace
of St. James or of Madrid, and hastened back
breathlessly to the far-off point where, metaphor-
ically speaking, pick-axe and spade had dropped
from their royal hands—that these heirs of the
ages should be unable to offer themselves the
comforts of up-to-date hotel life, and should enjoy
themselves "like babies" when they were invited
to the other kind of "Palace," to feast on buttered scones and watch the tango.

She simply could not bear the thought of their
privations; and neither, after a time, could Mr.

Hicks, who found the Prince more democratic than anyone he had ever known at Apex City, and was immensely interested by the fact that their spectacles came from the same optician.

But it was, above all, the artistic tendencies of the Prince and his mother which had conquered the Hickses. There was fascination in the thought that, among the rabble of vulgar uneducated royalties who overran Europe from Biarritz to the Engadine, gambling, tangoing, and sponging on no less vulgar plebeians, they, the unobtrusive and self-respecting Hickses, should have had the luck to meet this cultivated pair, who joined them in gentle ridicule of their own frivolous kinsfolk, and whose tastes were exactly those of the eccentric, unreliable and sometimes money-borrowing persons who had hitherto represented the higher life to the Hickses.

Now at last Mrs. Hicks saw the possibility of being at once artistic and luxurious, of surrendering herself to the joys of modern plumbing and yet keeping the talk on the highest level. "If the poor dear Princess *wants* to dine at the Nouveau Luxe why shouldn't we give her that pleasure?" Mrs. Hicks smilingly enquired; "and as for enjoying her buttered scones like a baby, as she says, I think it's the sweetest thing about her."

Coral Hicks did not join in this chorus; but she accepted, with her curious air of impartiality, the change in her parents' manner of life, and for the first time (as Nick observed) occupied herself

with her mother's toilet, with the result that Mrs.
Hicks's outline became firmer, her garments
soberer in hue and finer in material; so that,
should anyone chance to detect the daughter's
likeness to her mother, the result was less likely
to be disturbing.

Such precautions were the more needful—Lansing could not but note—because of the different
standards of the society in which the Hickses now
moved. For it was a curious fact that admission
to the intimacy of the Prince and his mother—
who continually declared themselves to be the
pariahs, the outlaws, the Bohemians among
crowned heads—nevertheless involved not only
living in Palace Hotels but mixing with those who
frequented them. The Prince's aide-de-camp—an
agreeable young man of easy manners—had smilingly hinted that their Serene Highnesses, though
so thoroughly democratic and unceremonious,
were yet accustomed to inspecting in advance the
names of the persons whom their hosts wished to
invite with them; and Lansing noticed that Mrs.
Hicks's lists, having been "submitted," usually
came back lengthened by the addition of numerous
wealthy and titled guests. Their Highnesses
never struck out a name; they welcomed with enthusiasm and curiosity the Hickses' oddest and
most inexplicable friends, at most putting off
some of them to a later day on the plea that it
would be "cosier" to meet them on a more private
occasion; but they invariably added to the list

many friends of their own, with the gracious hint
that they wished these latter (though socially so
well-provided for) to have the "immense privilege" of knowing the Hickses. And thus it happened that when October gales necessitated laying
up the *Ibis,* the Hickses, finding again in Rome
the august travellers from whom they had parted
the previous month in Athens, also found their
visiting-list enlarged by all that the capital contained of fashion.

It was true enough, as Lansing had not failed
to note, that the Princess Mother adored prehis-
toric art, and Russian music, and the paintings of
Gauguin and Matisse; but she also, and with a
beaming unconsciousness of perspective, adored
large pearls and powerful motors, caravan tea
and modern plumbing, perfumed cigarettes and
society scandals; and her son, while apparently
less sensible to these forms of luxury, adored his
mother, and was charmed to gratify her inclina-
tions without cost to himself—"Since poor Mam-
ma," as he observed, "is so courageous when we
are roughing it in the desert."

The smiling aide-de-camp, who explained these
things to Lansing, added with an intenser smile
that the Prince and his mother were under obligations, either social or cousinly, to most of the
titled persons whom they begged Mrs. Hicks to
invite; "and it seems to their Serene Highnesses," he added, "the most flattering return

they can make for the hospitality of their friends
to give them such an intellectual opportunity."

The dinner-table at which their Highnesses'
friends were seated on the evening in question represented, numerically, one of the greatest
intellectual opportunities yet afforded them.
Thirty guests were grouped about the flower-
wreathed board, from which Eldorada and Mr.
Beck had been excluded on the plea that the Princess Mother liked cosy parties and begged her
hosts that there should never be more than thirty
at table. Such, at least, was the reason given by
Mrs. Hicks to her faithful followers; but Lansing
had observed that, of late, the same skilled hand
which had refashioned the Hickses' social circle
usually managed to exclude from it the timid pres-
ences of the two secretaries. Their banishment
was the more displeasing to Lansing from the fact
that, for the last three months, he had filled Mr.
Buttles's place, and was himself their salaried
companion. But since he had accepted the post,
his obvious duty was to fill it in accordance with
his employers' requirements; and it was clear
even to Eldorada and Mr. Beck that he had, as
Eldorada ungrudgingly said, "Something of Mr.
Buttles's marvellous social gifts."

During the cruise his task had not been distasteful to him. He was glad of any definite
duties, however trivial, he felt more independent
as the Hickses' secretary than as their pampered
guest, and the large cheque which Mr. Hicks

handed over to him on the first of each month refreshed his languishing sense of self-respect.

He considered himself absurdly over-paid, but that was the Hickses' affair; and he saw nothing humiliating in being in the employ of people he liked and respected. But from the moment of the ill-fated encounter with the wandering Princes, his position had changed as much as that of his employers. He was no longer, to Mr. and Mrs. Hicks, a useful and estimable assistant, on the same level as Eldorada and Mr. Beck; he had become a social asset of unsuspected value, equalling Mr. Buttles in his capacity for dealing with the mysteries of foreign etiquette, and surpassing him in the art of personal attraction. Nick Lansing, the Hickses found, already knew most of the Princess Mother's rich and aristocratic friends. Many of them hailed him with enthusiastic ''Old Nicks'', and he was almost as familiar as His Highness's own aide-de-camp with all those secret ramifications of love and hate that made dinner-giving so much more of a science in Rome than at Apex City.

Mrs. Hicks, at first, had hopelessly lost her way in this labyrinth of subterranean scandals, rivalries and jealousies; and finding Lansing's hand within reach she clung to it with pathetic tenacity. But if the young man's value had risen in the eyes of his employers it had deteriorated in his own. He was condemned to play a part he had not bargained for, and it seemed to him more de-

grading when paid in bank-notes than if his retri-
bution had consisted merely in good dinners and
luxurious lodgings. The first time the smiling
aide-de-camp had caught his eye over a verbal slip
of Mrs. Hicks's, Nick had flushed to the forehead
and gone to bed swearing that he would chuck his
job the next day.

Two months had passed since then, and he was
still the paid secretary. He had contrived to let
the aide-de-camp feel that he was too deficient in
humour to be worth exchanging glances with; but
even this had not restored his self-respect, and
on the evening in question, as he looked about the
long table, he said to himself for the hundredth
time that he would give up his position on the
morrow.

Only—what was the alternative? The alternative, apparently, was Coral Hicks. He glanced
down the line of diners, beginning with the tall
lean countenance of the Princess Mother, with its
small inquisitive eyes perched as high as attic
windows under a frizzled thatch of hair and a
pediment of uncleaned diamonds; passed on to
the vacuous and overfed or fashionably haggard
masks of the ladies next in rank; and finally
caught, between branching orchids, a distant
glimpse of Miss Hicks.

In contrast with the others, he thought, she
looked surprisingly noble. Her large grave features made her appear like an old monument in a
street of Palace Hotels; and he marvelled at the

mysterious law which had brought this archaic face out of Apex City, and given to the oldest society of Europe a look of such mixed modernity.

Lansing perceived that the aide-de-camp, who was his neighbour, was also looking at Miss Hicks. His expression was serious, and even thoughtful; but, as his eyes met Lansing's he readjusted his official smile.

"I was admiring our hostess's daughter. Her absence of jewels is—er—an inspiration," he remarked in the confidential tone which Lansing had come to dread.

"Oh, Miss Hicks is full of inspirations," he returned curtly, and the aide-de-camp bowed with an admiring air, as if inspirations were rarer than pearls, as in his *milieu* they undoubtedly were. "She is the equal of any situation, I am sure," he replied; and then abandoned the subject with one of his automatic transitions.

After dinner, in the embrasure of a drawing-room window, he surprised Nick by returning to the same topic, and this time without thinking it needful to readjust his smile. His face remained serious, though his manner was studiously informal.

"I was admiring, at dinner, Miss Hicks's invariable sense of appropriateness. It must permit her friends to foresee for her almost any future, however exalted."

Lansing hesitated, and controlled his annoyance. Decidedly he wanted to know what was in his companion's mind.

"What do you mean by exalted?" he asked, with a smile of faint amusement.

"Well—equal to her marvellous capacity for shining in the public eye."

Lansing still smiled. "The question is, I suppose, whether her desire to shine equals her capacity."

The aide-de-camp stared. "You mean, she's not ambitious?"

"On the contrary; I believe her to be immeasurably ambitious."

"Immeasurably?" The aide-de-camp seemed to try to measure it. "But not, surely, beyond—" *"Beyond what we can offer,"* his eyes completed the sentence; and it was Lansing's turn to stare. The aide-de-camp faced the stare. *"Yes,"* his eyes concluded in a flash, while his lips let fall: "The Princess Mother admires her immensely." But at that moment a wave of Mrs. Hicks's fan drew them hurriedly from their embrasure.

"Professor Darchivio had promised to explain to us the difference between the Sassanian and Byzantine motives in Carolingian art; but the Manager has sent up word that the two new Creole dancers from Paris have arrived, and her Serene Highness wants to pop down to the ball-room and take a peep at them. . . . She's sure the Professor will understand. . . ."

"And accompany us, of course," the Princess irresistibly added.

Lansing's brief colloquy in the Nouveau Luxe window had lifted the scales from his eyes. Innumerable dim corners of memory had been flooded with light by that one quick glance of the aide-de-camp's: things he had heard, hints he had let pass, smiles, insinuations, cordialities, rumours of the improbability of the Prince's founding a family, suggestions as to the urgent need of replenishing the Teutoburger treasury. . . .

Miss Hicks, perforce, had accompanied her parents and their princely guests to the ballroom; but, as she did not dance, and took little interest in the sight of others so engaged, she remained aloof from the party, absorbed in an archæological discussion with the baffled but smiling *savant* who was to have enlightened the party on the difference between Sassanian and Byzantine ornament.

Lansing, also aloof, had picked out a post from which he could observe the girl: she wore a new look to him since he had seen her as the centre of all these scattered threads of intrigue. Yes; decidedly she was growing handsomer; or else she had learned how to set off her massive lines instead of trying to disguise them. As she held up her long eye-glass to glance absently at the dancers he was struck by the large beauty of her arm and the careless assurance of the gesture. There was nothing nervous or fussy about Coral Hicks; and he was not surprised that, plastically at least, the Princess Mother had discerned her possibilities.

Nick Lansing, all that night, sat up and stared at his future. He knew enough of the society into which the Hickses had drifted to guess that, within a very short time, the hint of the Prince's aide-de-camp would reappear in the form of a direct proposal. Lansing himself would probably —as the one person in the Hicks entourage with whom one could intelligibly commune—be entrusted with the next step in the negotiations: he would be asked, as the aide-de-camp would have said, "to feel the ground." It was clearly part of the state policy of Teutoburg to offer Miss Hicks, with the hand of its sovereign, an opportunity to replenish its treasury.

What would the girl do? Lansing could not guess; yet he dimly felt that her attitude would depend in a great degree upon his own. And he knew no more what his own was going to be than on the night, four months earlier, when he had flung out of his wife's room in Venice to take the midnight express for Genoa.

The whole of his past, and above all the tendency, on which he had once prided himself, to live in the present and take whatever chances it offered, now made it harder for him to act. He began to see that he had never, even in the closest relations of life, looked ahead of his immediate satisfaction. He had thought it rather fine to be able to give himself so intensely to the fullness of each moment instead of hurrying past it in pursuit of something more, or something else, in the manner of the over-scrupulous or the under-imaginative, whom he had always grouped together and equally pitied. It was not till he had linked his life with Susy's that he had begun to feel it reaching forward into a future he longed to make sure of, to fasten upon and shape to his own wants and purposes, till, by an imperceptible substitution, that future had become his real present, his all-absorbing moment of time.

Now the moment was shattered, and the power to rebuild it failed him. He had never before thought about putting together broken bits: he felt like a man whose house has been wrecked by an earthquake, and who, for lack of skilled labour, is called upon for the first time to wield a trowel and carry bricks. He simply did not know how.

Will-power, he saw, was not a thing one could suddenly decree oneself to possess. It must be built up imperceptibly and laboriously out of a succession of small efforts to meet definite objects, out of the facing of daily difficulties instead of cleverly eluding them, or shifting their burden on others. The making of the substance called character was a process about as slow and arduous as the building of the Pyramids; and the thing itself, like those awful edifices, was mainly useful to lodge one's descendants in, after they too were dust. Yet the Pyramid-instinct was the one which had made the world, made man, and caused his fugitive joys to linger like fading frescoes on imperishable walls. . . .

XXI

ON the drive back from her dinner at the
Nouveau Luxe, events had followed the
course foreseen by Susy.

She had promised Strefford to seek legal advice about her divorce, and he had kissed her; and
the promise had been easier to make than she had
expected, the kiss less difficult to receive.

She had gone to the dinner a-quiver with the
mortification of learning that her husband was
still with the Hickses. Morally sure of it though
she had been, the discovery was a shock, and she
measured for the first time the abyss between
fearing and knowing. No wonder he had not written—the modern husband did not have to: he had
only to leave it to time and the newspapers to
make known his intentions. Susy could imagine
Nick's saying to himself, as he sometimes used to
say when she reminded him of an unanswered
letter: "But there are lots of ways of answering
a letter—and writing doesn't happen to be mine."

Well—he had done it in his way, and she was
answered. For a minute, as she laid aside the
paper, darkness submerged her, and she felt herself dropping down into the bottomless anguish
of her dreadful vigil in the Palazzo Vanderlyn.

But she was weary of anguish: her healthy body
and nerves instinctively rejected it. The wave
was spent, and she felt herself irresistibly strug-
gling back to light and life and youth. He didn't
want her? Well, she would try not to want him!
There lay all the old expedients at her hand—the
rouge for her white lips, the atropine for her
blurred eyes, the new dress on her bed, the thought
of Strefford and his guests awaiting her, and of
the conclusions that the diners of the Nouveau
Luxe would draw from seeing them together.
Thank heaven no one would say: "Poor old Susy
—did you know Nick had chucked her?" They
would all say: "Poor old Nick! Yes, I daresay
she was sorry to chuck him; but Altringham's
mad to marry her, and what could she do?"

And once again events had followed the course
she had foreseen. Seeing her at Lord Altringham's table, with the Ascots and the old Duchess
of Dunes, the interested spectators could not but
regard the dinner as confirming the rumour of
her marriage. As Ellie said, people didn't wait
nowadays to announce their "engagements" till
the tiresome divorce proceedings were over. Ellie
herself, prodigally pearled and ermined, had
floated in late with Algie Bockheimer in her wake,
and sat, in conspicuous *tête-à-tête,* nodding and
signalling her sympathy to Susy. Approval
beamed from every eye: it was awfully exciting,
they all seemed to say, seeing Susy Lansing pull
it off! As the party, after dinner, drifted from

the restaurant back into the hall, she caught, in the smiles and hand-pressures crowding about her, the scarcely-repressed hint of official congratulations; and Violet Melrose, seated in a corner with Fulmer, drew her down with a wan jade-circled arm, to whisper tenderly: "It's most awfully clever of you, darling, not to be wearing any jewels."

In all the women's eyes she read the reflected lustre of the jewels she could wear when she chose: it was as though their glitter reached her from the far-off bank where they lay sealed up in the Altringham strong-box. What a fool she had been to think that Strefford would ever believe she didn't care for them!

The Ambassadress, a blank perpendicular person, had been a shade less affable than Susy could have wished; but then there was Lady Joan—and the girl was handsome, alarmingly handsome—to account for that: probably every one in the room had guessed it. And the old Duchess of Dunes was delightful. She looked rather like Strefford in a wig and false pearls (Susy was sure they were as false as her teeth); and her cordiality was so demonstrative that the future bride found it more difficult to account for than Lady Ascot's coldness, till she heard the old lady, as they passed into the hall, breathe in a hissing whisper to her nephew: "Streff, dearest, when you have a minute's time, and can drop in at my wretched little *pension,* I know you can explain in two words what I ought

to do to pacify those awful money-lenders. . . .
And you'll bring your exquisite American to see
me, won't you? . . . No, Joan Senechal's too fair
for my taste. . . . Insipid. . . "

Yes: the taste of it all was again sweet on her
lips. A few days later she began to wonder how
the thought of Strefford's endearments could have
been so alarming. To be sure he was not lavish
of them; but when he did touch her, even when he
kissed her, it no longer seemed to matter. An
almost complete absence of sensation had mercifully succeeded to the first wild flurry of her
nerves.

And so it would be, no doubt, with everything
else in her new life. If it failed to provoke any
acute reactions, whether of pain or pleasure, the
very absence of sensation would make for peace.
And in the meanwhile she was tasting what, she
had begun to suspect, was the maximum of bliss
to most of the women she knew: days packed with
engagements, the exhilaration of fashionable
crowds, the thrill of snapping up a jewel or a
bibelot or a new "model" that one's best friend
wanted, or of being invited to some private show,
or some exclusive entertainment, that one's best
friend couldn't get to. There was nothing, now,
that she couldn't buy, nowhere that she couldn't
go: she had only to choose and to triumph. And
for a while the surface-excitement of her life gave
her the illusion of enjoyment.

Strefford, as she had expected, had postponed
his return to England, and they had now been for
nearly three weeks together in their new, and
virtually avowed, relation. She had fancied that,
after all, the easiest part of it would be just the
being with Strefford—the falling back on their
old tried friendship to efface the sense of strangeness. But, though she had so soon grown used
to his caresses, he himself remained curiously unfamiliar: she was hardly sure, at times, that it
was the old Strefford she was talking to. It was
not that his point of view had changed, but that
new things occupied and absorbed him. In all the
small sides of his great situation he took an almost childish satisfaction; and though he still
laughed at both its privileges and its obligations,
it was now with a jealous laughter.

It amused him inexhaustibly, for instance, to
be made up to by all the people who had always
disapproved of him, and to unite at the same table
persons who had to dissemble their annoyance at
being invited together lest they should not be invited at all. Equally exhilarating was the capri-
cious favouring of the dull and dowdy on occasions when the brilliant and disreputable expected
his notice. It enchanted him, for example, to ask
the old Duchess of Dunes and Violet Melrose to
dine with the Vicar of Altringham, on his way to
Switzerland for a month's holiday, and to watch
the face of the Vicar's wife while the Duchess
narrated her last difficulties with book-makers

and money-lenders, and Violet proclaimed the rights of Love and Genius to all that had once been supposed to belong exclusively to Respectability and Dulness.

Susy had to confess that her own amusements were hardly of a higher order; but then she put up with them for lack of better, whereas Strefford, who might have had what he pleased, was completely satisfied with such triumphs.

Somehow, in spite of his honours and his opportunities, he seemed to have shrunk. The old Strefford had certainly been a larger person, and she wondered if material prosperity were always a beginning of ossification. Strefford had been much more fun when he lived by his wits. Sometimes, now, when he tried to talk of politics, or assert himself on some question of public interest, she was startled by his limitations. Formerly, when he was not sure of his ground, it had been his way to turn the difficulty by glib nonsense or easy irony; now he was actually dull, at times almost pompous. She noticed too, for the first time, that he did not always hear clearly when several people were talking at once, or when he was at the theatre; and he developed a habit of saying over and over again: "Does so-and-so speak indistinctly? Or am I getting deaf, I wonder?" which wore on her nerves by its suggestion of a corresponding mental infirmity.

These thoughts did not always trouble her. The current of idle activity on which they were both gliding was her native element as well as his; and never had its tide been as swift, its waves as buoyant. In his relation to her, too, he was full of tact and consideration. She saw that he still remembered their frightened exchange of glances after their first kiss; and the sense of this little hidden spring of imagination in him was sometimes enough for her thirst.

She had always had a rather masculine punctuality in keeping her word, and after she had promised Strefford to take steps toward a divorce she had promptly set about doing it. A sudden reluctance prevented her asking the advice of friends like Ellie Vanderlyn, whom she knew to be in the thick of the same negotiations, and all she could think of was to consult a young American lawyer practising in Paris, with whom she felt she could talk the more easily because he was not from New York, and probably unacquainted with her history.

She was so ignorant of the procedure in such matters that she was surprised and relieved at his asking few personal questions; but it was a shock to learn that a divorce could not be obtained, either in New York or Paris, merely on the ground of desertion or incompatibility.

"I thought nowadays . . . if people preferred to live apart . . . it could always be managed," she stammered, wondering at her own ignorance, after the many conjugal ruptures she had assisted at.

The young lawyer smiled, and coloured slightly. His lovely client evidently intimidated him by her grace, and still more by her inexperience.

"It can be—generally," he admitted; "and especially so if . . . as I gather is the case . . . your husband is equally anxious. . . ."

"Oh, quite!" she exclaimed, suddenly humiliated by having to admit it.

"Well, then—may I suggest that, to bring matters to a point, the best way would be for you to write to him?"

She recoiled slightly. It had never occurred to her that the lawyers would not "manage it" without her intervention.

"Write to him . . . but what about?"

"Well, expressing your wish . . . to recover your freedom. . . . The rest, I assume," said the young lawyer, "may be left to Mr. Lansing."

She did not know exactly what he meant, and was too much perturbed by the idea of having to communicate with Nick to follow any other train of thought. How could she write such a letter? And yet how could she confess to the lawyer that she had not the courage to do so? He would, of course, tell her to go home and be reconciled. She hesitated perplexedly.

"Wouldn't it be better," she suggested, "if the letter were to come from—from your office?"

He considered this politely. "On the whole: no. If, as I take it, an amicable arrangement is necessary—to secure the requisite evidence—then a line from you, suggesting an interview, seems to me more advisable.''

"An interview? Is an interview necessary?" She was ashamed to show her agitation to this cautiously smiling young man, who must wonder at her childish lack of understanding; but the break in her voice was uncontrollable.

"Oh, please write to him—I can't! And I can't see him! Oh, can't you arrange it for me?" she pleaded.

She saw now that her idea of a divorce had been that it was something one went out—or sent out —to buy in a shop: something concrete and portable, that Strefford's money could pay for, and that it required no personal participation to obtain. What a fool the lawyer must think her! Stiffening herself, she rose from her seat.

"My husband and I don't wish to see each other again. . . . I'm sure it would be useless . . . and very painful."

"You are the best judge, of course. But in any case, a letter from you, a friendly letter, seems wiser . . . considering the apparent lack of evidence. . . ."

"Very well, then; I'll write," she agreed, and hurried away, scarcely hearing his parting injunction that she should take a copy of her letter.

That night she wrote. At the last moment it might have been impossible, if at the theatre little Breckenridge had not bobbed into her box. He was just back from Rome, where he had dined with the Hickses ("a bang-up show—they're really *lancés*—you wouldn't know them!"), and had met there Lansing, whom he reported as intending to marry Coral "as soon as things were settled". "You were dead right, weren't you, Susy," he snickered, "that night in Venice last summer, when we all thought you were joking about their engagement? Pity now you chucked our surprise visit to the Hickses, and sent Streff up to drag us back just as we were breaking in! You remember?"

He flung off the "Streff" airily, in the old way, but with a tentative side-glance at his host; and Lord Altringham, leaning toward Susy, said coldly: "Was Breckenridge speaking about me? I didn't catch what he said. Does he speak indistinctly—or am I getting deaf, I wonder?"

After that it seemed comparatively easy, when Strefford had dropped her at her hotel, to go upstairs and write. She dashed off the date and her address, and then stopped; but suddenly she remembered Breckenridge's snicker, and the words rushed from her. "Nick dear, it was July when you left Venice, and I have had no word from you since the note in which you said you had gone for a few days, and that I should hear soon again.

"You haven't written yet, and it is five months since you left me. That means, I suppose, that you want to take back your freedom and give me mine. Wouldn't it be kinder, in that case, to tell me so? It is worse than anything to go on as we

are now. I don't know how to put these things—
but since you seem unwilling to write to me perhaps you would prefer to send your answer to Mr.
Frederic Spearman, the American lawyer here.
His address is 100, Boulevard Haussmann. I
hope—"

She broke off on the last word. Hope? What
did she hope, either for him or for herself?
Wishes for his welfare would sound like a mockery—and she would rather her letter should seem
bitter than unfeeling. Above all, she wanted to
get it done. To have to re-write even those few
lines would be torture. So she left "I hope," and
simply added: "to hear before long what you
have decided."

She read it over, and shivered. Not one word
of the past—not one allusion to that mysterious
interweaving of their lives which had enclosed
them one in the other like the flower in its sheath!
What place had such memories in such a letter?
She had the feeling that she wanted to hide that
other Nick away in her own bosom, and with him
the other Susy, the Susy he had once imagined
her to be. . . . Neither of them seemed concerned
with the present business.

The letter done, she stared at the sealed envelope till its presence in the room became intolerable, and she understood that she must either tear
it up or post it immediately. She went down to
the hall of the sleeping hotel, and bribed the night-
porter to carry the letter to the nearest post office,

though he objected that, at that hour, no time would be gained. "I want it out of the house," she insisted: and waited sternly by the desk, in her dressing-gown, till he had performed the errand.

As she re-entered her room, the disordered writing-table struck her; and she remembered the lawyer's injunction to take a copy of her letter. A copy to be filed away with the documents in "Lansing *versus* Lansing!" She burst out laughing at the idea. What were lawyers made of, she wondered? Didn't the man guess, by the mere look in her eyes and the sound of her voice, that she would never, as long as she lived, forget a word of that letter—that night after night she would lie down, as she was lying down to-night, to stare wide-eyed for hours into the darkness, while a voice in her brain monotonously hammered out: "Nick dear, it was July when you left me . . ." and so on, word after word, down to the last fatal syllable?

XXII

STREFFORD was leaving for England.

Once assured that Susy had taken the first step toward freeing herself, he frankly regarded her as his affianced wife, and could see no reason for further mystery. She understood his impatience to have their plans settled; it would protect him from the formidable menace of the marriageable, and cause people, as he said, to stop meddling. Now that the novelty of his situation was wearing off, his natural indolence reasserted itself, and there was nothing he dreaded more than having to be on his guard against the innumerable plans that his well-wishers were perpetually making for him. Sometimes Susy fancied he was marrying her because to do so was to follow the line of least resistance.

"To marry me is the easiest way of not marrying all the others," she laughed, as he stood before her one day in a quiet alley of the Bois de Boulogne, insisting on the settlement of various preliminaries. "I believe I'm only a protection to you."

An odd gleam passed behind his eyes, and she instantly guessed that he was thinking: "And what else am I to you?"

She changed colour, and he rejoined, laughing also: "Well, you're that at any rate, thank the Lord!"

She pondered, and then questioned: "But in the interval—how are you going to defend yourself for another year?"

"Ah, you've got to see to that; you've got to take a little house in London. You've got to look after me, you know."

It was on the tip of her tongue to flash back: "Oh, if that's all you care—!" But caring was exactly the factor she wanted, as much as possible, to keep out of their talk and their thoughts. She could not ask him how much he cared without laying herself open to the same question; and that way terror lay. As a matter of fact, though Strefford was not an ardent wooer—perhaps from tact, perhaps from temperament, perhaps merely from the long habit of belittling and disintegrating every sentiment and every conviction—yet she knew he did care for her as much as he was capable of caring for anyone. If the element of habit entered largely into the feeling—if he liked her, above all, because he was used to her, knew her views, her indulgences, her allowances, knew he was never likely to be bored, and almost certain to be amused, by her; why, such ingredients, though not of the fieriest, were perhaps those most likely to keep his feeling for her at a pleasant temperature. She had had a taste of the tropics, and wanted more equable weather; but

the idea of having to fan his flame gently for a
year was unspeakably depressing to her. Yet all
this was precisely what she could not say. The
long period of probation, during which, as she
knew, she would have to amuse him, to guard him,
to hold him, and to keep off the other women, was
a necessary part of their situation. She was sure
that, as little Breckenridge would have said, she
could "pull it off"; but she did not want to think
about it. What she would have preferred would
have been to go away—no matter where—and not
see Strefford again till they were married. But
she dared not tell him that either.

"A little house in London—?" She wondered.

"Well, I suppose you've got to have some sort
of a roof over your head."

"I suppose so."

He sat down beside her. "If you like me well
enough to live at Altringham some day, won't you,
in the meantime, let me provide you with a smaller
and more convenient establishment?"

Still she hesitated. The alternative, she knew,
would be to live on Ursula Gillow, Violet Melrose,
or some other of her rich friends, any one of whom
would be ready to lavish the largest hospitality
on the prospective Lady Altringham. Such an arrangement, in the long run, would be no less humiliating to her pride, no less destructive to her
independence, than Altringham's little establishment. But she temporized. "I shall go over to

London in December, and stay for a while with
various people—then we can look about."

"All right; as you like." He obviously considered her hesitation ridiculous, but was too full
of satisfaction at her having started divorce proceedings to be chilled by her reply.

"And now, look here, my dear; couldn't I give
you some sort of a ring?"

"A ring?" She flushed at the suggestion.
"What's the use, Streff, dear? With all those
jewels locked away in London—"

"Oh, I daresay you'll think them old-fashioned.
And, hang it, why shouldn't I give you something new? I ran across Ellie and Bockheimer
yesterday, in the rue de la Paix, picking out sapphires. Do you like sapphires, or emeralds? Or
just a diamond? I've seen a thumping one. . . .
I'd like you to have it."

Ellie and Bockheimer! How she hated the con-
junction of the names! Their case always seemed
to her like a caricature of her own, and she felt
an unreasoning resentment against Ellie for having selected the same season for her unmating and
re-mating.

"I wish you wouldn't speak of them, Streff . . .
as if they were like us! I can hardly bear to sit
in the same room with Ellie Vanderlyn."

"Hullo? What's wrong? You mean because
of her giving up Clarissa?"

"Not that only. . . . You don't know. . . . I
can't tell you. . . ." She shivered at the memory,

and rose restlessly from the bench where they had
been sitting.

Strefford gave his careless shrug. "Well, my
dear, you can hardly expect me to agree, for after
all it was to Ellie I owed the luck of being so long
alone with you in Venice. If she and Algie hadn't
prolonged their honeymoon at the villa—"

He stopped abruptly, and looked at Susy. She
was conscious that every drop of blood had left
her face. She felt it ebbing away from her heart,
flowing out of her as if from all her severed art-
eries, till it seemed as though nothing were left
of life in her but one point of irreducible pain.

"Ellie—at your villa? What do you mean?
Was it Ellie and Bockheimer who—?"

Strefford still stared. "You mean to say you
didn't know?"

"Who came after Nick and me . . . ?" she
insisted.

"Why, do you suppose I'd have turned you out
otherwise? That beastly Bockheimer simply
smothered me with gold. Ah, well, there's one
good thing: I shall never have to let the villa
again! I rather like the little place myself, and
I daresay once in a while we might go there for
a day or two. . . . Susy, what's the matter?" he
exclaimed.

She returned his stare, but without seeing him.
Everything swam and danced before her eyes.

"Then she was *there* while I was posting all
those letters for her—?"

"Letters—what letters? What makes you look so frightfully upset?"

She pursued her thought as if he had not spoken. "She and Algie Bockheimer arrived there the very day that Nick and I left?"

"I suppose so. I thought she'd told you. Ellie always tells everybody everything."

"She would have told me, I daresay—but I wouldn't let her."

"Well, my dear, that was hardly my fault, was it? Though I really don't see—"

But Susy, still blind to everything but the dance of dizzy sparks before her eyes, pressed on as if she had not heard him. "It was their motor, then, that took us to Milan! It was Algie Bockheimer's motor!" She did not know why, but this seemed to her the most humiliating incident in the whole hateful business. She remembered Nick's reluctance to use the motor—she remembered his look when she had boasted of her "managing." The nausea mounted to her throat.

Strefford burst out laughing. "I say—you borrowed their motor? And you didn't know whose it was?"

"How could I know? I persuaded the chauffeur . . . for a little tip. . . . It was to save our railway fares to Milan . . . extra luggage costs so frightfully in Italy. . . ."

"Good old Susy! Well done! I can see you doing it—"

"Oh, how horrible—how horrible!" she groaned.

"Horrible? What's horrible?"

"Why, your not seeing . . . not feeling . . ." she began impetuously; and then stopped. How could she explain to him that what revolted her was not so much the fact of his having given the little house, as soon as she and Nick had left it, to those two people of all others—though the vision of them in the sweet secret house, and under the plane-trees of the terrace, drew such a trail of slime across her golden hours? No, it was not that from which she most recoiled, but from the fact that Strefford, living in luxury in Nelson Vanderlyn's house, should at the same time have secretly abetted Ellie Vanderlyn's love-affairs, and allowed her—for a handsome price—to shelter them under his own roof. The reproach trembled on her lip—but she remembered her own part in the wretched business, and the impossibility of avowing it to Strefford, and of revealing to him that Nick had left her for that very reason. She was not afraid that the discovery would diminish her in Strefford's eyes: he was untroubled by moral problems, and would laugh away her avowal, with a sneer at Nick in his new part of moralist. But that was just what she could not bear: that anyone should cast a doubt on the genuineness of Nick's standards, or should know how far below them she had fallen.

She remained silent, and Strefford, after a mo-

ment, drew her gently down to the seat beside him.
"Susy, upon my soul I don't know what you're
driving at. Is it me you're angry with—or yourself? And what's it all about? Are you disgusted
because I let the villa to a couple who weren't
married? But, hang it, they're the kind that pay
the highest price—and I had to earn my living
somehow! One doesn't run across a bridal pair
every day. . . ."

She lifted her eyes to his puzzled incredulous
face. Poor Streff! No, it was not with him that
she was angry. Why should she be? Even that
ill-advised disclosure had told her nothing she had
not already known about him. It had simply revealed to her once more the real point of view of
the people he and she lived among, had shown her
that, in spite of the superficial difference, he felt
as they felt, judged as they judged, was blind as
they were—and as she would be expected to be,
should she once again become one of them. What
was the use of being placed by fortune above such
shifts and compromises, if in one's heart one still
condoned them? And she would have to—she
would catch the general note, grow blunted as
those other people were blunted, and gradually
come to wonder at her own revolt, as Strefford
now honestly wondered at it. She felt as though
she were on the point of losing some new-found
treasure, a treasure precious only to herself, but
beside which all he offered her was nothing, the

triumph of her wounded pride nothing, the security of her future nothing.

"What is it, Susy?" he asked, with the same puzzled gentleness.

Ah, the loneliness of never being able to make him understand! She had felt lonely enough when the flaming sword of Nick's indignation had shut her out from their Paradise; but there had been a cruel bliss in the pain. Nick had not opened her eyes to new truths, but had waked in her again something which had lain unconscious under years of accumulated indifference. And that re-awakened sense had never left her since, and had somehow kept her from utter loneliness because it was a secret shared with Nick, a gift she owed to Nick, and which, in leaving her, he could not take from her. It was almost, she suddenly felt, as if he had left her with a child.

"My dear girl," Strefford said, with a resigned glance at his watch, "you know we're dining at the Embassy. . . ."

At the Embassy? She looked at him vaguely: then she remembered. Yes, they were dining that night at the Ascots', with Strefford's cousin, the Duke of Dunes, and his wife, the handsome irreproachable young Duchess; with the old gambling Dowager Duchess, whom her son and daughter-in-law had come over from England to see; and with other English and French guests of a rank and standing worthy of the Duneses. Susy knew that her inclusion in such a dinner could mean but one thing: it was her definite recognition as Altringham's future wife. She was "the little American" whom one had to ask when one invited him, even on ceremonial occasions. The family had accepted her; the Embassy could but follow suit.

"It's late, dear; and I've got to see someone on business first," Strefford reminded her patiently.

"Oh, Streff—I can't, I can't!" The words broke from her without her knowing what she was saying. "I can't go with you—I can't go to the Embassy. I can't go on any longer like this. . . ." She lifted her eyes to his in desperate appeal. "Oh, understand—do please understand!" she wailed, knowing, while she spoke, the utter impossibility of what she asked.

Strefford's face had gradually paled and hardened. From sallow it turned to a dusky white, and lines of obstinacy deepened between the ironic eyebrows and about the weak amused mouth.

"Understand? What do you want me to understand?" He laughed. "That you're trying to chuck me—already?"

She shrank at the sneer of the "already," but instantly remembered that it was the only thing he could be expected to say, since it was just because he couldn't understand that she was flying from him.

"Oh, Streff—if I knew how to tell you!"

"It doesn't so much matter about the how. *Is* that what you're trying to say?"

Her head drooped, and she saw the dead leaves whirling across the path at her feet, lifted on a sudden wintry gust.

"The reason," he continued, clearing his throat with a stiff smile, "is not quite as important to me as the fact."

She stood speechless, agonized by his pain. But still, she thought, he had remembered the dinner at the Embassy! The thought gave her courage to go on.

"It wouldn't do, Streff. I'm not a bit the kind of person to make you happy."

"Oh, leave that to me, please, won't you?"

"No, I can't. Because I should be unhappy too."

He flicked at the leaves as they whirled past. "You've taken a rather long time to find it out." She saw that his new-born sense of his own consequence was making him suffer even more than his wounded affection; and that again gave her courage.

"If I've taken long it's all the more reason why I shouldn't take longer. If I've made a mistake it's you who would have suffered from it. . . ."

"Thanks," he said, "for your extreme solicitude."

She looked at him helplessly, penetrated by the despairing sense of their inaccessibility to each other. Then she remembered that Nick, during their last talk together, had seemed as inaccessible, and wondered if, when human souls try to get too near each other, they do not inevitably become mere blurs to each other's vision. She would have liked to say this to Streff—but he would not have understood it either. The sense of loneliness once more enveloped her, and she groped in vain for a word that should reach him.

"Let me go home alone, won't you?" she appealed to him.

"Alone?"

She nodded. "To-morrow—to-morrow. . . ."

He tried, rather valiantly, to smile. "Hang to-morrow! Whatever is wrong, it needn't prevent my seeing you home." He glanced toward the taxi that awaited them at the end of the deserted drive.

"No, please. You're in a hurry; take the taxi. I want immensely a long long walk by myself . . . through the streets, with the lights coming out. . . ."

He laid his hand on her arm. "I say, my dear, you're not ill?"

"No; I'm not ill. But you may say I am, to-night at the Embassy."

He released her and drew back. "Oh, very well," he answered coldly; and she understood by his tone that the knot was cut, and that at that moment he almost hated her. She turned away,

hastening down the deserted alley, flying from
him, and knowing, as she fled, that he was still
standing there motionless, staring after her,
wounded, humiliated, uncomprehending. It was
neither her fault nor his. . . .

XXIII

A S she fled on toward the lights of the streets a breath of freedom seemed to blow into her face.

Like a weary load the accumulated hypocrisies of the last months had dropped from her: she was herself again, Nick's Susy, and no one else's. She sped on, staring with bright bewildered eyes at the stately façades of the La Muette quarter, the perspectives of bare trees, the awakening glitter of shop-windows holding out to her all the things she would never again be able to buy. . . .

In an avenue of shops she paused before a milliner's window, and said to herself: "Why shouldn't I earn my living by trimming hats?" She met work-girls streaming out under a doorway, and scattering to catch trams and omnibuses; and she looked with newly-wakened interest at their tired independent faces. "Why shouldn't I earn my living as well as they do?" she thought. A little farther on she passed a Sister of Charity with softly trotting feet, a calm anonymous glance, and hands hidden in her capacious sleeves. Susy looked at her and thought: "Why shouldn't I be a Sister, and have no money to worry about, and trot about under a white coif helping poor people?"

All these strangers on whom she smiled in passing, and glanced back at enviously, were free from the necessities that enslaved her, and would not have known what she meant if she had told them that she must have so much money for her dresses, so much for her cigarettes, so much for bridge and cabs and tips, and all kinds of extras, and that at that moment she ought to be hurrying back to a dinner at the British Embassy, where her permanent right to such luxuries was to be solemnly recognized and ratified.

The artificiality and unreality of her life overcame her as with stifling fumes. She stopped at a street-corner, drawing long panting breaths as if she had been running a race. Then, slowly and aimlessly, she began to saunter along a street of small private houses in damp gardens that led to the Avenue du Bois. She sat down on a bench. Not far off, the Arc de Triomphe raised its august bulk, and beyond it a river of lights streamed down toward Paris, and the stir of the city's heart-beats troubled the quiet in her bosom. But not for long. She seemed to be looking at it all from the other side of the grave; and as she got up and wandered down the Champs Elysées, half empty in the evening lull between dusk and dinner, she felt as if the glittering avenue were really changed into the Field of Shadows from which it takes its name, and as if she were a ghost among ghosts.

Halfway home, a weakness of loneliness over-

came her, and she seated herself under the trees
near the Rond Point. Lines of motors and car-
riages were beginning to animate the converging
thoroughfares, streaming abreast, crossing, winding in and out of each other in a tangle of hurried
pleasure-seeking. She caught the light on jewels
and shirt-fronts and hard bored eyes emerging
from dim billows of fur and velvet. She seemed to
hear what the couples were saying to each other,
she pictured the drawing-rooms, restaurants,
dance-halls they were hastening to, the breathless
routine that was hurrying them along, as Time,
the old vacuum-cleaner, swept them away with the
dust of their carriage-wheels. And again the loneliness vanished in a sense of release. . . .

At the corner of the Place de la Concorde she
stopped, recognizing a man in evening dress who
was hailing a taxi. Their eyes met, and Nelson
Vanderlyn came forward. He was the last person
she cared to run across, and she shrank back involuntarily. What did he know, what had he
guessed, of her complicity in his wife's affairs?
No doubt Ellie had blabbed it all out by this
time; she was just as likely to confide her love-
affairs to Nelson as to anyone else, now that the
Bockheimer prize was landed.

"Well—well—well—so I've caught you at it!
Glad to see you, Susy, my dear." She found her
hand cordially clasped in Vanderlyn's, and his
round pink face bent on her with all its old ur-
banity. Did nothing matter, then, in this world

she was fleeing from, did no one love or hate or remember?

"No idea you were in Paris—just got here myself," Vanderlyn continued, visibly delighted at the meeting. "Look here, don't suppose you're out of a job this evening by any chance, and would come and cheer up a lone bachelor, eh? No? You are? Well, that's luck for once! I say, where shall we go? One of the places where they dance, I suppose? Yes, I twirl the light fantastic once in a while myself. Got to keep up with the times! Hold on, taxi! Here—I'll drive you home first, and wait while you jump into your toggery. Lots of time." As he steered her toward the carriage she noticed that he had a gouty limp, and pulled himself in after her with difficulty.

"Mayn't I come as I am, Nelson? I don't feel like dancing. Let's go and dine in one of those nice smoky little restaurants by the Place de la Bourse."

He seemed surprised but relieved at the suggestion, and they rolled off together. In a corner at Baugé's they found a quiet table, screened from the other diners, and while Vanderlyn adjusted his eyeglasses to study the *carte* Susy stole a long look at him. He was dressed with even more than his usual formal trimness, and she detected, in an ultra-flat wrist-watch and discreetly expensive waistcoat buttons, an attempt at smartness altogether new. His face had undergone the same change: its familiar look of worn optimism had been, as it were, done up to match his clothes, as though a sort of moral cosmetic had made him pinker, shinier and sprightlier without really rejuvenating him. A thin veil of high spirits had merely been drawn over his face, as the shining strands of hair were skilfully brushed over his baldness.

"Here! *Carte des vins*, waiter! What champagne, Susy?" He chose, fastidiously, the best the cellar could produce, grumbling a little at the *bourgeois* character of the dishes. "Capital food of its kind, no doubt, but coarsish, don't you think? Well, I don't mind . . . it's rather a jolly change from the Luxe cooking. A new sensation —I'm all for new sensations, ain't you, my dear?" He re-filled their champagne glasses, flung an arm sideways over his chair, and smiled at her with a foggy benevolence.

As the champagne flowed his confidences flowed with it.

"Suppose you know what I'm here for—this divorce business? We wanted to settle it quietly, without a fuss, and of course Paris is the best place for that sort of job. Live and let live; no questions asked. None of your dirty newspapers. Great country, this. No hypocrisy . . . they understand Life over here!"

Susy gazed and listened. She remembered that people had thought Nelson would make a row when he found out. He had always been addicted to truculent anecdotes about unfaithful wives, and

the very formula of his perpetual ejaculation—
"Caught you at it, eh?"—seemed to hint at a constant preoccupation with such ideas. But now it
was evident that, as the saying was, he had "swallowed his dose" like all the others. No strong
blast of indignation had momentarily lifted him
above his normal stature: he remained a little man
among little men, and his eagerness to rebuild his
life with all the old smiling optimism reminded
Susy of the patient industry of an ant remaking
its ruined ant-heap.

"Tell you what, great thing, this liberty! Everything's changed nowadays; why shouldn't marriage be too? A man can get out of a business
partnership when he wants to; but the parsons
want to keep us noosed 'up to each other for life
because we've blundered into a church one day and
said 'Yes' before one of 'em. No, no—that's too
easy. We've got beyond *that*. Science, and all
these new discoveries. . . . I say the Ten Commandments were made for man, and not man for
the Commandments; and there ain't a word
against divorce in 'em, anyhow! That's what I
tell my poor old mother, who builds everything on
her Bible. 'Find me the place where it says: *Thou
shalt not sue for divorce.*' It makes her wild,
poor old lady, because she can't; and she doesn't
know how they happen to have left it out. . . . I
rather think Moses left it out because he knew
more about human nature than these snivelling
modern parsons do. Not that they'll always bear

investigating either; but I don't care about that.
Live and let live, eh, Susy? Haven't we all got a
right to our Affinities? I hear you're following
our example yourself. First-rate idea: I don't
mind telling you I saw it coming on last summer
at Venice. Caught you at it, so to speak! Old
Nelson ain't as blind as people think. Here, let's
open another bottle to the health of Streff and
Mrs. Streff!''

She caught the hand with which he was signalling to the *sommelier*. This flushed and garrulous
Nelson moved her more poignantly than a more
heroic figure. ''No more champagne, please, Nelson. Besides,'' she suddenly added, ''it's not
true.''

He stared. ''Not true that you're going to
marry Altringham?''

''No.''

''By George—then what on earth did you
chuck Nick for? Ain't you got an Affinity, my
dear?''

She laughed and shook her head.

''Do you mean to tell me it's all Nick's doing,
then?''

''I don't know. Let's talk of you instead, Nelson. I'm glad you're in such good spirits. I
rather thought—''

He interrupted her quickly. ''Thought I'd cut
up a rumpus—do some shooting? I know—people
did.'' He twisted his moustache, evidently proud
of his reputation. ''Well, maybe I did see red for

a day or two—but I'm a philosopher, first and last.
Before I went into banking I'd made and lost two
fortunes out West. Well, how did I build 'em up
again? Not by shooting anybody—even myself.
By just buckling to, and beginning all over again.
That's how . . . and that's what I am doing now.
Beginning all over again. . . ." His voice
dropped from boastfulness to a note of wistful
melancholy, the look of strained jauntiness fell
from his face like a mask, and for an instant she
saw the real man, old, ruined, lonely. Yes, that
was it: he was lonely, desperately lonely, founder-
ing in such deep seas of solitude that any presence out of the past was like a spar to which he
clung. Whatever he knew or guessed of the part
she had played in his disaster, it was not callous-
ness that had made him greet her with such for-
giving warmth, but the same sense of smallness,
insignificance and isolation which perpetually
hung like a cold fog on her own horizon. Suddenly she too felt old—old and unspeakably tired.

"It's been nice seeing you, Nelson. But now I
must be getting home."

He offered no objection, but asked for the bill,
resumed his jaunty air while he scattered *largesse*
among the waiters, and sauntered out behind her
after calling for a taxi.

They drove off in silence. Susy was thinking:
"And Clarissa?" but dared not ask. Vanderlyn
lit a cigarette, hummed a dance-tune, and stared

out of the window. Suddenly she felt his hand
on hers.

"Susy—do you ever see her?"

"See—Ellie?"

He nodded, without turning toward her.

"Not often . . . sometimes. . . ."

"If you do, for God's sake tell her I'm happy
. . . happy as a king . . . tell her you could see
for yourself that I was. . . ." His voice broke in
a little gasp. "I . . . I'll be damned if . . . if
she shall ever be unhappy about me . . . if I can
help it. . . ." The cigarette dropped from his
fingers, and with a sob he covered his face.

"Oh, poor Nelson — poor Nelson," Susy
breathed. While their cab rattled across the Place
du Carrousel, and over the bridge, he continued to
sit beside her with hidden face. At last he pulled
out a scented handkerchief, rubbed his eyes with
it, and groped for another cigarette.

"I'm all right! Tell her that, will you, Susy?
There are some of our old times I don't suppose I
shall ever forget; but they make me feel kindly to
her, and not angry. I didn't know it would be so,
beforehand—but it is . . . And now the thing's
settled I'm as right as a trivet, and you can tell
her so. . . . Look here, Susy . . ." he caught her
by the arm as the taxi drew up at her hotel. . . .
"Tell her I *understand,* will you? I'd rather like
her to know that. . . ."

"I'll tell her, Nelson," she promised; and
climbed the stairs alone to her dreary room.

Susy's one fear was that Strefford, when he returned the next day, should treat their talk of the previous evening as a fit of "nerves" to be jested away. He might, indeed, resent her behaviour too deeply to seek to see her at once; but his easygoing modern attitude toward conduct and convictions made that improbable. She had an idea that what he had most minded was her dropping so unceremoniously out of the Embassy Dinner.

But, after all, why should she see him again? She had had enough of explanations during the last months to have learned how seldom they explain anything. If the other person did not understand at the first word, at the first glance even, subsequent elucidations served only to deepen the obscurity. And she wanted above all—and especially since her hour with Nelson Vanderlyn— to keep herself free, aloof, to retain her hold on her precariously recovered self. She sat down and wrote to Strefford—and the letter was only a little less painful to write than the one she had despatched to Nick. It was not that her own feelings were in any like measure engaged; but because, as the decision to give up Strefford affirmed itself, she remembered only his kindness, his forbearance, his good humour, and all the other qualities she had always liked in him; and because she felt ashamed of the hesitations which must cause him so much pain and humiliation. Yes: humiliation chiefly. She knew that what she had to say would hurt his pride, in whatever way she framed her renunciation; and her pen wavered, hating its task. Then she remembered Vanderlyn's words about his wife: "There are some of our old times I don't suppose I shall ever forget—" and a phrase of Grace Fulmer's that she had but half grasped at the time: "You haven't been married long enough to understand how trifling such things seem in the balance of one's memories."

Here were two people who had penetrated farther than she into the labyrinth of the wedded state, and struggled through some of its thorniest passages; and yet both, one consciously, the other half-unaware, testified to the mysterious fact which was already dawning on her: that the influence of a marriage begun in mutual understanding is too deep not to reassert itself even in the moment of flight and denial.

"The real reason is that you're not Nick" was what she would have said to Strefford if she had dared to set down the bare truth; and she knew that, whatever she wrote, he was too acute not to read that into it.

"He'll think it's because I'm still in love with Nick . . . and perhaps I am. But even if I were, the difference doesn't seem to lie there, after all, but deeper, in things we've shared that seem to be meant to outlast love, or to change it into something different." If she could have hoped to make Strefford understand that, the letter would have been easy enough to write—but she knew just at what point his imagination would fail, in what obvious and superficial inferences it would rest.

"Poor Streff—poor me!" she thought as she sealed the letter.

After she had despatched it a sense of blankness descended on her. She had succeeded in driving from her mind all vain hesitations, doubts, returns upon herself: her healthy system naturally rejected them. But they left a queer emptiness in which her thoughts rattled about as thoughts might, she supposed, in the first moments after death—before one got used to it. To get used to being dead: that seemed to be her immediate business. And she felt such a novice at it—felt so horribly alive! How had those others learned to do without living? Nelson—well, he was still in the throes; and probably never would understand, or be able to communicate, the lesson when he had mastered it. But Grace Fulmer—she suddenly remembered that Grace was in Paris, and set forth to find her.

XXIV

NICK LANSING had walked out a long way into the Campagna. His hours were seldom his own, for both Mr. and Mrs. Hicks were becoming more and more addicted to sudden and somewhat imperious demands upon his time; but on this occasion he had simply slipped away after luncheon, and taking the tram to the Porta Salaria, had wandered on thence in the direction of the Ponte Nomentano.

He wanted to get away and think; but now that he had done it the business proved as unfruitful as everything he had put his hand to since he had left Venice. Think—think about what? His future seemed to him a negligible matter since he had received, two months earlier, the few lines in which Susy had asked him for her freedom.

The letter had been a shock—though he had fancied himself so prepared for it—yet it had also, in another sense, been a relief, since, now that at last circumstances compelled him to write to her, they also told him what to say. And he had said it as briefly and simply as possible, telling her that he would put no obstacle in the way of her release, that he held himself at her lawyer's disposal to answer any further communication—and that he would never forget their days together, or cease to bless her for them.

That was all. He gave his Roman banker's address, and waited for another letter; but none came. Probably the "formalities," whatever they were, took longer than he had supposed; and being in no haste to recover his own liberty, he did not try to learn the cause of the delay. From that moment, however, he considered himself virtually free, and ceased, by the same token, to take any interest in his own future. His life seemed as flat as a convalescent's first days after the fever has dropped.

The only thing he was sure of was that he was not going to remain in the Hickses' employ: when they left Rome for Central Asia he had no intention of accompanying them. The part of Mr. Buttles' successor was becoming daily more intolerable to him, for the very reasons that had probably made it most gratifying to Mr. Buttles. To be treated by Mr. and Mrs. Hicks as a paid oracle, a paraded and petted piece of property, was a good deal more distasteful than he could have imagined any relation with these kindly people could be. And since their aspirations had become frankly social he found his task, if easier, yet far less congenial than during his first months with them. He preferred patiently explaining to Mrs. Hicks, for the hundredth time, that Sassanian and Saracenic were not interchangeable terms, to unravelling for her the genealogies of

her titled guests, and reminding her, when she
"seated" her dinner-parties, that Dukes ranked
higher than Princes. No—the job was decidedly
intolerable; and he would have to look out for
another means of earning his living. But that was
not what he had really got away to think about.
He knew he should never starve; he had even
begun to believe again in his book. What he
wanted to think of was Susy—or rather, it was
Susy that he could not help thinking of, on whatever train of thought he set out.

Again and again he fancied he had established
a truce with the past: had come to terms—the
terms of defeat and failure—with that bright
enemy called happiness. And, in truth, he had
reached the point of definitely knowing that he
could never return to the kind of life that he and
Susy had embarked on. It had been the tragedy
of their relation that loving her roused in him
ideals she could never satisfy. He had fallen in
love with her because she was, like himself,
amused, unprejudiced and disenchanted; and he
could not go on loving her unless she ceased to be
all these things. From that circle there was no
issue, and in it he desperately revolved.

If he had not heard such persistent rumours of
her re-marriage to Lord Altringham he might
have tried to see her again; but, aware of the
danger and the hopelessness of a meeting, he was,
on the whole, glad to have a reason for avoiding
it. Such, at least, he honestly supposed to be his

state of mind until he found himself, as on this occasion, free to follow out his thought to its end. That end, invariably, was Susy; not the bundle of qualities and defects into which his critical spirit had tried to sort her out, but the soft blur of identity, of personality, of eyes, hair, mouth, laugh, tricks of speech and gesture, that were all so solely and profoundly her own, and yet so mysteriously independent of what she might do, say, think, in crucial circumstances. He remembered her once saying to him: "After all, you were right when you wanted me to be your mistress," and the indignant stare of incredulity with which he had answered her. Yet in these hours it was the palpable image of her that clung closest, till, as invariably happened, his vision came full circle, and feeling her on his breast he wanted her also in his soul.

Well—such all-encompassing loves were the rarest of human experiences; he smiled at his presumption in wanting no other. Wearily he turned, and tramped homeward through the winter twilight. . . .

At the door of the hotel he ran across the Prince of Teutoburg's aide-de-camp. They had not met for some days, and Nick had a vague feeling that if the Prince's matrimonial designs took definite shape he himself was not likely, after all, to be their chosen exponent. He had surprised, now and then, a certain distrustful coldness under the Princess Mother's cordial glance, and had con-

cluded that she perhaps suspected him of being
an obstacle to her son's aspirations. He had no
idea of playing that part, but was not sorry to
appear to; for he was sincerely attached to Coral
Hicks, and hoped for her a more human fate than
that of becoming Prince Anastasius's consort.

This evening, however, he was struck by the
beaming alacrity of the aide-de-camp's greeting.
Whatever cloud had hung between them had
lifted: the Teutoburg clan, for one reason or another, no longer feared or distrusted him. The
change was conveyed in a mere hand-pressure, a
brief exchange of words, for the aide-de-camp was
hastening after a well-known dowager of the old
Roman world, whom he helped into a large coro-
netted brougham which looked as if it had been
extracted, for some ceremonial purpose, from a
museum of historic vehicles. And in an instant it
flashed on Lansing that this lady had been the
person chosen to lay the Prince's offer at Miss
Hicks's feet.

The discovery piqued him; and instead of making straight for his own room he went up to Mrs.
Hicks's drawing-room.

The room was empty, but traces of elaborate tea
pervaded it, and an immense bouquet of stiff
roses lay on the centre table. As he turned away,
Eldorada Tooker flushed and tear-stained,
abruptly entered.

"Oh, Mr. Lansing—we were looking every-
where for you."

"Looking for me?"

"Yes. Coral especially . . . she wants to see you. She wants you to come to her own sitting-room."

She led him across the ante-chamber and down the passage to the separate suite which Miss Hicks inhabited. On the threshold Eldorada gasped out emotionally: "You'll find her looking lovely—" and jerked away with a sob as he entered.

Coral Hicks was never lovely: but she certainly looked unusually handsome. Perhaps it was the long dress of black velvet which, outlined against a shaded lamp, made her strong build seem slenderer, or perhaps the slight flush on her dusky cheek: a bloom of womanhood hung upon her which she made no effort to dissemble. Indeed, it was one of her originalities that she always gravely and courageously revealed the utmost of whatever mood possessed her.

"How splendid you look!" he said, smiling at her.

She threw her head back and gazed him straight in the eyes. "That's going to be my future job."

"To look splendid?"

"Yes."

"And wear a crown?"

"And wear a crown. . . ."

They continued to consider each other without speaking. Nick's heart contracted with pity and perplexity.

"Oh, Coral—it's not decided?"

She scrutinized him for a last penetrating moment; then she looked away. "I'm never long deciding."

He hesitated, choking with contradictory impulses, and afraid to formulate any, lest they should either mislead or pain her.

"Why didn't you tell me?" he questioned lamely; and instantly perceived his blunder.

She sat down, and looked up at him under brooding lashes—had he ever noticed the thickness of her lashes before?

"Would it have made any difference if I had told you?"

"Any difference—?"

"Sit down by me," she commanded. "I want to talk to you. You can say now whatever you might have said sooner. I'm not married yet: I'm still free."

"You haven't given your answer?"

"It doesn't matter if I have."

The retort frightened him with the glimpse of what she still expected of him, and what he was still so unable to give.

"That means you've said yes?" he pursued, to gain time.

"Yes or no—it doesn't matter. I had to say something. What I want is your advice."

"At the eleventh hour?"

"Or the twelfth." She paused. "What shall I

do?'' she questioned, with a sudden accent of helplessness.

He looked at her as helplessly. He could not say: "Ask yourself—ask your parents." Her next word would sweep away such frail hypocrisies. Her "What shall I do?" meant "What are *you* going to do?" and he knew it, and knew that she knew it.

"I'm a bad person to give any one matrimonial advice," he began, with a strained smile; "but I had such a different vision for you."

"What kind of a vision?" She was merciless.

"Merely what people call happiness, dear."

" 'People call'—you see you don't believe in it yourself! Well, neither do I—in that form, at any rate."

He considered. "I believe in trying for it—even if the trying's the best of it."

"Well, I've tried, and failed. And I'm twenty-two, and I never was young. I suppose I haven't enough imagination." She drew a deep breath. "Now I want something different." She appeared to search for the word. "I want to be—prominent," she declared.

"Prominent?"

She reddened swarthily. "Oh, you smile—you think it's ridiculous: it doesn't seem worth while to you. That's because you've always had all those things. But I haven't. I know what father pushed up from, and I want to push up as high again—higher. No, I haven't got much imagination. I've always liked Facts. And I find I shall like the fact of being a Princess—choosing the people I associate with, and being up above all these European grandees that father and mother bow down to, though they think they despise them. You can be up above these people by just being yourself; you know how. But I need a platform—a sky-scraper. Father and mother slaved to give me my education. They thought education was the important thing; but, since we've all three of us got mediocre minds, it has just landed us among mediocre people. Don't you suppose I see through all the sham science and sham art and sham everything we're surrounded with? That's why I want to buy a place at the very top, where I shall be powerful enough to get about me the people I want, the big people, the right people, and to help them. I want to promote culture, like those Renaissance women you're always talking about. I want to do it for Apex City; do you understand? And for father and mother too. I want all those titles carved on my tombstone. *They're* facts, anyhow! Don't laugh at me. . . ." She broke off with one of her clumsy smiles, and moved away from him to the other end of the room.

He sat looking at her with a curious feeling of admiration. Her harsh positivism was like a tonic to his disenchanted mood, and he thought: "What a pity!"

Aloud he said: "I don't feel like laughing at you. You're a great woman."

"Then I shall be a great Princess."

"Oh—but you might have been something so much greater!"

Her face flamed again. "Don't say that!"

He stood up involuntarily, and drew near her.

"Why not?"

"Because you're the only man with whom I can imagine the other kind of greatness."

It moved him—moved him unexpectedly. He got as far as saying to himself: "Good God, if she were not so hideously rich—" and then of yielding for a moment to the persuasive vision of all that he and she might do with those very riches which he dreaded. After all, there was nothing mean in her ideals—they were hard and material, in keeping with her primitive and massive person; but they had a certain grim nobility. And when she spoke of "the other kind of greatness" he knew that she understood what she was talking of, and was not merely saying something to draw him on, to get him to commit himself. There was not a drop of guile in her, except that which her very honesty distilled.

"The other kind of greatness?" he repeated.

"Well, isn't that what you said happiness was? I wanted to be happy . . . but one can't choose."

He went up to her. "No, one can't choose. And how can anyone give you happiness who hasn't got it himself?'' He took her hands, feeling how large, muscular and voluntary they were, even as they melted in his palms.

"My poor Coral, of what use can I ever be to you? What you need is to be loved.''

She drew back and gave him one of her straight strong glances: "No,'' she said gallantly, "but just to love.''

PART III

XXV

IN the persistent drizzle of a Paris winter morning Susy Lansing walked back alone from the
school at which she had just deposited the four
eldest Fulmers to the little house in Passy where,
for the last two months, she had been living with
them.

She had on ready-made boots, an old water-
proof and a last year's hat; but none of these
facts disturbed her, though she took no particular
pride in them. The truth was that she was too
busy to think much about them. Since she had
assumed the charge of the Fulmer children, in
the absence of both their parents in Italy, she had
had to pass through such an arduous apprenticeship of motherhood that every moment of her
waking hours was packed with things to do at
once, and other things to remember to do later.
There were only five Fulmers; but at times they
were like an army with banners, and their power
of self-multiplication was equalled only by the
manner in which they could dwindle, vanish, grow
mute, and become as it were a single tumbled
brown head bent over a book in some corner of
the house in which nobody would ever have
thought of hunting for them—and which, of

course, were it the *bonne's* room in the attic, or the
subterranean closet where the trunks were kept,
had been singled out by them for that very reason.

These changes from ubiquity to invisibility
would have seemed to Susy, a few months earlier,
one of the most maddening of many characteristics not calculated to promote repose. But now she
felt differently. She had grown interested in her
charges, and the search for a clue to their methods,
whether tribal or individual, was as exciting to her
as the development of a detective story.

What interested her most in the whole stirring
business was the discovery that they *had* a
method. These little creatures, pitched upward
into experience on the tossing waves of their parents' agitated lives, had managed to establish a
rough-and-ready system of self-government.
Junie, the eldest (the one who already chose her
mother's hats, and tried to put order in her wardrobe) was the recognized head of the state. At
twelve she knew lots of things which her mother
had never thoroughly learned, and Susy, her temporary mother, had never even guessed at: she
spoke with authority on all vital subjects, from
castor-oil to flannel under-clothes, from the fair
sharing of stamps or marbles to the number of
helpings of rice-pudding or jam which each child
was entitled to.

There was hardly any appeal from her verdict;
yet each of her subjects revolved in his or her own
orbit of independence, according to laws which

Junie acknowledged and respected; and the inter-
preting of this mysterious charter of rights and
privileges had not been without difficulty for Susy.

Besides this, there were material difficulties to
deal with. The six of them, and the breathless
bonne who cooked and slaved for them all, had but
a slim budget to live on; and, as Junie remarked,
you'd have thought the boys ate their shoes, the
way they vanished. They ate, certainly, a great
deal else, and mostly of a nourishing and expensive kind. They had definite views about the
amount and quality of their food, and were capable of concerted rebellion when Susy's catering
fell beneath their standard. All this made her
life a hurried and harassing business, but never—
what she had most feared it would be—a dull or
depressing one.

It was not, she owned to herself, that the society
of the Fulmer children had roused in her any abstract passion for the human young. She knew—
had known since Nick's first kiss—how she would
love any child of his and hers; and she had cher-
ished poor little Clarissa Vanderlyn with a shrinking and wistful solicitude. But in these rough
young Fulmers she took a positive delight, and
for reasons that were increasingly clear to her.
It was because, in the first place, they were all intelligent; and because their intelligence had been
fed only on things worth caring for. However
inadequate Grace Fulmer's bringing-up of her increasing tribe had been, they had heard in her

company nothing trivial or dull: good music, good
books and good talk had been their daily food, and
if at times they stamped and roared and crashed
about like children unblessed by such privileges,
at others they shone with the light of poetry and
spoke with the voice of wisdom.

That had been Susy's discovery: for the first
time she was among awakening minds which had
been wakened only to beauty. From their cramped
and uncomfortable household Grace and Nat Fulmer had managed to keep out mean envies, vulgar
admirations, shabby discontents; above all the din
and confusion the great images of beauty had
brooded, like those ancestral figures that stood
apart on their shelf in the poorest Roman households.

No, the task she had undertaken for want of a
better gave Susy no sense of a missed vocation:
"mothering" on a large scale would never, she
perceived, be her job. Rather it gave her, in odd
ways, the sense of being herself mothered, of taking her first steps in the life of immaterial values
which had begun to seem so much more substantial
than any she had known.

On the day when she had gone to Grace Fulmer
for counsel and comfort she had little guessed that
they would come to her in this form. She had
found her friend, more than ever distracted and
yet buoyant, riding the large untidy waves of her
life with the splashed ease of an amphibian. Grace
was probably the only person among Susy's

friends who could have understood why she could
not make up her mind to marry Altringham; but
at the moment Grace was too much absorbed in her
own problems to pay much attention to her
friend's, and, according to her wont, she immediately "unpacked" her difficulties.

Nat was not getting what she had hoped out of
his European opportunity. Oh, she was enough
of an artist herself to know that there must be
fallow periods—that the impact of new impressions seldom produced immediate results. She
had allowed for all that. But her past experience
of Nat's moods had taught her to know just when
he was assimilating, when impressions were fruc-
tifying in him. And now they were not, and he
knew it as well as she did. There had been too
much rushing about, too much excitement and
sterile flattery . . . Mrs. Melrose? Well, yes, for
a while . . . the trip to Spain had been a love-
journey, no doubt. Grace spoke calmly, but the
lines of her face sharpened: she had suffered, oh
horribly, at his going to Spain without her. Yet
she couldn't, for the children's sake, afford to miss
the big sum that Ursula Gillow had given her for
her fortnight at Ruan. And her playing had
struck people, and led, on the way back, to two or
three profitable engagements in private houses in
London. Fashionable society had made "a little
fuss" about her, and it had surprised and pleased
Nat, and given her a new importance in his eyes.
"He was beginning to forget that I wasn't only a

nursery-maid, and it's been a good thing for him
to be reminded . . . but the great thing is that
with what I've earned he and I can go off to
southern Italy and Sicily for three months. You
know I know how to manage . . . and, alone with
me, Nat will settle down to work: to observing,
feeling, soaking things in. It's the only way. Mrs.
Melrose wants to take him, to pay all the expenses
again—well she shan't. *I'll* pay them." Her worn
cheek flushed with triumph. "And you'll see what
wonders will come of it. . . . Only there's the
problem of the children. Junie quite agrees that
we can't take them. . . ."

Thereupon she had unfolded her idea. If Susy
was at a loose end, and hard up, why shouldn't she
take charge of the children while their parents
were in Italy? For three months at most—Grace
could promise it shouldn't be longer. They
couldn't pay her much, of course, but at least she
would be lodged and fed. "And, you know, it will
end by interesting you—I'm sure it will," the
mother concluded, her irrepressible hopefulness
rising even to this height, while Susy stood before
her with a hesitating smile.

Take care of five Fulmers for three months!
The prospect cowed her. If there had been only
Junie and Geordie, the oldest and youngest of the
band, she might have felt less hesitation. But
there was Nat, the second in age, whose motor-
horn had driven her and Nick out to the hill-side on
their fatal day at the Fulmers' and there were

the twins, Jack and Peggy, of whom she had kept memories almost equally disquieting. To rule this uproarious tribe would be a sterner business than trying to beguile Clarissa Vanderlyn's ladylike leisure; and she would have refused on the spot, as she had refused once before, if the only possible alternatives had not come to seem so much less bearable, and if Junie, called in for advice, and standing there, small, plain and competent, had not said in her quiet grown-up voice: "Oh, yes, I'm sure Mrs. Lansing and I can manage while you're away—especially if she reads aloud well."

Reads aloud well! The stipulation had enchanted Susy. She had never before known children who cared to be read aloud to; she remembered with a shiver her attempts to interest Clarissa in anything but gossip and the fashions, and the tone in which the child had said, showing Strefford's trinket to her father: "Because I said I'd rather have it than a book."

And here were children who consented to be left for three months by their parents, but on condition that a good reader was provided for them!

"Very well—I will! But what shall I be expected to read to you?" she had gaily questioned; and Junie had answered, after one of her sober pauses of reflection: "The little ones like nearly everything; but Nat and I want poetry particularly, because if we read it to ourselves we so often pronounce the puzzling words wrong, and then it sounds so horrid."

"Oh, I hope I shall pronounce them right," Susy murmured, stricken with self-distrust and humility.

Apparently she did; for her reading was a success, and even the twins and Geordie, once they had grown used to her, seemed to prefer a ringing page of Henry V, or the fairy scenes from the Midsummer Night's Dream, to their own more specialized literature, though that had also at times to be provided.

There were, in fact, no lulls in her life with the Fulmers; but its commotions seemed to Susy less meaningless, and therefore less fatiguing, than those that punctuated the existence of people like Altringham, Ursula Gillow, Ellie Vanderlyn and their train; and the noisy uncomfortable little house at Passy was beginning to greet her with the eyes of home when she returned there after her tramps to and from the children's classes. At any rate she had the sense of doing something useful and even necessary, and of earning her own keep, though on so modest a scale; and when the children were in their quiet mood, and demanded books or music (or, even, on one occasion, at the surprising Junie's instigation, a collective visit to the Louvre, where they recognized the most unlikely pictures, and the two elders emitted startling technical judgments, and called their companion's attention to details she had not observed); on these occasions, Susy had a surprised sense of being drawn back into her brief life with

Nick, or even still farther and deeper, into those visions of Nick's own childhood on which the trivial later years had heaped their dust.

It was curious to think that if he and she had remained together, and she had had a child—the vision used to come to her, in her sleepless hours, when she looked at little Geordie, in his cot by her bed—their life together might have been very much like the life she was now leading, a small obscure business to the outer world, but to themselves how wide and deep and crowded!

She could not bear, at that moment, the thought of giving up this mystic relation to the life she had missed. In spite of the hurry and fatigue of her days, the shabbiness and discomfort of everything, and the hours when the children were as "horrid" as any other children, and turned a conspiracy of hostile faces to all her appeals; in spite of all this she did not want to give them up, and had decided, when their parents returned, to ask to go back to America with them. Perhaps, if Nat's success continued, and Grace was able to work at her music, they would need a kind of governess-companion. At any rate, she could picture no future less distasteful.

She had not sent to Mr. Spearman Nick's answer to her letter. In the interval between writing to him and receiving his reply she had broken with Strefford; she had therefore no object in seeking her freedom. If Nick wanted his, he knew he had only to ask for it; and his silence, as the weeks passed, woke a faint hope in her. The hope flamed high when she read one day in the newspapers a vague but evidently "inspired" allusion to the possibility of an alliance between his Serene Highness the reigning Prince of Teutoburg-Waldhain and Miss Coral Hicks of Apex City; it sank to ashes when, a few days later, her eye lit on a paragraph wherein Mr. and Mrs. Mortimer Hicks "requested to state" that there was no truth in the report.

On the foundation of these two statements Susy raised one watch-tower of hope after another, feverish edifices demolished or rebuilt by every chance hint from the outer world wherein Nick's name figured with the Hickses'. And still, as the days passed and she heard nothing, either from him or from her lawyer, her flag continued to fly from the quaking structures.

Apart from the custody of the children there was indeed little to distract her mind from these persistent broodings. She winced sometimes at the thought of the ease with which her fashionable friends had let her drop out of sight. In the perpetual purposeless rush of their days, the feverish making of winter plans, hurrying off to the Riviera or St. Moritz, Egypt or New York, there was no time to hunt up the vanished or to wait for the laggard. Had they learned that she had broken her "engagement" (how she hated the word!) to Strefford, and had the fact gone about that she was once more only a poor hanger-on, to be taken up when it was convenient, and ignored in the intervals? She did not know; though she fancied Strefford's newly-developed pride would prevent his revealing to any one what had passed between them. For several days after her abrupt flight he had made no sign; and though she longed to write and ask his forgiveness she could not find the words. Finally it was he who wrote: a short note, from Altringham, typical of all that was best in the old Strefford. He had gone down to Altringham, he told her, to think quietly over their last talk, and try to understand what she had been driving at. He had to own that he couldn't; but that, he supposed, was the very head and front of his offending. Whatever he had done to displease her, he was sorry for; but he asked, in view of his invincible ignorance, to be allowed not to regard his offence as a cause for a final break. The possibility of that, he found, would make him even more unhappy than he had foreseen; as she knew, his own happiness had always been his first object in life, and he therefore begged her to suspend her decision a little longer. He expected to be in Paris within another two months, and before arriving he would write again, and ask her to see him.

The letter moved her but did not make her waver. She simply wrote that she was touched by his kindness, and would willingly see him if he came to Paris later; though she was bound to tell him that she had not yet changed her mind, and did not believe it would promote his happiness to have her try to do so.

He did not reply to this, and there was nothing further to keep her thoughts from revolving endlessly about her inmost hopes and fears.

On the rainy afternoon in question, tramping home from the *"cours"* (to which she was to return at six), she had said to herself that it was two months that very day since Nick had known she was ready to release him—and that after such a delay he was not likely to take any further steps. The thought filled her with a vague ecstasy. She had had to fix an arbitrary date as the term of her anguish, and she had fixed that one; and behold she was justified. For what could his silence mean but that he too. . . .

On the hall-table lay a typed envelope with the Paris postage-mark. She opened it carelessly, and saw that the letter-head bore Mr. Spearman's office address. The words beneath spun round before her eyes. . . . "Has notified us that he is at your disposal . . . carry out your wishes . . . arriving in Paris . . . fix an appointment with his lawyers . . ."

Nick—it was Nick the words were talking of! It was the fact of Nick's return to Paris that was being described in those preposterous terms! She sank down on the bench beside the dripping umbrella-stand and stared vacantly before her. It had fallen at last—this blow in which she now saw that she had never really believed! And yet she had imagined she was prepared for it, had expected it, was already planning her future life in view of it—an effaced impersonal life in the service of somebody else's children—when, in reality, under that thin surface of abnegation and acceptance, all the old hopes had been smouldering red-hot in their ashes! What was the use of any self-discipline, any philosophy, any experience, if the lawless self underneath could in an instant consume them like tinder?

She tried to collect herself—to understand what had happened. Nick was coming to Paris—coming not to see her but to consult his lawyer! It meant, of course, that he had definitely resolved to claim his freedom; and that, if he had made up his mind to this final step, after more than six months of inaction and seeming indifference, it could be only because something unforeseen and decisive had happened to him. Feverishly, she put together again the stray scraps of gossip and the newspaper paragraphs that had reached her in the last months. It was evident that Miss Hicks's projected marriage with the Prince of Teutoburg-Waldhain had been broken off at the last moment; and broken off because she intended to marry Nick. The announcement of his arrival in Paris and the publication of Mr. and Mrs. Hicks's formal denial of their daughter's betrothal coincided too closely to admit of any other inference. Susy tried to grasp the reality of these assembled facts, to picture to herself their actual tangible results. She thought of Coral Hicks bearing the name of Mrs. Nick Lansing—*her* name, Susy's own!—and entering drawing-rooms with Nick in her wake, gaily welcomed by the very people who, a few months before, had welcomed Susy with the same warmth. In spite of Nick's growing dislike of society, and Coral's attitude of intellectual superiority, their wealth would fatally draw them back into the world to which Nick was attached by all his habits and associations. And no doubt it would amuse him to re-enter that world as a dispenser of hospitality, to play the part of host where he had so long been a guest; just as Susy had once fancied it would amuse her to re-enter it as Lady Altringham. . . . But, try as she would, now that the reality was so close on her, she could not visualize it or relate it to herself. The mere juxtaposition of the two names—Coral, Nick—which in old times she had so often laughingly coupled, now produced a blur in her brain.

She continued to sit helplessly beside the hall-table, the tears running down her cheeks. The appearance of the *bonne* aroused her. Her youngest charge, Geordie, had been feverish for a day or two; he was better, but still confined to the nursery, and he had heard Susy unlock the house-door, and could not imagine why she had not come straight up to him. He now began to manifest his indignation in a series of racking howls, and Susy, shaken out of her trance, dropped her cloak and umbrella and hurried up.

"Oh, that child!" she groaned.

Under the Fulmer roof there was little time or space for the indulgence of private sorrows. From morning till night there was always some immediate practical demand on one's attention; and Susy was beginning to see how, in contracted households, children may play a part less romantic but not less useful than that assigned to them in fiction, through the mere fact of giving their parents no leisure to dwell on irremediable grievances. Though her own apprenticeship to family life had been so short, she had already acquired the knack of rapid mental readjustment, and as she hurried up to the nursery her private cares were dispelled by a dozen problems of temperature, diet and medicine.

Such readjustment was of course only momentary; yet each time it happened it seemed to give her more firmness and flexibility of temper. "What a child I was myself six months ago!" she thought, wondering that Nick's influence, and the tragedy of their parting, should have done less to mature and steady her than these few weeks in a house full of children.

Pacifying Geordie was not easy, for he had long since learned to use his grievances as a pretext for keeping the offender at his beck with a continuous supply of stories, songs and games. "You'd better be careful never to put yourself in the wrong with Geordie," the astute Junie had warned Susy at the outset, "because he's got such a memory, and he won't make it up with you till you've told him every fairy-tale he's ever heard before."

But on this occasion, as soon as he saw her, Geordie's indignation melted. She was still in the doorway, compunctious, abject and racking her dazed brain for his favourite stories, when she saw, by the smoothing out of his mouth and the sudden serenity of his eyes, that he was going to give her the delicious but not wholly reassuring shock of being a good boy.

Thoughtfully he examined her face as she knelt down beside the cot; then he poked out a finger and pressed it on her tearful cheek.

"Poor Susy got a pain too," he said, putting his arms about her; and as she hugged him close, he added philosophically: "Tell Geordie a new story, darling, and 'oo'll forget all about it."

XXVI

NICK Lansing arrived in Paris two days after his lawyer had announced his coming to Mr. Spearman.

He had left Rome with the definite purpose of freeing himself and Susy; and though he was not pledged to Coral Hicks he had not concealed from her the object of his journey. In vain had he tried to rouse in himself any sense of interest in his own future. Beyond the need of reaching a definite point in his relation to Susy his imagination could not travel. But he had been moved by Coral's confession, and his reason told him that he and she would probably be happy together, with the temperate happiness based on a community of tastes and an enlargement of opportunities. He meant, on his return to Rome, to ask her to marry him; and he knew that she knew it. Indeed, if he had not spoken before leaving it was with no idea of evading his fate, or keeping her longer in suspense, but simply because of the strange apathy that had fallen on him since he had received Susy's letter. In his incessant self-communings he dressed up this apathy as a discretion which forbade his engaging Coral's future till his own was assured. But in truth he knew that Coral's future was already engaged, and his with it: in Rome the fact had seemed natural and even inevitable.

In Paris, it instantly became the thinnest of unrealities. Not because Paris was not Rome, nor because it was Paris; but because hidden away somewhere in that vast unheeding labyrinth was the half-forgotten part of himself that was Susy. . . . For weeks, for months past, his mind had been saturated with Susy: she had never seemed more insistently near him than as their separation lengthened, and the chance of reunion became less probable. It was as if a sickness long smoul-dering in him had broken out and become acute, enveloping him in the Nessus-shirt of his memories. There were moments when, to his memory, their actual embraces seemed perfunctory, acci-dental, compared with this deep deliberate im-print of her soul on his.

Yet now it had become suddenly different. Now that he was in the same place with her, and might at any moment run across her, meet her eyes, hear her voice, avoid her hand—now that pene-trating ghost of her with which he had been living was sucked back into the shadows, and he seemed, for the first time since their parting, to be again in her actual presence. He woke to the fact on the morning of his arrival, staring down from his hotel window on a street she would perhaps walk through that very day, and over a limitless huddle of roofs, one of which covered her at that hour. The abruptness of the transition startled him; he had not known that her mere geographical nearness would take him by the throat in that way. What would it be, then, if she were to walk into the room?

Thank heaven that need never happen! He was sufficiently informed as to French divorce proceedings to know that they would not necessitate a confrontation with his wife; and with ordinary luck, and some precautions, he might escape even a distant glimpse of her. He did not mean to remain in Paris more than a few days; and during that time it would be easy—knowing, as he did, her tastes and Altringham's—to avoid the places where she was likely to be met. He did not know where she was living, but imagined her to be staying with Mrs. Melrose, or some other rich friend, or else lodged, in prospective affluence, at the Nouveau Luxe, or in a pretty flat of her own. Trust Susy—ah, the pang of it—to "manage"!

His first visit was to his lawyer's; and as he walked through the familiar streets each approaching face, each distant figure seemed hers. The obsession was intolerable. It would not last, of course; but meanwhile he had the exposed sense of a fugitive in a nightmare, who feels himself the only creature visible in a ghostly and besetting multitude. The eye of the metropolis seemed fixed on him in an immense unblinking stare.

At the lawyer's he was told that, as a first step

to freedom, he must secure a domicile in Paris.
He had of course known of this necessity: he had
seen too many friends through the Divorce Court,
in one country or another, not to be fairly familiar
with the procedure. But the fact presented a different aspect as soon as he tried to relate it to
himself and Susy: it was as though Susy's personality were a medium through which events still
took on a transfiguring colour. He found the
"domicile" that very day: a tawdrily furnished
rez-de-chaussée, obviously destined to far different uses. And as he sat there, after the *concierge*
had discreetly withdrawn with the first quarter's
payment in her pocket, and stared about him at
the vulgar plushy place, he burst out laughing
at what it was about to figure in the eyes of the
law: a Home, and a Home desecrated by his own
act! The Home in which he and Susy had reared
their precarious bliss, and seen it crumble at the
brutal touch of his unfaithfulness and his cruelty
—for he had been told that he must be cruel to her
as well as unfaithful! He looked at the walls hung
with sentimental photogravures, at the shiny
bronze "nudes," the moth-eaten animal-skins and
the bedizened bed—and once more the unreality,
the impossibility, of all that was happening to him
entered like a drug into his veins.

To rouse himself he stood up, turned the key
on the hideous place, and returned to his lawyer's.
He knew that in the hard dry atmosphere of the
office the act of giving the address of the flat

would restore some kind of reality to the phan-
tasmal transaction. And with wonder he watched
the lawyer, as a matter of course, pencil the street
and the number on one of the papers enclosed in
a folder on which his own name was elaborately
engrossed.

As he took leave it occurred to him to ask where
Susy was living. At least he imagined that it had
just occurred to him, and that he was making the
enquiry merely as a measure of precaution, in
order to know what quarter of Paris to avoid; but
in reality the question had been on his lips since
he had first entered the office, and lurking in his
mind since he had emerged from the railway station that morning. The fact of not knowing where
she lived made the whole of Paris a meaningless
unintelligible place, as useless to him as the face
of a huge clock that has lost its hour hand.

The address in Passy surprised him: he had
imagined that she would be somewhere in the
neighborhood of the Champs Elysées or the Place
de l'Etoile. But probably either Mrs. Melrose or
Ellie Vanderlyn had taken a house at Passy. Well
—it was something of a relief to know that she
was so far off. No business called him to that
almost suburban region beyond the Trocadéro,
and there was much less chance of meeting her
than if she had been in the centre of Paris.

All day he wandered, avoiding the fashionable
quarters, the streets in which private motors glittered five deep, and furred and feathered sil-

houettes glided from them into tea-rooms, picture-galleries and jewellers' shops. In some such scenes Susy was no doubt figuring: slenderer, finer, vivider, than the other images of clay, but imitating their gestures, chattering their jargon, winding her hand among the same pearls and sables. He struck away across the Seine, along the quays to the Cité, the net-work of old Paris, the great grey vaults of St. Eustache, the swarming streets of the Marais. He gazed at monuments, dawdled before shop-windows, sat in squares and on quays, watching people bargain, argue, philander, quarrel, work-girls stroll past in linked bands, beggars whine on the bridges, derelicts doze in the pale winter sun, mothers in mourning hasten by taking children to school, and street-walkers beat their weary rounds before the cafés.

The day drifted on. Toward evening he began to grow afraid of his solitude, and to think of dining at the Nouveau Luxe, or some other fashionable restaurant where he would be fairly sure to meet acquaintances, and be carried off to a theatre, a *boîte* or a dancing-hall. Anything, anything now, to get away from the maddening round of his thoughts. He felt the same blank fear of solitude as months ago in Genoa. . . . Even if he were to run across Susy and Altringham, what of it? Better get the job over. People had long since ceased to take on tragedy airs about divorce: dividing couples dined together to the last, and met afterward in each other's houses, happy in the consciousness that their respective remarriages had provided two new centres of entertainment. Yet most of the couples who took their re-matings so philosophically had doubtless had their hour of enchantment, of belief in the immortality of loving; whereas he and Susy had simply and frankly entered into a business contract for their mutual advantage. The fact gave the last touch of incongruity to his agonies and exaltations, and made him appear to himself as grotesque and superannuated as the hero of a romantic novel.

He stood up from a bench on which he had been lounging in the Luxembourg gardens, and hailed a taxi. Dusk had fallen, and he meant to go back to his hotel, take a rest, and then go out to dine. But instead, he threw Susy's address to the driver, and settled down in the cab, resting both hands on the knob of his umbrella and staring straight ahead of him as if he were accomplishing some tiresome duty that had to be got through with before he could turn his mind to more important things.

"It's the easiest way," he heard himself say.

At the street-corner—her street-corner—he stopped the cab, and stood motionless while it rattled away. It was a short vague street, much farther off than he had expected, and fading away at the farther end in a dusky blur of hoardings overhung by trees. A thin rain was beginning to fall, and it was already night in this inadequately lit suburban quarter. Lansing walked

down the empty street. The houses stood a few
yards apart, with bare-twigged shrubs between,
and gates and railings dividing them from the
pavement. He could not, at first, distinguish their
numbers; but presently, coming abreast of a
street-lamp, he discovered that the small shabby
façade it illuminated was precisely the one he
sought. The discovery surprised him. He had
imagined that, as frequently happened in the out-
lying quarters of Passy and La Muette, the mean
street would lead to a stately private hotel, built
upon some bowery fragment of an old country-
place. It was the latest whim of the wealthy to
establish themselves on these outskirts of Paris,
where there was still space for verdure; and he
had pictured Susy behind some pillared house-
front, with lights pouring across glossy turf to
sculptured gateposts. Instead, he saw a six-win-
dowed house, huddled among neighbours of its
kind, with the family wash fluttering between
meagre bushes. The arc-light beat ironically on
its front, which had the worn look of a tired work-
woman's face; and Lansing, as he leaned against
the opposite railing, vainly tried to fit his vision
of Susy into so humble a setting.

The probable explanation was that his lawyer
had given him the wrong address; not only the
wrong number but the wrong street. He pulled
out the slip of paper, and was crossing over to
decipher it under the lamp, when an errand-boy
appeared out of the obscurity, and approached

the house. Nick drew back, and the boy, unlatch-
ing the gate, ran up the steps and gave the bell
a pull.

Almost immediately the door opened; and there
stood Susy, the light full upon her, and upon a
red-cheeked child against her shoulder. The space
behind them was dark, or so dimly lit that it
formed a black background to her vivid figure.
She looked at the errand-boy without surprise,
took his parcel, and after he had turned away,
lingered a moment in the door, glancing down the
empty street.

That moment, to her watcher, seemed quicker
than a flash yet as long as a life-time. There she
was, a stone's throw away, but utterly unconscious of his presence: his Susy, the old Susy, and
yet a new Susy, curiously transformed, trans-
figure'd almost, by the new attitude in which he
beheld her.

In the first shock of the vision he forgot his
surprise at her being in such a place, forgot to
wonder whose house she was in, or whose was the
sleepy child in her arms. For an instant she stood
out from the blackness behind her, and through
the veil of the winter night, a thing apart, an un-
conditioned vision, the eternal image of the
woman and the child; and in that instant everything within him was changed and renewed. His
eyes were still absorbing her, finding again the
familiar curves of her light body, noting the thin-
ness of the lifted arm that upheld the little boy,

the droop of the shoulder he weighed on, the brooding way in which her cheek leaned to his even while she looked away; then she drew back, the door closed, and the street-lamp again shone on blankness.

"But she's mine!" Nick cried, in a fierce triumph of recovery. . . .

His eyes were so full of her that he shut them to hold in the crowding vision.

It remained with him, at first, as a complete picture; then gradually it broke up into its component parts, the child vanished, the strange house vanished, and Susy alone stood before him, his own Susy, only his Susy, yet changed, worn, tempered—older, even—with sharper shadows under the cheek-bones, the brows drawn, the joint of the slim wrist more prominent.   It was not thus that his memory had evoked her, and he recalled, with a remorseful pang, the fact that something in her look, her dress, her tired and drooping attitude, suggested poverty, dependence, seemed to make her after all a part of the shabby house in which, at first sight, her presence had seemed so incongruous.

"But she looks *poor!*" he thought, his heart tightening. And instantly it occurred to him that these must be the Fulmer children whom she was living with while their parents travelled in Italy. Rumours of Nat Fulmer's sudden ascension had reached him, and he had heard that the couple had lately been seen in Naples and Palermo. No one had mentioned Susy's name in connection with them, and he could hardly tell why he had arrived at this conclusion, except perhaps because it seemed natural that, if Susy were in trouble, she should turn to her old friend Grace.

But why in trouble? What trouble? What could have happened to check her triumphant career?

"That's what I mean to find out!" he exclaimed.

His heart was beating with a tumult of new hopes and old memories. The sight of his wife, so remote in mien and manner from the world in which he had imagined her to be re-absorbed, changed in a flash his own relation to life, and flung a mist of unreality over all that he had been trying to think most solid and tangible. Nothing now was substantial to him but the stones of the street in which he stood, the front of the house which hid her, the bell-handle he already felt in his grasp. He started forward, and was halfway to the threshold when a private motor turned the corner, the twin glitter of its lamps carpeting the wet street with gold to Susy's door.

Lansing drew back into the shadow as the motor swept up to the house. A man jumped out, and the light fell on Strefford's shambling figure, its lazy disjointed movements so unmistakably the same under his fur coat, and in the new setting of prosperity.

Lansing stood motionless, staring at the door.

Strefford rang, and waited. Would Susy appear
again? Perhaps she had done so before only because she had been on the watch. . . .

But no: after a slight delay a *bonne* appeared
—the breathless maïd-of-all-work of a busy household—and at once effaced herself, letting the visitor in. Lansing was sure that not a word passed
between the two, of enquiry on Lord Altringham's
part, or of acquiescence on the servant's. There
could be no doubt that he was expected.

The door closed on him, and a light appeared
behind the blind of the adjoining window. The
maid had shown the visitor into the sitting-room
and lit the lamp. Upstairs, meanwhile, Susy was
no doubt running skilful fingers through her
tumbled hair and daubing her pale lips with red.
Ah, how Lansing knew every movement of that
familiar rite, even to the pucker of the brow and
the pouting thrust-out of the lower lip! He was
seized with a sense of physical sickness as the
succession of remembered gestures pressed upon
his eyes. . . . And the other man? The other
man, inside the house, was perhaps at that very
instant smiling over the remembrance of the same
scene!

At the thought, Lansing plunged away into the
night.

XXVII

SUSY and Lord Altringham sat in the little drawing-room, divided from each other by a table carrying a smoky lamp and heaped with tattered school-books.

In another half hour the *bonne*, despatched to fetch the children from their classes, would be back with her flock; and at any moment Geordie's imperious cries might summon his slave up to the nursery. In the scant time allotted them, the two sat, and visibly wondered what to say.

Strefford, on entering, had glanced about the dreary room, with its piano laden with tattered music, the children's toys littering the lame sofa, the bunches of dyed grass and impaled butterflies flanking the cast-bronze clock. Then he had turned to Susy and asked simply: "Why on earth are you here?"

She had not tried to explain; from the first, she had understood the impossibility of doing so. And she would not betray her secret longing to return to Nick, now that she knew that Nick had taken definite steps for his release. In dread lest Strefford should have heard of this, and should announce it to her, coupling it with the news of Nick's projected marriage, and lest, hearing her

323

fears thus substantiated, she should lose her self-control, she had preferred to say, in a voice that she tried to make indifferent: "The 'proceedings,' or whatever the lawyers call them, have begun. While they're going on I like to stay quite by myself. . . . I don't know why. . . ."

Strefford, at that, had looked at her keenly "Ah," he murmured; and his lips were twisted into their old mocking smile. "Speaking of proceedings," he went on carelessly, "what stage have Ellie's reached, I wonder? I saw her and Vanderlyn and Bockheimer all lunching cheerfully together to-day at Larue's."

The blood rushed to Susy's forehead. She remembered her tragic evening with Nelson Vanderlyn, only two months earlier, and thought to herself: "In time, then, I suppose, Nick and I. . . ."

Aloud she said: "I can't imagine how Nelson and Ellie can ever want to see each other again. And in a restaurant, of all places!"

Strefford continued to smile. "My dear, you're incorrigibly old-fashioned. Why should two people who've done each other the best turn they could by getting out of each other's way at the right moment behave like sworn enemies ever afterward? It's too absurd; the humbug's too flagrant. Whatever our generation has failed to do, it's got rid of humbug; and that's enough to immortalize it. I daresay Nelson and Ellie never liked each other better than they do to-day.

Twenty years ago, they'd have been afraid to confess it; but why shouldn't they now?"

Susy looked at Strefford, conscious that under his words was the ache of the disappointment she had caused him; and yet conscious also that that very ache was not the overwhelming penetrating emotion he perhaps wished it to be, but a pang on a par with a dozen others; and that even while he felt it he foresaw the day when he should cease to feel it. And she thought to herself that this certainty of oblivion must be bitterer than any certainty of pain.

A silence had fallen between them. He broke it by rising from his seat, and saying with a shrug: "You'll end by driving me to marry Joan Senechal."

Susy smiled. "Well, why not? She's lovely."

"Yes; but she'll bore me."

"Poor Streff! So should I—"

"Perhaps. But nothing like as soon—" He grinned sardonically. "There'd be more margin." He appeared to wait for her to speak. "And what else on earth are *you* going to do?" he concluded, as she still remained silent.

"Oh, Streff, I couldn't marry you for a reason like that!" she murmured at length.

"Then marry me, and find your reason afterward."

Her lips made a movement of denial, and still in silence she held out her hand for good-bye. He clasped it, and then turned away; but on the threshold he paused, his screwed-up eyes fixed on her wistfully.

The look moved her, and she added hurriedly: "The only reason I can find is one for *not* marrying you. It's because I can't yet feel unmarried enough."

"Unmarried enough? But I thought Nick was doing his best to make you feel that."

"Yes. But even when he has—sometimes I think even that won't make any difference."

He still scrutinized her hesitatingly, with the gravest eyes she had ever seen in his careless face.

"My dear, that's rather the way I feel about you," he said simply as he turned to go.

That evening after the children had gone to bed Susy sat up late in the cheerless sitting-room. She was not thinking of Strefford but of Nick. He was coming to Paris—perhaps he had already arrived. The idea that he might be in the same place with her at that very moment, and without her knowing it, was so strange and painful that she felt a violent revolt of all her strong and joy-loving youth. Why should she go on suffering so unbearably, so abjectly, so miserably? If only she could see him, hear his voice, even hear him say again such cruel and humiliating words as he had spoken on that dreadful day in Venice— even that would be better than this blankness, this utter and final exclusion from his life! He had been cruel to her, unimaginably cruel: hard, arrogant, unjust; and had been so, perhaps, deliberately, because he already wanted to be free. But she was ready to face even that possibility, to humble herself still farther than he had humbled her—she was ready to do anything, if only she might see him once again.

She leaned her aching head on her hands and pondered. Do anything? But what could she do? Nothing that should hurt him, interfere with his liberty, be false to the spirit of their pact: on that she was more than ever resolved. She had made a bargain, and she meant to stick to it, not for any abstract reason, but simply because she happened to love him in that way. Yes —but to see him again, only once!

Suddenly she remembered what Strefford had said about Nelson Vanderlyn and his wife. "Why should two people who've just done each other the best turn they could behave like sworn enemies ever after?" If in offering Nick his freedom she had indeed done him such a service as that, perhaps he no longer hated her, would no longer be unwilling to see her. . . . At any rate, why should she not write to him on that assumption, write in a spirit of simple friendliness, suggesting that they should meet and "settle things"? The business-like word "settle" (how she hated it) would prove to him that she had no secret designs upon his liberty; and besides he was too unprejudiced, too modern, too free from what Strefford

called humbug, not to understand and accept such
a suggestion. After all, perhaps Strefford was
right; it was something to have rid human relations of hypocrisy, even if, in the process, so many
exquisite things seemed somehow to have been
torn away with it. . . .

She ran up to her room, scribbled a note, and
hurried with it through the rain and darkness to
the post-box at the corner. As she returned
through the empty street she had an odd feeling
that it was not empty—that perhaps Nick was
already there, somewhere near her in the night,
about to follow her to the door, enter the house,
go up with her to her bedroom in the old way. It
was strange how close he had been brought by the
mere fact of her having written that little note to
him!

In the bedroom, Geordie lay in his crib in ruddy
slumber, and she blew out the candle and un-
dressed softly for fear of waking him.

Nick Lansing, the next day, received Susy's
letter, transmitted to his hotel from the lawyer's
office.

He read it carefully, two or three times over,
weighing and scrutinizing the guarded words.
She proposed that they should meet to ''settle
things.'' What things? And why should he
accede to such a request? What secret purpose
had prompted her? It was horrible that nowadays, in thinking of Susy, he should always sus-

pect ulterior motives, be meanly on the watch for
some hidden tortuousness. What on earth was
she trying to "manage" now, he wondered?

A few hours ago, at the sight of her, all his
hardness had melted, and he had charged himself
with cruelty, with injustice, with every sin of
pride against himself and her; but the appearance
of Strefford, arriving at that late hour, and so
evidently expected and welcomed, had driven back
the rising tide of tenderness.

Yet, after all, what was there to wonder at?
Nothing was changed in their respective situations. He had left his wife, deliberately, and for
reasons which no subsequent experience had
caused him to modify. She had apparently acquiesced in his decision, and had utilized it, as she
was justified in doing, to assure her own future.

In all this, what was there to wail or knock the
breast between two people who prided themselves
on looking facts in the face, and making their
grim best of them, without vain repinings? He
had been right in thinking their marriage an act
of madness. Her charms had overruled his judgment, and they had had their year . . . their mad
year . . . or at least all but two or three months
of it. But his first intuition had been right; and
now they must both pay for their madness. The
Fates seldom forget the bargains made with them,
or fail to ask for compound interest. Why not,
then, now that the time had come, pay up gal-

lantly, and remember of the episode only what had made it seem so supremely worth the cost?

He sent a pneumatic telegram to Mrs. Nicholas Lansing to say that he would call on her that afternoon at four. "That ought to give us time," he reflected drily, "to 'settle things,' as she calls it, without interfering with Strefford's afternoon visit."

XXVIII

HER husband's note had briefly said:
"To-day at four o'clock. N. L."

All day she pored over the words in an agony
of longing, trying to read into them regret, emotion, memories, some echo of the tumult in her
own bosom. But she had signed "Susy," and he
signed "N. L." That seemed to put an abyss between them. After all, she was free and he was
not. Perhaps, in view of his situation, she had
only increased the distance between them by her
unconventional request for a meeting.

She sat in the little drawing-room, and the cast-
bronze clock ticked out the minutes. She would
not look out of the window: it might bring bad
luck to watch for him. And it seemed to her that
a thousand invisible spirits, hidden demons of
good and evil, pressed about her, spying out her
thoughts, counting her heart-beats, ready to
pounce upon the least symptom of over-confidence
and turn it deftly to derision. Oh, for an altar
on which to pour out propitiatory offerings! But
what sweeter could they have than her smothered
heart-beats, her choked-back tears?

The bell rang, and she stood up as if a spring
had jerked her to her feet. In the mirror between

the dried grasses her face looked long pale inanimate. Ah, if he should find her too changed—! If there were but time to dash upstairs and put on a touch of red. . . .

The door opened; it shut on him; he was there.

He said: "You wanted to see me—"

She answered: "Yes." And her heart seemed to stop beating.

At first she could not make out what mysterious change had come over him, and why it was that in looking at him she seemed to be looking at a stranger; then she perceived that his voice sounded as it used to sound when he was talking to other people; and she said to herself, with a sick shiver of understanding, that she had become an "other person" to him.

There was a deathly pause; then she faltered out, not knowing what she said: "Nick—you'll sit down?"

He said: "Thanks," but did not seem to have heard her, for he continued to stand motionless, half the room between them. And slowly the uselessness, the hopelessness of his being there overcame her. A wall of granite seemed to have built itself up between them. She felt as if it hid her from him, as if with those remote new eyes of his he were staring into the wall and not at her. Suddenly she said to herself: "He's suffering more than I am, because he pities me, and is afraid to tell me that he is going to be married."

The thought stung her pride, and she lifted her head and met his eyes with a smile.

"Don't you think," she said, "it's more sensible—with everything so changed in our lives—that we should meet as friends, in this way? I wanted to tell you that you needn't feel—feel in the least unhappy about me."

A deep flush rose to his forehead. "Oh, I know—I know that—" he declared hastily; and added, with a factitious animation: "But thank you for telling me."

"There's nothing, is there," she continued, "to make our meeting in this way in the least embarrassing or painful to either of us, when both have found. . . ." She broke off, and held her hand out to him. "I've heard about you and Coral," she ended.

He just touched her hand with cold fingers, and let it drop. "Thank you," he said for the third time.

"You won't sit down?"

He sat down.

"Don't you think," she continued, "that the new way of . . . of meeting as friends . . . and talking things over without ill-will . . . is much pleasanter and more sensible, after all?"

He smiled. "It's immensely kind of you—to feel that."

"Oh, I do feel it!" She stopped short, and wondered what on earth she had meant to say

next, and why she had so abruptly lost the thread
of her discourse.

In the pause she heard him cough slightly and
clear his throat. "Let me say, then," he began,
"that I'm glad too—immensely glad that your
own future is so satisfactorily settled."

She lifted her glance again to his walled face,
in which not a muscle stirred.

"Yes: it—it makes everything easier for you,
doesn't it?"

"For you too, I hope." He paused, and then
went on: "I want also to tell you that I perfectly
understand—"

"Oh," she interrupted, "so do I; your point of
view, I mean."

They were again silent.

"Nick, why can't we be friends—real friends?
Won't it be easier?" she broke out at last with
twitching lips.

"Easier—?"

"I mean, about talking things over—arrangements. There are arrangements to be made, I
suppose?"

"I suppose so." He hesitated. "I'm doing
what I'm told—simply following out instructions.
The business is easy enough, apparently. I'm
taking the necessary steps—"

She reddened a little, and drew a gasping
breath. "The necessary steps: what are they?
Everything the lawyers tell one is so confusing.
. . . I don't yet understand—how it's done."

"My share, you mean? Oh, it's very simple."
He paused, and added in a tone of laboured ease:
"I'm going down to Fontainebleau to-morrow—"

She stared, not understanding. "To Fontainebleau—?"

Her bewilderment drew from him his first frank
smile. "Well—I chose Fontainebleau—I don't
know why . . . except that we've never been
there together."

At that she suddenly understood, and the blood
rushed to her forehead. She stood up without
knowing what she was doing, her heart in her
throat. "How grotesque—how utterly disgust-
ing!"

He gave a slight shrug. "I didn't make the
laws. . . ."

"But isn't it too stupid and degrading that such
things should be necessary when two people want
to part—?" She broke off again, silenced by the
echo of that fatal *"want to part."* . . .

He seemed to prefer not to dwell farther on
the legal obligations involved.

"You haven't yet told me," he suggested, "how
you happen to be living here."

"Here—with the Fulmer children?" She
roused herself, trying to catch his easier note.
"Oh, I've simply been governessing them for a
few weeks, while Nat and Grace are in Sicily."
She did not say: "It's because I've parted with
Strefford." Somehow it helped her wounded

pride a little to keep from him the secret of her precarious independence.

He looked his wonder. "All alone with that bewildered *bonne?* But how many of them are there? Five? Good Lord!" He contemplated the clock with unseeing eyes, and then turned them again on her face.

"I should have thought a lot of children would rather get on your nerves."

"Oh, not *these* children. They're so good to me."

"Ah, well, I suppose it won't be for long."

He sent his eyes again about the room, which his absent-minded gaze seemed to reduce to its dismal constituent elements, and added, with an obvious effort at small talk: "I hear the Fulmers are not hitting it off very well since his success. Is it true that he's going to marry Violet Melrose?"

The blood rose to Susy's face. "Oh, never, never! He and Grace are travelling together now."

"Oh, I didn't know. People say things. . . ." He was visibly embarrassed with the subject, and sorry that he had broached it. ,

"Some of the things that people say are true. But Grace doesn't mind. She says she and Nat belong to each other. They can't help it, she thinks, after having been through such a lot together."

"Dear old Grace!"

He had risen from his chair, and this time she made no effort to detain him. He seemed to have recovered his self-composure, and it struck her painfully, humiliatingly almost, that he should have spoken in that light way of the expedition to Fontainebleau on the morrow. . . . Well, men were different, she supposed; she remembered having felt that once before about Nick.

It was on the tip of her tongue to cry out: "But wait—wait! I'm not going to marry Strefford after all!"—but to do so would seem like an appeal to his compassion, to his indulgence; and that was not what she wanted. She could never forget that he had left her because he had not been able to forgive her for "managing"—and not for the world would she have him think that this meeting had been planned for such a purpose.

"If he doesn't see that I *am* different, in spite of appearances . . . and that I never was what he said I was that day—if in all these months it hasn't come over him, what's the use of trying to make him see it now?" she mused. And then, her thoughts hurrying on: "Perhaps he's suffering too—I believe he *is* suffering—at any rate, he's suffering for me, if not for himself. But if he's pledged to Coral, what can he do? What would he think of me if I tried to make him break his word to her?"

There he stood—the man who was "going to Fontainebleau to-morrow"; who called it "taking the necessary steps!" Who could smile as he made the careless statement! A world seemed to divide them already: it was as if their parting were already over. All the words, cries, arguments beating loud wings in her dropped back into silence. The only thought left was: "How much longer does he mean to go on standing there?"

He may have read the question in her face, for turning back from an absorbed contemplation of the window curtains he said: "There's nothing else—?"

"Nothing else?"

"I mean: you spoke of things to be settled—"

She flushed, suddenly remembering the pretext she had used to summon him.

"Oh," she faltered, "I didn't know . . . I thought there might be. . . . But the lawyers, I suppose. . . ."

She saw the relief on his contracted face. "Exactly. I've always thought it was best to leave it to them. I assure you"—again for a moment the smile strained his lips— "I shall do nothing to interfere with a quick settlement."

She stood motionless, feeling herself turn to stone. He appeared already a long way off, like a figure vanishing down a remote perspective.

"Then—good-bye," she heard him say from its farther end.

"Oh,—good-bye," she faltered, as if she had not had the word ready, and was relieved to have him supply it.

He stopped again on the threshold, looked back

at her, began to speak. "I've—" he said; then he repeated "Good-bye," as though to make sure he had not forgotten to say it; and the door closed on him.

It was over; she had had her last chance and missed it. Now, whatever happened, the one thing she had lived and longed for would never be. He had come, and she had let him go again. . . .

How had it come about? Would she ever be able to explain it to herself? How was it that she, so fertile in strategy, so practised in feminine arts, had stood there before him, helpless, inarticulate, like a school-girl a-choke with her first love-longing? If he was gone, and gone never to return, it was her own fault, and none but hers. What had she done to move him, detain him, make his heart beat and his head swim as hers were beating and swimming? She stood aghast at her own inadequacy, her stony inexpressiveness. . . .

And suddenly she lifted her hands to her throbbing forehead and cried out: "But this is love! This must be love!"

She had loved him before, she supposed; for what else was she to call the impulse that had drawn her to him, taught her how to overcome his scruples, and whirled him away with her on their mad adventure? Well, if that was love, this was something so much larger and deeper that the other feeling seemed the mere dancing of her blood in tune with his. . . .

But, no! Real love, great love, the love that poets sang, and privileged and tortured beings lived and died of, that love had its own superior expressiveness, and the sure command of its means. The petty arts of coquetry were no farther from it than the numbness of the untaught girl. Great love was wise, strong, powerful, like genius, like any other dominant form of human power. It knew itself, and what it wanted, and how to attain its ends.

Not great love, then . . . but just the common humble average of human love was hers. And it had come to her so newly, so overwhelmingly, with a face so grave, a touch so startling, that she had stood there petrified, humbled at the first look of its eyes, recognizing that what she had once taken for love was merely pleasure and spring-time, and the flavour of youth.

"But how was I to know? And now it's too late!" she wailed.

XXIX

THE inhabitants of the little house in Passy were of necessity early risers; but when Susy jumped out of bed the next morning no one else was astir, and it lacked nearly an hour of the call of the *bonne's* alarm-clock.

For a moment Susy leaned out of her dark room into the darker night. A cold drizzle fell on her face, and she shivered and drew back. Then, lighting a candle, and shading it, as her habit was, from the sleeping child, she slipped on her dressing-gown and opened the door. On the threshold she paused to look at her watch. Only half-past five! She thought with compunction of the unkindness of breaking in on Junie Fulmer's slumbers; but such scruples did not weigh an ounce in the balance of her purpose. Poor Junie would have to oversleep herself on Sunday, that was all.

Susy stole into the passage, opened a door, and cast her light on the girl's face.

"Junie! Dearest Junie, you must wake up!"

Junie lay in the abandonment of youthful sleep; but at the sound of her name she sat up with the promptness of a grown person on whom domestic burdens have long weighed.

"Which one of them is it?" she asked, one foot already out of bed.

341

"Oh, Junie dear, no . . . it's nothing wrong with the children . . . or with anybody," Susy stammered, on her knees by the bed.

In the candlelight, she saw Junie's anxious brow darken reproachfully.

"Oh, Susy, then why—? I was just dreaming we were all driving about Rome in a great big motor-car with father and mother!"

"I'm so sorry, dear. What a lovely dream! I'm a brute to have interrupted it—"

She felt the little girl's awakening scrutiny. "If there's nothing wrong with anybody, why are you crying, Susy? Is it *you* there's something wrong with? What has happened?"

"Am I crying?" Susy rose from her knees and sat down on the counterpane. "Yes, it *is* me. And I had to disturb you."

"Oh, Susy, darling, what is it?" Junie's arms were about her in a flash, and Susy grasped them in burning fingers.

"Junie, listen! I've got to go away at once—to leave you all for the whole day. I may not be back till late this evening; late to-night; I can't tell. I promised your mother I'd never leave you; but I've got to—I've got to."

Junie considered her agitated face with fully awakened eyes. "Oh, I won't tell, you know, you old brick," she said with simplicity.

Susy hugged her. "Junie, Junie, you darling! But that wasn't what I meant. Of course you may tell—you *must* tell. I shall write to your mother myself. But what worries me is the idea of having to go away—away from Paris—for the whole day, with Geordie still coughing a little, and no one but that silly Angèle to stay with him while you're out—and no one but you to take yourself and the others to school. But Junie, Junie, I've *got* to do it!" she sobbed out, clutching the child tighter.

Junie Fulmer, with her strangely mature perception of the case, and seemingly of every case that fate might call on her to deal with, sat for a moment motionless in Susy's hold. Then she freed her wrists with an adroit twist, and leaning back against the pillows said judiciously: "You'll never in the world bring up a family of your own if you take on like this over other people's children."

Through all her turmoil of spirit the observation drew a laugh from Susy. "Oh, a family of my own—I don't deserve one, the way I'm behaving to *you!*"

Junie still considered her. "My dear, a change will do you good: you need it," she pronounced.

Susy rose with a laughing sigh. "I'm not at all sure it will! But I've got to have it, all the same. Only I *do* feel anxious—and I can't even leave you my address!"

Junie still seemed to examine the case.

"Can't you even tell me where you're going?" she ventured, as if not quite sure of the delicacy of asking.

"Well—no, I don't think I can; not till I get

back. Besides, even if I could it wouldn't be much use, because I couldn't give you my address there. I don't know what it will be."

"But what does it matter, if you're coming back to-night?"

"Of course I'm coming back! How could you possibly imagine I should think of leaving you for more than a day?"

"Oh, I shouldn't be afraid—not much, that is, with the poker, and Nat's water-pistol," emended Junie, still judicious.

Susy again enfolded her vehemently, and then turned to more practical matters. She explained that she wished if possible to catch an eight-thirty train from the Gare de Lyon, and that there was not a moment to lose if the children were to be dressed and fed, and full instructions written out for Junie and Angèle, before she rushed for the underground.

While she bathed Geordie, and then hurried into her own clothes, she could not help wondering at her own extreme solicitude for her charges. She remembered, with a pang, how often she had deserted Clarissa Vanderlyn for the whole day, and even for two or three in succession—poor little Clarissa, whom she knew to be so unprotected, so exposed to evil influences. She had been too much absorbed in her own greedy bliss to be more than intermittently aware of the child; but now, she felt, no sorrow however ravaging, no happiness however absorbing, would ever again isolate her from her kind.

And then these children were so different! The exquisite Clarissa was already the predestined victim of her surroundings: her budding soul was divided from Susy's by the same barrier of incomprehension that separated the latter from Mrs. Vanderlyn. Clarissa had nothing to teach Susy but the horror of her own hard little appetites; whereas the company of the noisy argumentative Fulmers had been a school of wisdom and abnegation.

As she applied the brush to Geordie's shining head and the handkerchief to his snuffling nose, the sense of what she owed him was so borne in on Susy that she interrupted the process to catch him to her bosom.

"I'll have *such* a story to tell you when I get back to-night, if you'll promise me to be good all day," she bargained with him; and Geordie, always astute, bargained back: "Before I promise, I'd like to know *what* story."

At length all was in order. Junie had been enlightened, and Angèle stunned, by the minuteness of Susy's instructions; and the latter, waterproofed and stoutly shod, descended the doorstep, and paused to wave at the pyramid of heads yearning to her from an upper window.

It was hardly light, and still raining, when she turned into the dismal street. As usual, it was empty; but at the corner she perceived a hesitating taxi, with luggage piled beside the driver. Perhaps it was some early traveller, just arriving, who would release the carriage in time for her to catch it, and thus avoid the walk to the *métro,* and the subsequent strap-hanging; for it was the workpeople's hour. Susy raced toward the vehicle, which, overcoming its hesitation, was beginning to move in her direction. Observing this, she stopped to see where it would discharge its load. Thereupon the taxi stopped also, and the load discharged itself in front of her in the shape of Nick Lansing.

The two stood staring at each other through the rain till Nick broke out: "Where are you going? I came to get you."

"To get me? To get me?" she repeated. Beside the driver she had suddenly remarked the old suit-case from which her husband had obliged her to extract Strefford's cigars as they were leaving Como; and everything that had happened since seemed to fall away and vanish in the pang and rapture of that memory.

"To get you; yes. Of course." He spoke the words peremptorily, almost as if they were an order. "Where were you going?" he repeated.

Without answering, she turned toward the house. He followed her, and the laden taxi closed the procession.

"Why are you out in such weather without an umbrella?" he continued, in the same severe tone, drawing her under the shelter of his.

"Oh, because Junie's umbrella is in tatters, and I had to leave her mine, as I was going away for the whole day." She spoke the words like a person in a trance.

"For the whole day? At this hour? Where?" They were on the doorstep, and she fumbled automatically for her key, let herself in, and led the way to the sitting-room. It had not been tidied up since the night before. The children's school books lay scattered on the table and sofa, and the empty fireplace was grey with ashes. She turned to Nick in the pallid light.

"I was going to see you," she stammered, "I was going to follow you to Fontainebleau, if necessary, to tell you . . . to prevent you. . . ."

He repeated in the same aggressive tone: "Tell me what? Prevent what?"

"Tell you that there must be some other way . . . some decent way . . . of our separating . . . without that horror . . . that horror of your going off with a woman. . . ."

He stared, and then burst into a laugh. The blood rushed to her face. She had caught a familiar ring in his laugh, and it wounded her. What business had he, at such a time, to laugh in the old way?

"I'm sorry; but there *is* no other way, I'm afraid. No other way but one," he corrected himself.

She raised her head sharply. "Well?"

"That you should be the woman.—Oh, my

dear!'' He had dropped his mocking smile, and
was at her side, her hands in his. ''Oh, my dear,
don't you see that we've both been feeling the
same thing, and at the same hour? You lay
awake thinking of it all night, didn't you? So did
I. Whenever the clock struck, I said to myself:
'She's hearing it too.' And I was up before daylight, and packed my traps—for I never want to
set foot again in that awful hotel where I've lived
in hell for the last three days. And I swore to
myself that I'd go off with a woman by the first
train I could catch—and so I mean to, my dear.''

She stood before him numb. Yes, numb: that
was the worst of it! The violence of the reaction
had been too great, and she could hardly understand what he was saying. Instead, she noticed
that the tassel of the window-blind was torn off
again (oh, those children!), and vaguely wondered
if his luggage were safe on the waiting taxi. One
heard such stories. . . .

His voice came back to her. ''Listen!'' he
was entreating. ''You must see yourself that
it can't be. We're married—isn't that all that
matters? Oh, I know—I've behaved like a brute:
a cursèd arrogant ass! You couldn't wish that
ass a worse kicking than I've given him! But
that's not the point, you see. The point is that
we're *married*. . . . Married. . . . Doesn't it
mean something to you, something—inexorable?
It does to me. I didn't dream it would—in just
that way. But all I can say is that I suppose the

people who don't feel it aren't really married—
and they'd better separate; much better. As for
us—"

Through her tears she gasped out: "That's
what I felt . . . that's what I said to Streff. . . ."

He was upon her with a great embrace. "My
darling! My darling! You *have* told him?"

"Yes," she panted. "That's why I'm living
here." She paused. "And you've told Coral?"

She felt his embrace relax. He drew away a
little, still holding her, but with lowered head.

"No . . . I . . . haven't."

"Oh, Nick! But then—?"

He caught her to him again, resentfully. "Well
—then what? What do you mean? What earthly
difference does it make?"

"But if you've told her you were going to marry
her—" (Try as she would, her voice was full of
silver chimes.)

"Marry her? Marry her?" he echoed. "But
how could I? What does marriage mean anyhow?
If it means anything at all it means—*you!* And
I can't ask Coral Hicks just to come and live with
me, can I?"

Between crying and laughing she lay on his
breast, and his hand passed over her hair.

They were silent for a while; then he began
again: "You said it yourself yesterday, you
know."

She strayed back from sunlit distances. "Yesterday?"

"Yes: that Grace Fulmer says you can't separate two people who've been through a lot of things—"

"Ah, been through them together—it's not the things, you see, it's the togetherness," she interrupted.

"The togetherness—that's it!" He seized on the word as if it had just been coined to express their case, and his mind could rest in it without farther labour.

The door-bell rang, and they started. Through the window they saw the taxi-driver gesticulating enquiries as to the fate of the luggage.

"He wants to know if he's to leave it here," Susy laughed.

"No—no! You're to come with me," her husband declared.

"Come with you?" She laughed again at the absurdity of the suggestion.

"Of course: this very instant. What did you suppose? That I was going away without you? Run up and pack your things," he commanded.

"My things? My things? But I can't leave the children!"

He stared, between indignation and amusement. "Can't leave the children? Nonsense! Why, you said yourself you were going to follow me to Fontainebleau—"

She reddened again, this time a little painfully. "I didn't know what I was doing. . . . I had to find you . . . but I should have come back this evening, no matter what happened."

"No matter what?"

She nodded, and met his gaze resolutely.

"No; but really—"

"Really, I can't leave the children till Nat and Grace come back. I promised I wouldn't."

"Yes; but you didn't know then. . . . Why on earth can't their nurse look after them?"

"There isn't any nurse but me."

"Good Lord!"

"But it's only for two weeks more," she pleaded.

"Two weeks! Do you know how long I've been without you?" He seized her by both wrists, and drew them against his breast. "Come with me at least for two days—*Susy!*" he entreated her.

"Oh," she cried, "that's the very first time you've said my name!"

"Susy, Susy, then—my Susy—Susy! And you've only said mine once, you know."

"Nick!" she sighed, at peace, as if the one syllable were a magic seed that flung out great branches to envelop them.

"Well, then, Susy, be reasonable. Come!"

"Reasonable—oh, reasonable!" she sobbed through laughter.

"Unreasonable, then! That's even better."

She freed herself, and drew back gently. "Nick, I swore I wouldn't leave them; and I can't. It's not only my promise to their mother—it's what

they've been to me themselves. You don't know
. . . You can't imagine the things they've taught
me. They're awfully naughty at times, because
they're so clever; but when they're good they're
the wisest people I know." She paused, and a
sudden inspiration illuminated her. "But why
shouldn't we take them with us?" she exclaimed.

Her husband's arms fell away from her, and he
stood dumfounded.

"Take them with us?"

"Why not?"

"All five of them?"

"Of course—I couldn't possibly separate them.
And Junie and Nat will help us to look after the
young ones."

"Help *us?*" he groaned.

"Oh, you'll see; they won't bother you. Just
leave it to me; I'll manage—" The word stopped
her short, and an agony of crimson suffused her
from brow to throat. Their eyes met; and without
a word he stooped and laid his lips gently on the
stain of red on her neck.

"Nick," she breathed, her hands in his.

"But those children—"

Instead of answering, she questioned: "Where
are we going?"

His face lit up.

"Anywhere, dearest, that you choose."

"Well—I choose Fontainebleau!" she exulted.

"So do I! But we can't take all those children
to an hotel at Fontainebleau, can we?" he ques-

tioned weakly. "You see, dear, there's the mere
expense of it—"

Her eyes were already travelling far ahead of
him. "The expense won't amount to much. I've
just remembered that Angèle, the *bonne,* has a
sister who is cook there in a nice old-fashioned
pension which must be almost empty at this time
of year. I'm sure I can ma—arrange easily," she
hurried on, nearly tripping again over the fatal
word. "And just think of the treat it will be to
them! This is Friday, and I can get them let off
from their afternoon classes, and keep them in the
country till Monday. Poor darlings, they haven't
been out of Paris for months! And I daresay the
change will cure Geordie's cough—Geordie's the
youngest," she explained, surprised to find herself, even in the rapture of reunion, so absorbed
in the welfare of the Fulmers.

She was conscious that her husband was surprised also; but instead of prolonging the argument he simply questioned: "Was Geordie the
chap you had in your arms when you opened the
front door the night before last?"

She echoed: "I opened the front door the night
before last?"

"To a boy with a parcel."

"Oh," she sobbed, "you were there! You were
watching?"

He held her to him, and the currents flowed between them warm and full as on the night of their
moon over Como.

In a trice, after that, she had the matter in hand and her forces marshalled. The taxi was paid, Nick's luggage deposited in the vestibule, and the children, just piling down to breakfast, were summoned in to hear the news.

It was apparent that, seasoned to surprises as they were, Nick's presence took them aback. But when, between laughter and embraces, his identity, and his right to be where he was, had been made clear to them, Junie dismissed the matter by asking him in her practical way: "Then I suppose we may talk about you to Susy now?"—and thereafter all five addressed themselves to the vision of their imminent holiday.

From that moment the little house became the centre of a whirlwind. Treats so unforeseen, and of such magnitude, were rare in the young Fulmers' experience, and had it not been for Junie's steadying influence Susy's charges would have got out of hand. But young Nat, appealed to by Nick on the ground of their common manhood, was induced to forego celebrating the event on his motor horn (the very same which had tortured the New Hampshire echoes), and to assert his authority over his juniors; and finally a plan began to emerge from the chaos, and each child to fit into it like a bit of a picture puzzle.

Susy, riding the whirlwind with her usual firmness, nevertheless felt an undercurrent of anxiety. There had been no time as yet, between her and Nick, to revert to money matters; and where there was so little money it could not, obviously, much matter. But that was the more reason for being secretly aghast at her intrepid resolve not to separate herself from her charges. A three days' honey-moon with five children in the party—and children with the Fulmer appetite—could not but be a costly business; and while she settled details, packed them off to school, and routed out such nondescript receptacles as the house contained in the way of luggage, her thoughts remained fixed on the familiar financial problem.

Yes—it was cruel to have it rear its hated head even through the bursting boughs of her new spring; but there it was, the perpetual serpent in her Eden, to be bribed, fed, sent to sleep with such scraps as she could beg, borrow or steal for it. And she supposed it was the price that fate meant her to pay for her blessedness, and was surer than ever that the blessedness was worth it. Only, how was she to compound the business with her new principles?

With the children's things to pack, luncheon to be got ready, and the Fontainebleau *pension* to be telephoned to, there was little time to waste on moral casuistry; and Susy asked herself with a certain irony if the chronic lack of time to deal with money difficulties had not been the chief cause of her previous lapses. There was no time to deal with this question either; no time, in short, to do anything but rush forward on a great gale of plans and preparations, in the course of which she whirled Nick forth to buy some *charcuterie* for luncheon, and telephone to Fontainebleau.

Once he was gone—and after watching him safely round the corner—she too got into her wraps, and transferring a small packet from her dressing-case to her pocket, hastened out in a different direction.

XXX

IT took two brimming taxi-cabs to carry the Nicholas Lansings to the station on their second honey-moon. In the first were Nick, Susy and the luggage of the whole party (little Nat's motor horn included, as a last concession, and because he had hitherto forborne to play on it); and in the second, the five Fulmers, the *bonne,* who at the eleventh hour had refused to be left, a cage-full of canaries, and a foundling kitten who had murderous designs on them; all of which had to be taken because, if the *bonne* came, there would be nobody left to look after them.

At the corner Susy tore herself from Nick's arms and held up the procession while she ran back to the second taxi to make sure that the *bonne* had brought the house-key. It was found of course that she hadn't but that Junie had; whereupon the caravan got under way again, and reached the station just as the train was starting; and there, by some miracle of good nature on the part of the guard, they were all packed together into an empty compartment—no doubt, as Susy remarked, because train officials never failed to spot a newly-married couple, and treat them kindly.

The children, sentinelled by Junie, at first gave promise of superhuman goodness; but presently their feelings overflowed, and they were not to be quieted till it had been agreed that Nat should blow his motor-horn at each halt, while the twins called out the names of the stations, and Geordie, with the canaries and kitten, affected to change trains.

Luckily the halts were few; but the excitement of travel, combined with over-indulgence in the chocolates imprudently provided by Nick, over-whelmed Geordie with a sudden melancholy that could be appeased only by Susy's telling him stories till they arrived at Fontainebleau.

The day was soft, with mild gleams of sunlight on decaying foliage; and after luggage and live-stock had been dropped at the *pension* Susy con-fessed that she had promised the children a scamper in the forest, and buns in a tea-shop af-terward. Nick placidly agreed, and darkness had long fallen, and a great many buns been consumed, when at length the procession turned down the street toward the *pension,* headed by Nick with the sleeping Geordie on his shoulder, while the others, speechless with fatigue and food, hung heavily on Susy.

It had been decided that, as the *bonne* was of the party, the children might be entrusted to her for the night, and Nick and Susy establish them-selves in an adjacent hotel. Nick had flattered himself that they might remove their possessions

there when they returned from the tea-room; but
Susy, manifestly surprised at the idea, reminded
him that her charges must first be given their
supper and put to bed. She suggested that he
should meanwhile take the bags to the hotel, and
promised to join him as soon as Geordie was
asleep.

She was a long time coming, but waiting for her
was sweet, even in a deserted hotel reading-room
insufficiently heated by a sulky stove; and after
he had glanced through his morning's mail, hurriedly thrust into his pocket as he left Paris, he
sank into a state of drowsy beatitude. It was all
the maddest business in the world, yet it did not
give him the sense of unreality that had made
their first adventure a mere golden dream; and he
sat and waited with the security of one in whom
dear habits have struck deep roots. In this mood
of acquiescence even the presence of the five Fulmers seemed a natural and necessary consequence
of all the rest; and when Susy at length appeared,
a little pale and tired, with the brooding inward
look that busy mothers bring from the nursery,
that too seemed natural and necessary, and part
of the new order of things.

They had wandered out to a cheap restaurant
for dinner; now, in the damp December night, they
were walking back to the hotel under a sky full of
rain-clouds. They seemed to have said everything
to each other, and yet barely to have begun what

they had to tell; and at each step they took, their heavy feet dragged a great load of bliss.

In the hotel almost all the lights were already out; and they groped their way to the third floor room which was the only one that Susy had found cheap enough. A ray from a street-lamp struck up through the unshuttered windows; and after Nick had revived the fire they drew their chairs close to it, and sat quietly for a while in the dark.

Their silence was so sweet that Nick could not make up his mind to break it; not to do so gave his tossing spirit such a sense of permanence, of having at last unlimited time before him in which to taste his joy and let its sweetness stream through him. But at length he roused himself to say: "It's queer how things coincide. I've had a little bit of good news in one of the letters I got this morning."

Susy took the announcement serenely. "Well, you *would*, you know," she commented, as if the day had been too obviously designed for bliss to escape the notice of its dispensers.

"Yes," he continued with a thrill of pardonable pride. "During the cruise I did a couple of articles on Crete—oh, just travel-impressions, of course; they couldn't be more. But the editor of the *New Review* has accepted them, and asks for others. And here's his cheque, if you please! So you see you might have let me take the jolly room downstairs with the pink curtains. And it makes me awfully hopeful about my book."

He had expected a rapturous outburst, and perhaps some reassertion of wifely faith in the glorious future that awaited *The Pageant of Alexander;* and deep down under the lover's well-being the author felt a faint twinge of mortified vanity when Susy, leaping to her feet, cried out, ravenously and without preamble: "Oh, Nick, Nick—let me see how much they've given you!"

He flourished the cheque before her in the firelight. "A couple of hundred, you mercenary wretch!"

"Oh, oh—" she gasped, as if the good news had been almost too much for her tense nerves; and then surprised him by dropping to the ground, and burying her face against his knees.

"Susy, my Susy," he whispered, his hand on her shaking shoulder. "Why, dear, what is it? You're not crying?"

"Oh, Nick, Nick—two hundred? Two hundred dollars? Then I've got to tell you—oh now, at once!"

A faint chill ran over him, and involuntarily his hand drew back from her bowed figure.

"Now? Oh, why now?" he protested. "What on earth does it matter now—whatever it is?"

"But it does matter—it matters more than you can think!"

She straightened herself, still kneeling before him, and lifted her head so that the firelight behind her turned her hair into a ruddy halo.

"Oh, Nick, the bracelet—Ellie's bracelet. . . . I've never returned it to her," she faltered out.

He felt himself recoiling under the hands with which she clutched his knees. For an instant he did not remember what she alluded to; it was the mere mention of Ellie Vanderlyn's name that had fallen between them like an icy shadow. What an incorrigible fool he had been to think they could ever shake off such memories, or cease to be the slaves of such a past!

"The bracelet?—Oh, yes," he said, suddenly understanding, and feeling the chill mount slowly to his lips.

"Yes, the bracelet . . . Oh, Nick, I meant to give it back at once; I did—I *did;* but the day you went away I forgot everything else. And when I found the thing, in the bottom of my bag, weeks afterward, I thought everything was over between you and me, and I had begun to see Ellie again, and she was kind to me—and how could I?" To save his life he could have found no answer, and she pressed on: "And so this morning, when I saw you were frightened by the expense of bringing all the children with us, and when I felt I couldn't leave them, and couldn't leave you either, I remembered the bracelet; and I sent you off to telephone while I rushed round the corner to a little jeweller's where I'd been before, and pawned it so that you shouldn't have to pay for the children. . . . But now, darling, you see, if you've got all that money, I can get it out of pawn at once, can't I, and send it back to her?"

She flung her arms about him, and he held her fast, wondering if the tears he felt were hers or his. Still he did not speak; but as he clasped her close she added, with an irrepressible flash of her old irony: "Not that Ellie will understand why I've done it. She's never yet been able to make out why you returned her scarf-pin."

For a long time she continued to lean against him, her head on his knees, as she had done on the terrace of Como on the last night of their honeymoon. She had ceased to talk, and he sat silent also, passing his hand quietly to and fro over her hair. The first rapture had been succeeded by soberer feelings. Her confession had broken up the frozen pride about his heart, and humbled him to the earth; but it had also roused forgotten things, memories and scruples swept aside in the first rush of their reunion. He and she belonged to each other for always: he understood that now. The impulse which had first drawn them together again, in spite of reason, in spite of themselves almost, that deep-seated instinctive need that each had of the other, would never again wholly let them go. Yet as he sat there he thought of Strefford, he thought of Coral Hicks. He had been a coward in regard to Coral, and Susy had been sincere and courageous in regard to Strefford. Yet his mind dwelt on Coral with tenderness, with compunction, with remorse; and he was almost sure that Susy had already put Strefford utterly out of her mind.

It was the old contrast between the two ways of loving, the man's way and the woman's; and after a moment it seemed to Nick natural enough that Susy, from the very moment of finding him again, should feel neither pity nor regret, and that Strefford should already be to her as if he had never been. After all, there was something Providential in such arrangements.

He stooped closer, pressed her dreaming head between his hands, and whispered: "Wake up; it's bedtime."

She rose; but as she moved away to turn on the light he caught her hand and drew her to the window. They leaned on the sill in the darkness, and through the clouds, from which a few drops were already falling, the moon, labouring upward, swam into a space of sky, cast her troubled glory on them, and was again hidden.

THE END

VIRAGO MODERN CLASSICS

The first Virago Modern Classic, *Frost in May* by Antonia White, was published in 1978. It launched a list dedicated to the celebration of women writers and to the rediscovery and reprinting of their works. Its aim was, and is, to demonstrate the existence of a female tradition in fiction which is both enriching and enjoyable, and to broaden the sometimes narrow academic definition of a 'classic' which has often led to the neglect of a large number of interesting secondary works of fiction. In calling the series 'Modern Classics' we do not necessarily mean 'great' — although this is often the case. Published with new critical and biographical introductions, books are chosen for many reasons: sometimes for their importance in literary history; sometimes because they illuminate particular aspects of women's lives, both personal and public. They may be classics of comedy or storytelling; their interest can be historical, feminist, political or literary.

Initially the Virago Modern Classics concentrated on English novels and short stories published in the early decades of this century. As the series has grown it has broadened to include works of fiction from different centuries, different countries, cultures and literary traditions, many of which have been suggested by our readers.